THE HIGH COMMISSIONER

THE
HIGH
COMMISSIONER

A Novel by
JON CLEARY

William Morrow & Company, Inc.
New York   1966

4669

This is a work of fiction. Some positions and institutions are part of the story, but no one who has held any of the positions or worked in the institutions is meant to be represented in this book. All characters in the story have lived only in the writer's imagination.

THE HIGH COMMISSIONER

CHAPTER ONE

1

"We want you to go to London," said the Premier, "and arrest the High Commissioner for murder."

He sat back, one clawed finger stroking the beak of his nose, a baldheaded old eagle hawk who had made this office his eyrie for twenty-five years. He ran his tongue round his thin dry lips, as if tasting the shock that showed on Scobie Malone's face. He was seventy years old and fifty years of his hectic brawling life had been spent in politics. He knew and relished the value of shock.

"The Commissioner tells me you detectives are like nuns, you're usually only allowed out in pairs." He looked at Malone, then at Police Commissioner Leeds, his hooded eyes glistening with an old hawk's malicious humour. "Is that because you don't trust each other, Jack?"

John Leeds had been a policeman for forty years, Commissioner for ten, and he knew how to handle politicians. "Is that what you think of nuns, Mr. Premier?"

Flannery's laugh was more like a cough of mirth, as if it hurt him. "Are you trying to get me to lose the Catholic vote, Jack? Stone the bloody crows, I wouldn't mind betting you vote Liberal!" He looked back at Malone. "What do you vote, Sergeant?"

4669

Malone was still getting over the shock of the Premier's opening remark. After ten years in the force he was not unaccustomed to shocks; but nothing like this had ever been flung at him before. When Flannery had first spoken he had glanced quickly at the old man to see if he was joking; the ugly smile had told him that if there was a joke it was not intended for him. He was still dazed when Flannery spoke to him again, repeating his question. "What do you vote, Sergeant?"

He tried to collect his thoughts, but the question seemed so irrelevant at a time like this. "It depends, sir."

"Depends? What on?"

Malone saw Leeds' warning glance and retreated. "I'm not political-minded, sir. I vote by whim, I suppose."

Flannery stared at him, his eyes suddenly dark and glazed: twice he had come close to defeat on the vote of those who voted by whim, the floaters, the I-don't-knows of the opinion polls. Then abruptly he grinned, the surprisingly warm grin that had been winning him the women's vote for years. Malone, watching him, knew that, despite what the newspapers said, women were not always influenced by a politician's profile or his platform charm: a number of them, often enough to swing an election, voted for a father figure. But I'd have hated Flannery as a father, Malone thought: he'd have been using me as election bait before I was even weaned.

"Well, in a way, Sergeant, you're going to London to vote Labour. You want to tell him what's what, Jack?"

Leeds hesitated, then he leaned forward in his chair, both hands resting on his knees. Whenever Malone had been with the Commissioner, the latter had struck him as one of the most relaxed men he had ever met; Leeds gave the impression that time and circumstance were part of *his* pattern, not the other way round, as it was with Malone and the rest of the world. But not today: today Leeds was stiff and bony

[12]

with concern, even anxiety. But he was not going to confide in Malone, only give him the case facts:

"The Australian High Commissioner in London, as you know, is John Quentin. Or rather that's his name now. It was John Corliss. Under that name he lived here in Sydney before the war and worked for the Water Board as an assistant surveyor. He married a German refugee girl named Freda Wiseman and they lived out in Coogee. He murdered her on December 8, 1941, then disappeared. By the time the murder was discovered the newspapers were full of Pearl Harbor and the story got no play at all. Corliss just went into smoke and we were never able to trace him." He glanced at Flannery, who sat watching him with the look of malicious humour varnished on the mottled skull of his face. "Not until now."

Malone waited for Flannery to say something, but the Premier remained silent. He looked back at Leeds. "How did you get on to him, sir? I mean that Quentin and Corliss are the same man?"

Leeds looked at Flannery. There was an atmosphere between the two older men that had something to do with the room in which the three men sat. Malone was not insensitive to atmosphere: crime coarsened you, whether you were dealing in it or trying to prevent it, but it also heightened your perception of certain elements in which you moved. And one of them was atmosphere: the criminal or the policeman who was insensitive to it was never a lasting success in his job. Malone knew he himself would not be here if the Commissioner thought he was a failure.

He glanced around the room while the other two men fenced in their silent secret duel. It was a big office and it had all the homely charm of a battle room; which was what it was. This was where Flannery planned his campaigns to demolish the enemy: the official Opposition, the pressure groups, even members of his own party who showed too much ambition. A single painting, faded and fly-spotted, was his concession to the arts: painted by a third-rate artist it depicted a hold-up of a mail coach by bushrangers: Flannery had been known to remark that it often gave him inspiration. A glass-fronted bookcase stood beneath the painting, its three shelves lined with leather-bound official volumes; on top of two volumes of Hansard lay a copy of *They're a Weird Mob*: Flannery had been getting the lowdown on the citizens he led. The three other walls were studded with political *graffiti*, honorary membership for Flannery in a score of organizations, testimonials from others. Between the framed scrolls, like frozen moments of the old politician's life, were half a dozen photographs. Laying a foundation stone, the warm vote-catching grin as firmly in place as the stone he had just laid; shaking hands with the Prime Minister, both of them suffering from the spasm known as politicians' bonhomie; standing like a little old bird of prey among the fat unsuspecting pigeons of his Cabinet, several of whom had since been shot down. Everything smelled overpoweringly of politics: the room, the atmosphere between the Premier and the Commissioner of Police. And yet Leeds had never been a political policeman; for him corruption was a worse crime than murder. Murder, Malone had heard him say to a class of police trainees, was rarely cold-blooded; corruption always was. Malone looked back at Flannery, who considered corruption a necessity of political life.

The old man tapped the claw of his finger on a folder that lay on his desk. "It's all in here, Sergeant. Documented like a White Paper. It doesn't matter who got us started, the point is their tip was right. It happened six months ago and I've had a man working on it ever since."

"Someone from Headquarters?" Malone looked at Leeds, but it was Flannery who answered.

"Not from *Police* Headquarters. From Party Headquarters. One of our political research officers. He enjoyed it, said it was a nice change from trying to guess voters' intentions." He coughed another laugh; but Leeds was the one who looked hurt this time.

Malone hesitated, still finding everything incredible. Then he stuck his neck out, asking to be sent to the Back of Beyond: a bush beat or early retirement was usually the fate of a too-inquisitive detective. They were trained to ask questions, but not of the political boss of the State.

"Why wasn't it turned over to our Murder Squad when you first got the tip, Mr. Premier?"

Leeds shot Malone a glance that was both a warning and a look of gratitude; he had obviously asked this same question and got nowhere. But Flannery had spent most of his life dealing with questions that he didn't feel he had to answer.

"We just wanted to be sure, Sergeant. I've got where I am today—" He waved at the room around him, home sweet home; he had a wife and a grown-up family somewhere in Sydney, but a politician's family in New South Wales was never expected to be in evidence. "I've got where I am by observing one principle—never libel anyone unless you're sure of your facts." He grinned to himself, no longer a warm grin, chewing on the bones of a hundred dead foes. "London is one of the two most important diplomatic posts Australia has. You don't accuse our High Commissioner, our country's ambassador there, you don't accuse *him* of murdering his wife unless you are absolutely one hundred per cent sure of your facts."

"And this"—Malone stumbled a little: he could just picture this part-time Maigret down at Trades Hall—"this political research officer, he's sure of all his facts?"

Flannery coughed again: mirth sounded like lung cancer. "In twenty years he's never been wrong in an election forecast, not even a by-election. He forecasts a conviction with this." The claw scratched the folder again. "Says he'll stake his life on it."

[15]

Malone couldn't help himself: "Seems to me, sir, he's staking someone else's life on it."

The hoods dropped a little lower over the agate eyes. Malone could feel the old hawk peeling the flesh away from him, opening him up to look at the heart of Malone, scrutinizing it to see if it had a political label on it, one that might be treasonable. Then the hoods lifted and he looked at Leeds. "I thought you said he was your best man, Jack."

"He's the best man for this job." Leeds was still sitting forward in his chair, still taut.

"He's only a detective-sergeant. I thought this would call for an inspector at least, maybe even a superintendent."

"You asked for secrecy." Leeds' gruff husky voice had a hint of sharpness in it; a spark of reaction showed in Flannery's unblinking eyes. "It might be difficult to account for the absence for a week or ten days of an inspector from the Murder Squad. Someone would be sure to start asking questions."

"The sergeant here asks questions."

Malone felt he was just part of the furniture of the room, part of the furniture of Flannery's bailiwick: he was there to be used. He could feel the temper rising in him, but he held it in check.

"If Sergeant Malone sounded a little critical of"—Leeds also stumbled—"of your research worker, I think it's a natural reaction. The real professional always suspects the amateur. I've heard you say that, sir, in the House."

"This feller of mine isn't an amateur."

"He's an amateur detective. Not even a private investigator. In any case, when Sergeant Malone has read that file, I'm sure he'll agree your man has done a good job." Leeds looked at Malone. "I've read it. Everything is there for an arrest."

"And a conviction," said Flannery.

"We never look that far," said Leeds, showing his inde-

[16]

pendence. "We'll arrest him on the warrant that's been issued, in the name of Corliss. The rest is up to the Crown Prosecutor."

Flannery looked at Malone again, still poking away at his insides. "This has to be kept quiet. Not a word to anyone, not even your wife."

"I'm not married, sir."

"Good. But don't quote me! I'm the patron saint of the Labour League of Married Women." He coughed and once again Malone got the warm grin. Flannery had decided to trust him: he began to lay the flesh back on, strip by strip. "How can we keep it covered up in your department, Jack?"

"He can apply for leave." Leeds turned to Malone. "Better make it compassionate leave, to explain the hurry. Have your grandmother dying or something."

"I haven't used that one since I was a kid at school."

"You'll go the long way round. Fly over to Perth and pick up a plane there for Darwin. In Darwin you can catch the plane for London. If any of the airport reporters saw you getting on a plane for London, here in Sydney, they'd want to know the ins and outs of it all. But going to Perth—well, that's where your grandmother is dying."

Malone, still a little bemused, couldn't resist one more question: "But why all the secrecy, sir?"

Leeds looked at Flannery again: *it's your question, you answer it.* Flannery didn't mind in the least: "Because if it's at all possible I'd like Quentin back here in Sydney before his arrest is announced. I want to have the pleasure of ringing up someone and telling him myself." For a moment malevolence made a ruin of his face. Malone stared at him and all at once thought: why, you old bastard, you're a murderer, too. "I've waited a long time for this."

Leeds interrupted, a little too sharply, as if he were trying to stop the old man from exposing himself any further. This was the sort of indecent exposure for which there was no legal penalty, yet it was more shocking than any sex perversion. "I'll impress on Sergeant Malone that there has to be absolute secrecy. He'll be back here within a week. And he'll have the High Commissioner with him."

Flannery sat nodding for a moment, a mote of sunlight from the window behind him rolling on the freckled dome of his bald head like a thin drop of yellow oil. "In a way I feel sorry for Quentin. I met him a couple of times down in Canberra. He's not a bad bloke at all."

Leeds stood up. One look at his face told Malone that the Commissioner had had enough of the room's atmosphere; he looked like a man choking for air. He reached out a hand for the file on the desk and Flannery, after a moment's hesitation, gave it to him.

"I want it done quickly and quietly as possible, Jack." Then he looked up at Malone. "Quentin may make a fuss. You may have to go to Scotland Yard, get them to bring him before an English court and get an extradition order. If that has to happen, get on the phone to the Commissioner here right away, before the London newspapers get wind of it. I don't want a certain someone to hear about it before I have the chance of telling him myself."

"I'll watch it, sir." Malone was sickened by the look on the old man's face.

"I just hope you can talk him into coming back without any fuss, any need for extradition. If he's got any sense of dignity he'll see it's better for him as High Commissioner to be arrested here in Sydney than in London. We've got to think of Australia's good name. Don't forget that, Sergeant."

2

"Australia's good name!" Leeds seemed to gasp for air as he and Malone came out into the bright early winter sunlight. He waved away the car that stood waiting for him at the curb, as if even its large interior would be too confining for him in his present state of mind. "You mind walking?"

"I started on the beat. I haven't lost the habit."

"You were practically begging to be put back on the beat, a couple of those questions you put to him."

"I'm not querying your judgment, sir, but do you think I'm the right man for this job?"

Leeds looked at the man beside him. Malone was tall, six feet, big in the shoulders and chest but not top-heavy; perhaps the well-shaped head, carried high, kept the feeling of balance. The face was too bony to be handsome but Leeds guessed women would find the eyes attractive: they were dark, almost Latin, and they were friendly. The mouth, too, was friendly: smiling was a natural exercise, not a studied social habit. Behind the façade Leeds knew there was a shrewd intelligence that could be relied upon in almost any circumstance. Malone gave the impression of being easygoing, but there was a competence about him that had marked him for promotion from his first days in the force.

"You're the man, all right," Leeds said. "What's worrying you?"

They walked up Macquarie Street, past the discreet tradesmen's signs of the doctors' brass plates. People went reluctantly, almost stealthily into the somber doorways, taking their cancers, their coronaries, their troubled minds, in with them. Why was it, Malone wondered, that people always looked as if they were *smuggling* their illnesses into doctors' consulting rooms? Or was it that he had suddenly become infected by secrecy, saw it even in the faces of strangers? He looked away from the doorways, at the outer edge of the pavement where the young girls, on their way to the Botanical Gardens in their lunch-hour break, went by, carrying their youth and vitality and beauty like bold banners: no secrecy there. God, he thought, how young and wonderful they look. Then wondered what had happened to him that he had begun to think of himself as old.

"I don't know, sir. This smells of politics and I've never been mixed up in that sort of thing before." He knew of the rivalry and antagonism that existed between State and Federal political parties. "Another thing. How did the High Commissioner get away with this for so long? Is the file on him really fair dinkum?"

"It's about as factual and unarguable as you can get. Take my word for it, Scobie. I checked it and rechecked it before I put us out on a limb. As for Quentin getting away with it for so long. This is a big empty country. Western Australia, where he's officially supposed to come from, I mean as Quentin, that's practically another country in itself. Perth is two thousand miles from Canberra or Sydney. On top of that, Australians never seem to take much interest in where their public men were born or how they grew up. Take Flannery, for instance. I'd bet not one per cent of this State's population could tell you anything about his early life. They couldn't care less. It's what you are today that counts in this country, not what you were."

Malone nodded, realizing for the first time his own ignorance of the men who, one way or another, had ruled his life: they were just names and faces and nothing more. But something else made him uneasy:

"What's behind all this?" he asked Leeds. "Why does the State Premier have a murder investigation conducted by one of his own political hacks? Why all the secrecy?"

Leeds took another breath of air. He was a big man, bigger than Malone, and usually he walked with a slow ambling roll, reminding one of a retired sea captain whose rough seas were behind him forever. But today he was battling the storm of his own feelings.

"It's pure political malice!" He looked at Malone fiercely from under the grey wire brushes of his brows. "Don't you quote me to anyone or you'll be working a bush beat before you know what hit you!"

"I have some faults, sir," said Malone, trying not to sound priggish, "but indiscretion is not one of them."

"Don't sound so blasted priggish."

"No, sir," said Malone, and grinned.

Leeds nodded, then abruptly his reddish face, that could so often be as threatening as a clenched fist, broke into a smile. He walked in silence for a few yards as they turned down Hunter Street towards Police Headquarters; then he appeared to relax, began to roll a little as he walked. "You're right, Scobie. That was one of the reasons I picked you for this job, your discretion."

A young couple, blind with love, came towards them; the two policemen walked round them, respecting their selfishness. Leeds, interrupted, fell silent for a few more yards, and Malone paced beside him, silently patient. Patience had never been one of Malone's early virtues, but he had learned to cultivate it, just as Flannery had learned to cultivate his warm sincere grin. Some virtues, Malone thought, were often only hypocrisy under another name.

"Pure political malice," Leeds repeated. "He's never forgiven the Prime Minister for crossing the floor back in the 1930's. You wouldn't remember that."

"In the 1930's I was still in short pants and both my grandmothers were still alive. I didn't even know such things as politicians existed. What happened?"

"The P.M. was a Labour man in those days, here in State politics. That was before he went down to Canberra, went into the Federal ring. There was a division in the House on some bill and he crossed the floor and voted with the Opposition. It brought the Government down."

"And Flannery's never forgiven him for it?"

"Scobie, woman hath no fury like that of a politician scorned." Leeds smiled; he was almost fully himself again.

"But how does he get back at the P.M.?"

"Quentin has been the P.M.'s protégé. Some people think

[21]

the P.M. has been grooming him to take over some day. Quentin had only been in Parliament two years when he was made a junior Minister. If there were any overseas junkets, he was always on them. Then when the last High Commissioner in London died suddenly, Quentin was sent there. It's a diplomatic post, but it's always filled by a politician. Either as a reward for past services or as a build-up for bigger things. Quentin is obviously meant for bigger things." Then he corrected himself: "Or was."

Malone felt the light beginning to filter through; the atmosphere in Flannery's office had fogged up his mind, but now he was out in the open again. "So with the Federal elections coming up in July, with the voting as close as they expect it to be—a nice juicy scandal could tip the scales, is that the idea?"

"Elections have been won and lost on less. All Labour has to do is query the P.M.'s judgment of the men he appoints. He's made one or two poor choices as Ministers. Add this one and Labour will ask if he really should be in charge of the country."

"Somehow it's a bastard of a way to decide a country's future."

"You should read more history, Scobie. That look of pain you sometimes see on a politician's face has been caused by a stab in the back. Some of the most honoured men in history were very good with the knife."

"But Flannery, he's not thinking of going into Federal politics, is he?"

"Of course not. He's king here in New South Wales. Why would he want to go down to Canberra, just be one of the princes? No, this is just a personal feud between him and the P.M."

"And Quentin—what's he? The shuttlecock?"

"He's a murderer, Scobie. That's all you have to think of him."

They had reached the entrance to the shabby old tenement that was Police Headquarters. Amid the blinding dazzle of the steel-and-glass cliffs that surrounded it, it looked like an ancient monument of dubious origin, perhaps the only building ever erected by the aborigines. The law in Australia had always been the poor cousin of government; what right had a copper to be comfortable? They went into the musty lobby and ascended in the antique lift that creaked like the machinery of law itself.

As they got out of the lift Leeds handed Malone the file. "Read that, then bring it back to me. Keep the carbon of it, you might need it in London, but don't let anyone here see it. It's top secret. At least it is for another week. Then I shouldn't be surprised if Flannery has posters made of it and stuck up all over Sydney."

Malone took the file and went looking for an empty office. Most of the staff were out at lunch, but he himself had no appetite for food just now. Disturbed by what he had witnessed and been told this morning, excited by the sudden prospect of his first trip abroad, he wanted only to get into this case at once. He found an empty room, sat down in one of the uncomfortable chairs, opened the file and began his acquaintance with John Quentin, born Corliss, ambassador and murderer.

3

In a comfortable chair in a luxury apartment on the other side of the world, Madame Cholon looked out at the soft London drizzle and nodded her head emphatically.

"The man to kill," she said, "is the Australian High Commissioner."

The three men with her said nothing. Two of them had learned not to answer her till she looked directly at them for comment; the third, Pallain, was still feeling his way with her. She stood up and, the silk legs of her tailored slacks hissing together, she crossed to stand at the window. Down the road the Science Museum bulked like a dark cliff through the grey rain; Kensington was slowly being washed off the map. She had been in England a month now and she hated its greyness, its wetness and its cold. She shivered and pulled up the collar of her cashmere cardigan.

"This conference is not going the way we want it." She spoke French, in a high soft voice, for the benefit of Pallain; she knew that he could speak Vietnamese, but she had never heard him speak anything but French or English. He was a snob, but she was sometimes that herself. "Something has to be done to disrupt it. This man Quentin is the one who is now dominating it, so he is the obvious one to be eliminated." Below her in the street an ice cream van went slowly by, its bell tinkling with ridiculous optimism in the cold grey day. What optimists the English were, always confident the sun was about to shine! She preferred the French, with their cynicism and their pessimism; one always knew where one stood with pessimists. She turned back to the three men, all of them with at least a strain of French blood in them. "Do you not agree?"

Pallain scratched the stubble of beard that always began to appear on his face at this time of day. He had more French in him than the other two men: his father had been a hairy sergeant from Carcassonne who had died in the mud at Dien Bien Phu, leaving behind him a twenty-year-old son whose birth he regretted as much as his own death. "I don't see the point of killing the Australian."

Madame Cholon sighed, not attempting to hide her impatience with Pallain's lack of imagination. Legs still hissing like singing snakes, she came back and sat down. "If he is killed, who is going to be accused of it? Not us, because no one knows of us. But everyone else with an interest in our country will be suspected. The Americans will accuse the Chinese and vice versa. The same with the South Vietnamese

[24]

and the Viet Cong, the Catholics and the Buddhists. Why, even General de Gaulle might be suspected!" Her smooth schoolgirl's face showed a schoolgirl's spiteful humour. "And as soon as suspicion sets in, that is the end of the usefulness of the conference. It will be adjourned, just like so many other conferences. The war may stumble on, but there will be no real government in Saigon, just as there has not been for the past two years. Anarchy is the climate we want."

"It may not be easy," said Pallain. "I mean, killing the Australian."

The other two men nodded. Truong Tho and Pham Chinh were both small men, and the French blood in them was two generations old and poor vintage at that. They were not strangers to murder, but they were strangers to London and the big city made them ill at ease and even a little frightened.

"I love to gamble," said Madame Cholon. "But I do not think the odds in this case have to be against us."

The three men knew whom the betting would be against: themselves, not Madame Cholon. Pallain said, "London has a very clean record when it comes to assassination."

"Then it is time its record was spoiled. The English are too smug about their dull way of life. Reading their newspapers, one would think the rest of the world was made up of barbarians."

Pallain hid his smile, recognizing a barbarian when he saw one and being afraid of her. "How soon do you want Quentin—er—eliminated?" He wanted to smile again, embarrassed by the gangster phrase. He had spent all his adult life with gangsters of one sort or another, but he read Racine and dreamed of a life among people such as Proust had known. "We shall have to make plans."

"Naturally," said Madame Cholon, her voice tart with contempt for the dullards she had to employ. In the street below she heard the tinkling of the ice cream van's bell, and in her homesick ear it sounded like an echo of the temple bells along the Mekong River. She looked out the window again, saw the thin explosion of sun behind the range of clouds far away to the west, and felt her own sudden flash of optimism. "One does not kill a man without making plans."

CHAPTER TWO

1

John James Quentin (Corliss):
Born: Tumbarumba, New South Wales, July 15, 1915.
Parents: Peter Corliss and Ida Fahey Corliss died in car accident October 12, 1925. Corliss, only child, then raised by aunt, Mira Fahey, spinster, who died January 22, 1934.

Corliss moved to Sydney February 1934, joined Metropolitan Water, Sewerage and Drainage Board as trainee surveyor.

Married Freda Wiseman, previously Weitzmann, August 20, 1936. No children of marriage. Weitzmann had arrived in Australia alone from Vienna January 1936. No relatives of hers have been traced.

Stabbed corpse of Freda Corliss discovered by neighbour December 9, 1941. One wound in right breast, inflicted by sewing scissors.

Corliss disappeared. Reappeared as John Quentin May 12, 1942, date of voluntary enlistment in Royal Australian Navy at Perth, Western Australia.

Married Sheila Redmond, daughter of Leslie Redmond and Elizabeth Cousins Redmond, both deceased, Perth, July 10, 1942. No children of marriage . . .

"Would you please fasten your seat belts? We shall be landing at London Airport—"

Malone closed the file and put it back in his briefcase. It was a comprehensive file, sixty pages thick, a monument to the diligence of the researcher. On the trip over Malone had read it three times, reading it at night when the passenger beside him, a talkative grandmother, had been asleep. She had got off at Zurich ("Then I'm going down to Rome. To see the Pope. I'm a Presbyterian myself, but we can't all be bigots, can we?"), and the seat beside Malone had since been empty. In this last half-hour, free from interruptions and the grandmother's inquisitive eye, he had been trying to memorize the summary that was attached to the file. The more he read, the more he could taste the relish with which the researcher had worked: he really had enjoyed the change from dry political statistics and trying to guess the voters' intentions. John Quentin (or Corliss) had been pinned to these pages like a dead butterfly.

But the researcher had, in the final analysis, failed. He had pinned a specimen to a board, described its history, illustrated some of its characteristics; but John Quentin was still no more than a name (or two names) and a collection of facts; the researcher had not discovered what made him tick. And Malone had begun to feel the first stirring of an unease that had not troubled him since he had been sent out, years ago, to make his first arrest. Over the years he had come to appreciate that the less you knew about a man, the less you were involved emotionally when it came time to bring him in. Now, however, a personality, like a faint watermark, was hidden behind the typed facts; and, despite himself, Malone was intrigued by it. And for a policeman that way could lead to headaches. Subjectivity, he had heard Leeds say, was as corrupting as money.

Twenty minutes later the immigration officer was looking at his passport. "Police officer? On duty, sir?"

Malone shook his head. "Holiday."

"Enjoy yourself."

"Thanks," said Malone, and wondered when he had last enjoyed an arrest. He could for a while hate a murderer who had committed a particularly horrible crime, the callous bashing of an old woman or the rape and killing of a young child; but later there would come the moments of doubt, the wonder at what had caused the flaw in the murderer. He didn't believe all of the psychiatrists' theories that the flaw in any man could be found in his childhood; he was old-fashioned enough to believe that some men were born bad. But why? he often asked himself, and left himself open to further questions that bothered him more than his colleagues suspected. He had often thought that he would have liked to work on the case of Cain. After that all other murder cases might have been simple.

The flight had been delayed for hours by storms in Zurich and now it was late afternoon as he rode in in the airport bus to London. He looked out at England, catching glimpses of it from the motorway. He had never dreamed of travelling the wide world; well aware of his insularity and able to smile at himself, he had always been content with Australia and what it offered him. He was no explorer. Columbus, Magellan, Cook were men who probably would never have been happy while there was an horizon to draw them. Up till now, at thirty-one, horizons had meant little to him.

But England now was not something beyond the horizon; it was here around him. He could feel his excitement and interest growing; it was a pity that he was going to have no more than a day or two here. Perversely he began to hope that Quentin might fight the warrant, might ask for extradition procedure. It would play hell with Australia's good name, but it would at least give Malone time to look at London. Then he cursed himself for his lack of patriotism. He was as hypocritical as Flannery.

[29]

He checked in at a hotel in Cromwell Road in Kensington. The affable Irish porter showed him to his room, talking a torrent all the way. "Ah, we get a lot of Aussies here at the hotel, sir. It must be a grand country, the numbers of you that are always coming over here." Malone looked at the porter, but the latter wasn't being sarcastic, only Irish. "Would you be on business, sir?"

"No, holiday." Malone took out his notebook and looked at an address. "Is Belgrave Square far from here?"

The porter put down the bags. "Not far, sir. Was it an embassy you were wanting?" He had an Irishman's frank curiosity: no one in Mullinahone had had any secrets.

"No. Just friends."

The porter's eyebrows went up. "It's a posh area, that it is, sir."

"I have posh friends."

The Irishman recognized the rebuff: some Aussies were just like the bloody English, keeping everything to themselves. He gave Malone directions on how to get to Belgrave Square and went out of the room, wondering why a man who stayed in a thirty-bob bed-and-breakfast room and who gave only a shilling tip should have posh friends in Belgravia.

Malone, a relaxed man who could sleep anywhere, even in an economy-class airplane seat, was not tired by the long flight from Australia. He showered, changed into the light grey suit he had brought as a concession to the English summer, looked at his watch and decided to go and see Quentin at once. He had already made up his mind that he would confront Quentin with the arrest warrant at his home and not at his office at Australia House. He had never arrested a public official before and he did not want to be too public about it. Seven o'clock. The High Commissioner would probably be home now, doing whatever ambassadors did in their off-duty moments, having a bath, having a drink, wondering why they hadn't taken up something easy like mountaineering or gun-running. It must be a bastard of a life, Malone thought: even the small diplomacies of a policeman's life were difficult enough. But soon it would be over for Quentin.

Riding in the taxi towards Belgravia Malone tried to rehearse what he would say to Quentin; and after a while gave up. How did you face a man, secure in a new life and a new identity, almost impregnable behind the importance of his office, with a crime that was distant in time and place, ten thousand miles and twenty-three years from here and now? "Your Excellency, in regard to an ancient murder . . ." Malone gazed out of the window of the taxi, trying to make his mind a blank, trusting that the right words would come by instinct when the moment arrived. Habit, sometimes, was a comfort.

The taxi pulled in before the big four-storied house. Malone got out and, conditioned by another habit, paid the driver the exact amount on the meter.

"You Aussies," said the driver, an economist from Bethnal Green. "I bet you don't have any balance of payments deficit."

Malone, who had never tipped a taxi driver in his life, looked at the man blankly. "Get lost," said the latter, and drove off, gnashing his gears instead of his teeth.

Malone shrugged, beginning to appreciate why someone had once written that the English were incomprehensible, and turned towards the house. He was surprised at its size; he was a long way from the five-room house in Erskineville where he had grown up. Then he looked at the other houses in the square and saw that some of them were even bigger; this square was a manifestation of living that he had only read about. This was diplomatic territory; above almost every entrance there jutted a white flagpole, like a single blunt-tipped mammoth's tusk; the huge front doors had the magnificent discouragement of a butler's façade. The heavily elegant cliff-faces of the houses hid secrets that exercized the British government; but none of them held such a secret as this house behind him. He turned, hesitated, then pressed the bell firmly.

2

The door was opened by a butler, something Malone had never experienced in his life before. He had all the appearance of the butlers Malone had seen in films: tall, portly, his aristocratic nose pushed back by a smell not apparent to men with less sensitive olfactory organs. But when he spoke his rich purple voice had a foreign tinge to it, and at once Malone thought he had come to the wrong address.

"Is this the home of the Australian High Commissioner?"

"It is, sir. May we ask whom you wish to see?" Monarchs and butlers, Malone thought: who else has the right to speak in the royal plural?

"The High Commissioner. My name is Malone and I have a special message for him from the Premier of New South Wales."

The butler looked suspiciously at him, then stood aside, opening the door wider. Malone stepped into an entrance hall and waited while the butler, like a bishop on his way to the altar, did a slow march towards the rear of the house. Though the hall was only sparsely furnished, Malone was at once aware that he was on the close outskirts of luxury. Through a half-open door he caught a glimpse of a room that reminded him of illustrations he had seen in *Vogue*, a periodical that had once been delivered by mistake to the Murder Squad and reduced the officers there to a state of depressed inferiority. He turned his head and saw himself in a huge gilt-frame mirror: he looked at the stranger there who seemed so out of place. He shifted his feet nervously in the thick carpet of the hall, feeling as awkward as a three-legged colt. Suddenly he wanted this business of Quentin over and done with quickly. He would come back in his old age and look at London.

The butler came back down the hall with a girl. He stood aside, watchful as an old sea lion; images kept flashing through Malone's mind, but he could not see the butler as just a man like himself. The girl came forward.

"I am the High Commissioner's secretary." She, too, had a slight accent. Stone the bloody crows, Malone thought, whatever happened to the Australian accent? "What was it you wanted?"

"I have a personal message from the Premier of New South Wales." He had no such thing; but he had not expected it to be so difficult to get in to see Quentin.

"A letter?"

"No, it's verbal."

"I'm sorry, but the High Commissioner is busy. Could you not come to Australia House tomorrow?"

Malone shook his head, trying not to appear too stubborn. He liked the look of the girl: tall, good-looking, blonde, and with a poise about her that he had looked for in the girls he had known and had so rarely found. But he sensed her impatience with him and he was aware of the cold disapproving eye of the butler. "The message is urgent and important."

The girl looked at the butler, and Malone read the message that passed between them. They think I'm some crank! He was appalled at the idea, remembering his own impatience as a policeman with cranks. His hand moved towards his pocket to take out his identification badge. Then his hand dropped back to his side and he smiled to himself at the situation and his own reaction to it.

"Perhaps if you told the High Commissioner that the message concerns Tumbarumba, he might see me."

"Tumbarumba?" The girl was now convinced she was dealing with a crank.

"It's a town, not a disease." This comes of employing foreigners, Malone thought; and began to feel more xenophobic by the minute. He had always been tolerant of the foreign migrants who had come to Australia, even those he had had to arrest; but now these two foreigners, the girl and the butler, were beginning to annoy him with their attitude towards him. Deep inside him he knew that, regardless of their accents, they were only doing their job of trying to protect the High Commissioner from uninvited and unwanted guests. But they were also trying to prevent him from doing *his* job, one that he wanted finished as soon as possible. He was out of his depth here, in alien territory no matter that his country's ambassador lived here, and he wanted to be on the plane at once for Sydney, home and an atmosphere where he didn't have to be so secretive. He said sharply, "Just tell the High Commissioner that I've come from Tumbarumba."

The girl raised an eyebrow, as if recognizing for the first time that Malone was accustomed to some authority. Without a word, but with a nod of warning to the butler, she turned and went back along the hall. Malone and the butler stood watching each other in the huge mirror: they were posed in the gilt frame like a tableau titled "Suspicion." Then the girl came back.

"This way, Mr.—"

"Malone."

"Mr. Malone. The High Commissioner will see you." Her poise had been cracked a little; there was no mistaking the surprise she felt that the Ambassador had agreed to see this crank.

She led Malone down the hall, pushed open a door and stood aside. "Mr. Malone, sir, from Tumbarumba."

"We are not to be disturbed, Lisa," said the man standing in front of the marble-fronted fireplace. "By *anyone*."

The girl closed the door. Malone, feeling more awkward

[34]

than he had ever felt in his life before, stood watching the man across the room from him. He had checked on newspaper photographs of Quentin; but they had not done the man justice. He was taller than Malone had expected, and slimmer. His thick wavy hair, brushed close to his head, and his military moustache were grey, but somehow they did not add age to his lean high-cheeked face; Malone would have guessed him to be at least five to six years younger than the age that showed against him in the file. The wide sensitive mouth looked as if it knew the exercises of humour, and the dark blue eyes looked as if they, too, could smile with enjoyment. But not now: eyes and mouth were both stiff with suspicion.

"What is it, Mr. Malone?" Quentin's voice, Malone guessed, would normally have been deep and pleasant. Now it was strained, a little high: the Australian accent was evident, the vowels flattened. "My secretary said you were from Tumbarumba."

"I'm from Sydney, sir. Detective-sergeant Malone." He produced his badge, glad of the opportunity to do so; for the time being there was no longer any need for secrecy. "I'm sorry, Mr. Quentin, but I have a warrant for your arrest for the murder of your wife Freda."

Quentin, for all the stiff suspicion in his face, had been standing at ease before the fireplace. Now all at once he seemed to wilt: years piled into his face like grey blood and he looked his age and more. Behind his head an ormolu clock ticked like a bomb; but the bomb had already gone off. The lips, as grey now as the moustache above them, grimaced in a thin smile.

"Tumbarumba—what a password!"

"I had to try something, sir. Your secretary is quite a watchdog."

"But not quite good enough. I should have warned her about policemen." He put his hands together in front of his

[35]

face and bowed his head like a man in prayer. Malone had
seen many reactions to arrest and he had never got over his
embarrassment at some of them. He just hoped Quentin was
not going to start praying out loud. But then Quentin looked
up and his mouth was twisted in the same thin grimace of
a smile. "I've often wondered what I would say to you when
you came. Somehow it was a speech that never got written.
And I'm said to be a very good speaker."

"I'd save it for the trial, sir. I'm supposed to warn you—"

"I know, Sergeant. But anything I may say now won't
help you very much. You wouldn't be here unless you had a
watertight case. You don't go around arresting ambassadors
to keep up your monthly quota, do you?" He smiled without rancour. As quickly as he had wilted he was now becoming philosophical. His voice had deepened, come under control again; the Australian accent was still there but less evident, the vowels were being given their full value. He moved
towards a side table on which stood a decanter and glasses.
"A sherry? Or don't you drink on duty?"

"Where I grew up, sir, sherry isn't considered a drink.
It's something you flavour jelly or trifle with."

"You are looking a gift prisoner in the mouth, Sergeant.
But I admire your sense of occasion. Sherry is for vicars and
old ladies." He smiled again, a much warmer smile. He put
down the decanter without taking the stopper from it, pulled
a long tasseled cord hanging beside the fireplace. When he
turned back the smile had waned. "I must have grown up
in the same sort of circles as you, Sergeant. A pity I ever left
them. I wonder what Tumbarumba is like now?"

There was a knock at the door and the butler opened it.
Quentin ordered Scotch, then turned back to Malone as the
door closed again. He stared at the detective for a long moment, then moved to a high-backed leather armchair and
sat down, slowly and a little wearily. He gestured at the room
about him, and Malone, looking about him for the first time,

[36]

saw that it was a small library. Books lined three of the walls: leather-bound volumes, large illustrated books, bright-jacketed novels, somber-titled non-fiction: Quentin, or someone in the house, had a wide taste in reading. The fourth wall held some sporting prints: spindle-shanked horses straddled hedges, a fighter in long underwear posed behind bare fists and a walrus moustache. On a small desk a woman looked with calm eyes from out of a silver frame: she looked out of place beneath the sporting prints, too much of a lady.

"This is my retreat. A diplomat doesn't get much time to himself and he needs somewhere where he can lock himself away for an hour or so every day, just so he can be himself. All day every day, and every night too, almost, you're being someone else. Mr. Australia, if you like, or whatever country you represent. You need some time each day just so you can check your own identity, make sure there's some of the original man left." He sighed and looked up at Malone, still standing awkwardly in the middle of the room. "I've spent almost twenty-four years trying to lose the original man. John Corliss, that is. How did you get on to him?"

Malone told him about the political research worker. "I don't know who gave them the tip-off. It could have been someone who recognized you from years ago."

Quentin nodded. "It's been a long wait. Somehow I always knew the day would come. I've changed in appearance. My hair went grey during the war, then afterwards I grew this moustache. But you never feel you've really changed, you see yourself from the inside—"

They were interrupted by the return of the butler with the drinks. "Madame asks will you be long, sir?"

"Not long, Joseph." Quentin waited till the butler had gone out of the room. He poured himself and Malone a drink each, both of them strong: he seemed to take for granted that Malone was as much in need of sustenance as himself.

[37]

Malone, grateful for the drink, didn't contradict him. "When this matter comes out into the open, Joseph is the one who's going to disapprove of me more than anyone else. There's no snob like a butler, and a Hungarian butler is the worst of the lot."

"I wondered about his accent. And your secretary's, too." Malone held up his glass, then lowered it. "Sorry. I was going to drink to your health."

Quentin smiled wryly. "Thank you. I'm glad they sent a man with some sensitivity." He raised his own glass and they drank silently to each other. Then Quentin said, "Yes, about my secretary. She's Dutch. A Dutch New Australian. She was out there for seven or eight years. Joseph's never been there and somehow I gather he's glad of the fact. I inherited him from my predecessor. I think he still expects to be asked some day to serve witchetty grubs and fried ants." He sipped his drink, then took a swift gulp, put down the glass and looked up at Malone. "I'm just talking, Sergeant. Putting off the evil moment or whatever it is. What's the next move?"

Malone told him. "We'd like it if it can be done as quietly as possible. I can get an extradition order from the court here if you insist—"

Quentin waved a long-fingered hand. "There won't be any need for that. I'll go quietly, as the saying is."

"Could you be ready to leave tomorrow?"

Quentin's chin shot up. "*When?* Sergeant, don't you read the newspapers? I'm in the middle of a conference, an important one—"

"I know, sir." Malone sipped his own drink, hating more and more each minute this task he had been given. He still stood in the middle of the room, feeling as insecure as if he were the one who was being arrested. "But I'm afraid I haven't been given much discretion in the matter. They want you back in Sydney at once."

[38]

"Who does? The police? Or is it Flannery?" Malone hesitated, then nodded. Quentin barked angrily and went on: "That malicious conniving old bastard! You know why he's doing this, don't you?"

"I had it explained to me."

"Not by him, I'll bet!" Quentin got up and began to walk about the room, angrily, agitatedly; all his poise had left him, the past had caught him up, was riding his back like a savage monkey. The ormolu clock struck the half-hour and was echoed somewhere out in the hall by a deeper note. Quentin stopped, looked at the clock, then shrugged, as if time meant nothing now. But when he spoke again, his voice was still harsh, the flat accent back again. This was the voice he must have had twenty-odd years ago, Malone thought: the original man was always there in the tongue. "He'd be too shrewd to commit himself that far in front of a stranger. You are a stranger to him, aren't you?"

"Very much so." And glad to stay that way: Malone took another drink, washing away a taste that had been with him all the way from Sydney.

Quentin turned and looked directly at Malone. "Sergeant, I can't afford to leave here for at least another four or five days. This conference, you know what it's about, trying to settle a cease-fire in Vietnam, it's much more important than me or Flannery." He hesitated, then his voice hoarsened: "Or even my dead first wife."

Malone put down his glass on a nearby table. It was time to show some authority, to get started for home. "I appreciate all that. But it's not my decision—"

"Whose is it?"

Malone hesitated. "The Commissioner's, I suppose."

"Get on to him, phone him. Tell him I promise to come quietly, but I must stay here till this conference is finished."

"How do you know it will be finished in four or five days?"

Quentin gestured, a motion that already suggested lack

[39]

of real hope. "If it isn't—well, Vietnam then will have about as much future as I have. We'll both have reached the end of our roads."

"Why is it so important that you stay?"

Quentin was patient. "I'm Australia's leading representative at the conference. In the normal course of events it would be our Minister for External Affairs, but he's still in Canberra, ill. None of the other Cabinet Ministers know as much about Southeast Asia as I do—some of them know nothing about it. So I was pitched into the job." There was a note of regret in his voice: Malone couldn't tell whether he regretted being handed the job or being taken away from it. He looked at Malone, still patient, sounding as if it were a long time since he had talked to an ordinary man in the street: "How much do you know about international politics?"

"Not much," Malone admitted. "A policeman's problems are usually too close to home. It's hard to get any sort of perspective. Or find time to be interested, come to that."

"That's the way it is with about ninety per cent of the world's population. They read the papers, but they don't really care. A nice juicy murder—" He stopped and shook his head as if he had suddenly been hit a blow. "That's what they'll get next week, isn't it?"

It was Malone's turn to be patient: "You were explaining to me about this conference."

"Oh yes. Yes. Well—" He drew in his breath, regained control of himself: his powers of recovery were quick and remarkable. "There are several interests who don't want a cease-fire in Vietnam. If this conference could be interrupted, adjourned, even called off altogether, nothing would please them more. I'm not boasting, Sergeant, but I think I'm the one at this conference that the other delegates are listening to. Everybody at it has opinions, but too many of them are waiting for someone else to make the moves that might bring about peace terms. For better or worse, I look like being the man. By the end of this week I think I can swing them to some sort of terms for a cease-fire, one that should satisfy both sides. For the time being, anyway. In another year or two they may be back at each other's throats again. Maybe even America and China will be in there in a full-scale war. I don't know. But we'll have bought some more time, thrown the military mind out of step while we try and see if the diplomatic mind can accomplish anything. Diplomacy has been down-graded these last few years since the generals have been given so much say in certain countries. I think it's time we showed it's not a dead method of working." There was a knock on the door, but he ignored it. "That's what I want to buy from your Commissioner—some time."

Before Malone could answer, the door opened. "I'm sorry, John, but shall I have Lisa call them and tell them we can't come?"

The woman who stood in the doorway was the most beautiful Malone had ever seen: the photograph on the desk had not done her justice. Perhaps it had something to do with the way she was dressed; none of the girls he had known back home had ever looked so elegant. She was not tall, but she gave the impression of tallness; she held herself erect, almost with a touch of imperiousness. He could only guess at her age, but he knew she must be in her early forties: she had married Quentin twenty-three years ago. But the erosion of age had not yet got at her, you knew she would look as beautiful as this for another ten years at least. The dark auburn hair, shining like metal; the complexion that looked as if it would be impregnable to the slow ivy-growth of wrinkles; the hazel eyes with their heavy lids: Malone, looking at her, knew she would protect those assets with a fierce pride, fighting age with more determination than most women. Then she smiled at him and the image of imperious-

[41]

ness and pride was suddenly gone, as if it had been no more than a trick of eyesight.

"I hope you will excuse me for interrupting—"

"Darling, this is Mr. Malone. From Canberra." Malone looked at Quentin, but the latter had moved forward to take the woman's hand. "This is my wife, Mr. Malone."

Malone put out his hand. "Pleased to meet you, Mrs. Quentin."

Sheila Quentin gave him her hand and smiled again. "And I'm pleased to meet you, Mr. Malone. Are you here to stay in London or just visiting?"

"Just visiting," said Malone, and glanced at Quentin.

"He's here till the end of the conference." Quentin was relaxed, almost casual; Malone could have been a minor government official who had called to pay his respects. "He's been sent with some new advice."

"Oh? Are you an expert on Vietnam, Mr. Malone?"

"Not exactly." Malone wondered what Quentin's game was, but he decided to play along for the time being. It was a question he would not have dared to offer advice on: when you were arrested for murder, how and when did you tell your wife? "You might say I'm a legal expert. I know how far you can go in the prevention of certain things."

Quentin's lips twitched, but he didn't smile. "We'll be another ten minutes, darling, no more. There's no need to have Lisa call."

"Good night, Mr. Malone. Perhaps we'll meet again before you leave London." She went out, her long green gown rustling like dead leaves in the quiet room.

The silence lasted for almost a minute after the door closed. Malone had become accustomed to silences; it was remarkable the number of men who remained dumb when you arrested them for a serious crime. But Quentin was not dumb because of his arrest: he was staring at the closed door, obviously wondering what effect his arrest would have on

[42]

his wife, whether she would be struck dumb or would collapse in loud hysterics. Somehow Malone did not think there would be any hysterics from Mrs. Quentin: there would be something more terrible, a cold rage at himself for what he represented, for what he had done to her husband. He had seen the look that had passed between the Quentins: they were deeply in love with each other. And he knew from experience that a woman in love never saw the merits of justice.

At last Quentin said, "You're wondering why I didn't tell her who you really are? I've been rehearsing the words on and off for years. *Darling, this is the policeman who's come to arrest me for the murder of my first wife, the one you know nothing about.* I'm a politician and a diplomat, Sergeant, supposedly skilled in all the uses of words. How do you deliver such a message to the wife you love dearly?"

Malone shook his head. He had had many awkward and distressing messages to deliver, but never to someone he loved: he dealt in tragedy, but remained outside it: he was like the heroin dealer who lived the good clean life. "I don't want to have to tell her myself—"

"You won't have to. When the time comes, I'll tell her. I'm not a coward." Then he bit his lip and turned away. "Or maybe I am. Always have been."

"Do you still want me to phone the Commissioner? I mean, I don't want to take you away from this conference if you feel—"

Quentin looked at his watch. "It'll be almost five o'clock in the morning out there. Do you want to phone him at his home?"

"How soon could I get through?"

"I can get you a priority." He smiled wryly; from now on all jokes would be against himself. "I may not have that privilege much longer."

Malone checked Leeds' home phone number from his

[43]

notebook and gave it to Quentin. The latter picked up the phone and dialled. "This is the Australian High Commissioner at—" He gave his own number. "I want a top-priority person-to-person call to Mr. John Leeds at—" He read from the notebook Malone held out to him. "Will you ring back, confirming and telling me how long it will be?"

He hung up the phone and Malone said, "If the Commissioner okays this, you know I can't let you out of my sight for those four or five days. Technically you're already under arrest."

"I wonder if I could get the P.M. to put up bail for me?" Again he smiled wryly; then he said, "You won't trust me?"

"Don't put it like that, Mr. Quentin."

"I'm sorry." He looked curiously at Malone. "I have the feeling you're not enjoying this assignment. Am I right?"

"There's a lot of police work I don't enjoy. We're not all bastards, you know." Malone held back. He was coming to like this man more than he should. Flannery had been right: *He's not a bad bloke at all.*

"I suppose it's like politics."

"And diplomacy, too?"

Quentin looked at him, then nodded. "Everything is compromise. Only the saints escape, and they never go into politics or diplomacy."

"Or police work," said Malone, and after a slight hesitation both men smiled at each other.

The phone rang and Quentin picked it up. After a few words he looked at Malone. "The call will be through in twenty minutes."

"I hope for your sake he's in a good humor at five o'clock in the morning."

"Not for my sake," said Quentin, hanging up the phone. "That's not why I'm asking for the extra time."

"Sorry," said Malone, and began to wonder what sort of

man Quentin had been twenty-three years ago when he had murdered his wife.

"I have to get dressed now. There's a reception at one of the African embassies. Do you want to come with me to that?"

"Am I dressed for it?"

Quentin looked at the very pale grey suit, the blue nylon shirt and the green-figured tie that looked like an aunt's present. "At the risk of offending you, Sergeant, I don't think you're dressed for *anything* in London. Where do you buy your clothes back home?"

Malone grinned: he had been criticized many times before for his lack of interest in clothes. "The first shop I come to. I've never been much of a dresser."

"I admire your modesty, but you certainly speak the truth. Have you ever worn tails?" Malone shook his head. "You're going to tonight. We're about the same size, you can wear my spare set. What size shoes do you take?"

"Eight and a half. I haven't got policemen's feet."

"The same size as mine. You can step into my shoes tonight, Sergeant, have a look at my world. You might understand why I'm going to be reluctant to leave it. It has its drawbacks, but I enjoy it."

Malone began to protest. "Look, I don't want to crowd you, sir—I'll wait outside—"

"I feel I owe you something, Sergeant—" He gestured at the phone. "If I'm to keep you here in London longer than you expected, I'll see you get more out of it than waiting around in doorways."

"What will your wife say? I mean about lending me your clothes? Won't she ask some awkward questions?"

"My wife trusts me, Sergeant. She never asks too many questions. A diplomat's wife learns not to." Then he sighed. "There'll be enough questions after I've told her who you really are."

[45]

CHAPTER THREE

1

"He has discovered the elixir of adolescence," said the donnish-looking Labour M.P. "Any day now I'm expecting him to call the House dining room the tuck shop."

"He is the sort of African who wears his colour on his sleeve," said the light-skinned Indian.

"Her intelligence, my dear, is second to anyone's you care to name," said the wife of the junior Foreign Office man.

"Australia, I'm told, is the world's largest suburb," said the man from Commonwealth Relations.

Malone almost popped the stud of his collar as he heard the last remark. He was about to move forward to break up Commonwealth Relations when a restraining hand caught his arm.

"Ignore them, Mr. Malone. Diplomatic receptions are very much like women's tea parties, only a little more elegant and epigrammatic." Lisa Pretorious stood beside him, her tanned shoulders and arms offset by the pale pink of her gown. A South American second secretary went by, all teeth and wink, and she gave him a cool smile that was both an acknowledgment and a rebuff. "Don't you go to them in Canberra?"

[46]

Malone shook his head. "I'm known back home for my undiplomatic behaviour, so I'm never invited."

"They should invite you. You look quite decorative in tails." She looked him up and down. "I'm quite proud to have you as my escort. When Mr. Quentin suggested it—"

"You thought I'd be wearing my own suit?" She nodded, and now it was his turn to look her up and down. "Don't you diplomatic types ever blush? You've just insulted me—"

"I'm not a diplomatic type, I'm just a private secretary. But one learns the tricks. Any diplomat who blushed would be out of a job at once."

"You could be a little more diplomatic in telling me I've got no taste."

"Mr. Malone, I was born in Holland and I've spent seven years in Australia—my formative years, if you like to call them that. What sort of training is that for subtlety?" Suddenly he laughed and she smiled in return. "That grey suit of yours is pretty awful, you know. You looked like an unsuccessful race course tipster. I think you should understand why I was so suspicious of you, why I didn't want you to see the High Commissioner."

"What's he like to work for?" Malone asked the question idly, just to keep the conversation going: he was enjoying the company of this good-looking, frank girl. Then he regretted the question: he was already becoming too interested in Quentin.

"The best boss I've ever had. I've been a doctor's receptionist, secretary to an advertising man, a guide on a conducted tour of Europe, oh, and several other things. I'd never done anything like this till I came to work for Mr. Quentin." She looked about the crowded room that moved like a wind-ruffled pool under the crystal sun of the huge chandelier. Conversation floated like a swarm of butterflies: words were coloured, had a polish and exoticism about them that Malone had never heard before. "I don't think

[47]

I'd want to do anything else now. I hope Mr. Quentin remains High Commissioner for years."

Across the room Malone saw Quentin and his wife moving slowly from group to group, from Africa to Asia to the Americas: everywhere they were greeted with genuine smiles of welcome. "Is he popular?"

She nodded. "He's considered to be the best man Australia's ever had in London. But I don't think they really appreciate that back home."

"No," he said, and tried not to load his voice. He looked at her, changing the subject quickly: "You're Dutch, but you think of Australia as home, do you?"

"My parents are settled there, in Melbourne. They'll never come back to Europe. So I look on Australia as home. One needs roots somewhere."

"I guess so," said Malone, and wondered where Quentin thought of his roots as being planted. Tumbarumba, Sydney, Perth, Canberra, London: the man had been on the run all his life.

Then a thin elderly woman, throttled by pearls, was squeezed out of the crowd like a magician's trick. She greeted Lisa with a hoarse whinny.

"Lady Porthleven, may I present Mr. Malone?"

"Pleased to meet you," said Malone.

"Oh, really?" Lady Porthleven looked surprised: no one had ever actually *told* her he was pleased to meet her. Then she drew Lisa back into the crowd with her, leaving Malone well aware of the fact that he was on the outside.

He looked about the room. Jewels glittered like angry eyes; decorations were bleeding wounds on breasts. A Pakistani and a Bolivian went by, continents arm in arm; Italy flirted with Iran, and an international bed was already beginning to bounce. A string quartet was playing somewhere in an alcove, working its laboured way through a medley:

[48]

even the requests at the Grand at Brighton had never been as demanding as this. The colours of the women's gowns, Western, Eastern, African, both pleased and pained the eye: Malone felt the effects of visual gluttony. He stood irresolute for a moment, suddenly tired, wanting to shout at the crowd to go to hell: no wonder Australians disliked bloody foreigners. Then he grinned and shook his head. He *was* an outsider here. He was discovering for the first time what it was like to be a foreigner.

"Don't get too involved over there," Leeds had said on the phone when the call had come through. "I'll see what Flannery says about the extra time Quentin has asked for. I'll try and talk him into it. But don't forget, Scobie—you're a policeman on duty for all those extra days."

"I know, sir. Polite but impersonal."

"That's the ticket. I'll call you back in four hours' time, let you know the score. Where will you be staying?" Malone had put his hand over the phone and repeated the question to Quentin. Then he had said, "Mr. Quentin says I can stay here at his house. They have several guest rooms."

"Don't be a guest, Scobie. Or anyway, don't act like one. But I guess you'll have to stay there to keep an eye on him. I'll ring you. This is getting to be a bigger bastard of a situation all the time."

Then Malone had followed Quentin upstairs, where Joseph, the butler, had taken him over. "This is your room, sir. Some very distinguished gentlemen have stayed here."

Malone had glanced about the room: even here he was in the midst of discreet elegance. It was a room designed for a male guest: antique pistols hung on one wall, the chair and the dressing-table accessories were leather-backed, even the air smelled as if it had been sprayed with some masculine air freshener. Only the carpet had a feminine luxury about it: Malone felt bogged down in its deep soft pile. An over-

[49]

night room for the rich and the distinguished: Malone remembered some of the closets with bed in which he had slept when sent to country towns on a case.

"The tone will be lowered tonight," Malone had said, but Joseph had said nothing: one didn't joke about a self-evident truth.

When he was dressed Malone had looked at himself in the long mirror and been impressed by what he saw. The coat was a little tight under the arms, but otherwise everything might have been tailored for him. Even the shoes had fit, but he had felt a momentary doubt when pulling them on: was this how you felt when stepping into a dead man's shoes?

He had gone downstairs and Quentin, his wife and Lisa Pretorious had been waiting in the hall for him.

"You look most distinguished, Mr. Malone," Sheila Quentin had said, and Malone had felt a youthful glow of pleasure: he had never expected in all his life to be called distinguished.

He had looked at Joseph, standing nearby, and winked; but the butler had not moved a muscle. *I should arrest that bastard,* Malone thought, *for insulting a police officer.* Then he had glanced at Quentin and the humour in him had been doused. The High Commissioner, handsome and distinguished though *he* was, looked exhausted, a man who had all at once begun to age. Looking at the tall grey-haired man in the beautifully cut dress suit, Malone felt he was looking at a corpse dressed for a wedding instead of a funeral: someone had got the dates wrong.

"Would you be kind enough to escort Miss Pretorious?" Sheila Quentin had said; and Malone had offered his arm to the cool lovely blonde who was looking at him with new, almost unbelieving, interest.

"If you'll have me," he said, as the Quentins had gone ahead of them out the front door to the waiting car.

"I wonder that Tumbarumba ever let you go," Lisa had said. He had looked quickly in front to see if the Quentins had heard the remark, but if they had neither of them showed any reaction. "I wouldn't have recognized you as the man I let in a while ago."

Her smile had taken the ice out of her remark. *But she knows I'm an outsider,* Malone had thought.

Now here at the reception he felt even more of an outsider. Then through an open arch he saw a waiter go past bearing a tray of food; his stomach reminded him he had not eaten for almost nine hours. He followed the waiter, easing his way through the groups of people with more politeness than he felt. He knew it was stupid to feel resentful because people didn't turn and welcome him with open arms. But he had been spoiled back in Sydney: there, even the crims had been friendly to him. Except when he came to arrest them.

The supper room was almost deserted but for a few disguised journalists pecking at the perks of the diplomatic social round, and two Negro men in evening dress.

"Enjoying yourself?" The older of the two men, tall and portly and cheerful, had a voice as rich as that of Quentin's butler; but he had none of the servant's snobbery, he was a man born to be friendly.

"Not much," said Malone with undiplomatic truthfulness; hunger always sharpened one's candour. Then he remembered that he was in an African embassy, that the men beside him were coloured. "Do you belong here?"

"I'm the Ambassador. I'm not enjoying it, either." He laughed, a deep gurgle of merriment that made jelly of his jowls. The younger Negro, lighter-skinned and thinner, smiled with more controlled humour. The Ambassador was piling a plate with food; he held a bouquet of crab, salad, tomato, celery. "But the food is good. Help yourself. Where are you from?"

"Australia," said Malone, and saw the younger Negro look at him with sudden interest.

"With Quentin? A splendid chap. I can even forgive him your White Australia policy. He'll be the one to make a success of this conference." He added a ribbon of mayonnaise to the bouquet in his hand. "If it's going to be a success."

"You don't think it will be?" Malone followed him round the table, using the Ambassador's plate as his own example: if a diplomat could be a hog, why not a plain policeman?

"Champagne? The wages of sin and diplomacy, Bollinger '55. Back in my country I'm expected to drink a concoction made out of tropical fruits. We call it Château-neuf-du-Papaya. Terrible stuff."

"Jungle juice," said the younger Negro in a soft American accent. "The Aussies used to make it and sell it to our guys in New Guinea."

"Really? I'm surprised you won the war. Well, now I have to find somewhere quiet to eat this." The Ambassador looked at the heaped plate, then winked a piebald eye at them both. "My father died of gluttony, a surfeit of underdone missionary. What a pity he didn't live to appreciate the fruits of independence."

He went rolling out of the room, chuckling to himself. Malone grinned and the younger Negro said, "His father went to Oxford, just as he did. Periodically he takes a course in atavism, to come down to the level of some of his politicians back home."

Malone steered clear of any racial comment: he wasn't sure that he was not being baited. "Do you work for him?"

"I'm like you, a guest here. The name is Jamaica."

"You're an American?"

Jamaica nodded. He might have been a handsome man had his face not been so *tight*: all his feeling towards the world was screwed in behind the closed defense of his face. The sculptured head, with its close-cropped hair and its stiff

[52]

dark features, reminded one of a helmet with its visor down: all Jamaica's pain, joy, hate and love would be his own secret.

"From Georgia." His voice was softly accented, but he had been gone a long time from Georgia. "I haven't seen you around before. Are you here just for the conference?"

Malone hesitated, then nodded. "I expect to be going back at the end of the week."

"You think it'll be finished by then?"

"Don't you?" Malone added Russian salad to his plate, hoping it would not indict him in the eyes of the American.

Jamaica shrugged. He wore his evening clothes with less ease than had the African; his jacket was too large and when he shrugged one shoulder slipped forward a little, as if he had dislocated it. *He's like me,* Malone thought, *he's wearing someone else's tail plumes.* "You know what conferences are like."

"I don't. This is my first."

Jamaica picked up a stick of celery, bit into it. Across the room the journalists watched attentively, their stares hidden behind their champagne glasses. Their dress suits were less expensive than those worn by the other guests, but they wore them with as much ease; most of them were middle-aged or elderly men who had been on this round for years. Malone, a policeman with little affection for newspapermen, looked at them and thought of them as vultures dressed as penguins. But Jamaica ignored them; all his attention was on Malone. The celery crackled in his mouth as he said, "Your man Quentin is a great one for compromise, isn't he?"

"You Americans don't like compromise, do you?"

"It was a European invention."

"You're wrong there, mate. I think it was the Chinese."

"The Chinese aren't interested in compromise now."

"That's the only thing you have in common. You two ought to get together." *Stone the crows, I'm talking like a bloody diplomat;* and Malone almost beamed with pleasure at his repartee. This was better than talking cricket scores and football results with the other blokes in the Murder Squad.

"You Australians aren't in a position to be too independent."

"No," said Malone, his plate at last full. "That's probably why Quentin is plumping for compromise."

"You'd better be careful." Jamaica's voice was even, toneless: you could read into it any emphasis you wished. Malone read a warning, close to a threat; and turned his head sharply to ask Jamaica what he meant. But the American was already walking away. "I'll see you around."

Malone stared after him. Why was the American so sour, what did he mean that Malone should be careful? Then Malone was aware of someone moving along the supper table towards him.

Across the room one of the journalists had taken a step forward, but had stopped when he saw the small Oriental woman in the yellow *ao dais* moving towards the Australian.

"Who's the woman?" the journalist whispered to one of his colleagues.

"Search me. But East is East and West is West—"

"Yes, I know. And quicker the twain should meet. But somehow I can't see them going for a concubine down in Chislehurst. And that's what she'd have to be. I already have a missus."

"We're backward here in Britain. We need a New Society."

At the supper table Malone had turned as the woman spoke to him. "You are an Australian, I believe? Are you here for the conference?"

Out of the corner of his eye Malone saw that Jamaica had halted for a moment beyond the doorway and looked back. Had he warned Malone to be careful of this woman? If so,

[54]

why? Malone looked down at the woman, tiny, beautiful, as dangerous-looking as a budgerigar.

"Sort of." He had never become adept at looking at a woman while pretending to look elsewhere; he gazed frankly at this woman with the schoolgirl's face. There was an innocence about her that seemed incongruous with the sophistication of the tight-fitting long gown she wore. The *ao dais* exposed almost nothing of her but a shimmer of leg, yet it was more revealing than any other gown Malone had seen tonight. But the woman had not cheapened herself: what her gown hinted at was not for sale at bargain prices. "My name's Malone. Pleased to meet you."

"Pleased to meet you—I have never heard that greeting before. It is so much friendlier than 'how do you do.' I am Madame Cholon." Malone put out his free hand. After a moment's hesitation Madame Cholon smiled and put her hand in his; it felt like the wing of a small bird and he pressed it with rough but gentle fingers. "You seem a very friendly man. One does not meet too many of those at receptions like this."

"I'm new here. I'll learn to be like the rest of them. Like something to eat?"

Eyed by the curious journalists, they moved out of the room on to a terrace that overlooked a large garden. Green lanterns bloomed in the trees and guests moved through the aqueous light like floating upright corpses. In the huge house the chatter of the reception buzzed like the sound of a plague of summer night insects; the effect was heightened by the sultry warmth of the evening. Beyond the garden London was only a dull gold reflection on the low clouds, silent as a faraway eruption.

"This road used to be called Millionaires' Row." Madame Cholon pointed to the house behind them, then to the mansions on either side. She picked with long-nailed fingers at a small bunch of grapes. "Then the embassies moved in

here. Governments are the only ones with money these days."
Malone noticed the sharp blade of resentment in her soft
high voice; this schoolgirl *could* be spiteful. "But then you
are a government man, are you not?"

"None of the money filters down as far as me."

"I have heard there is very little corruption in Australian
government. Where I come from, a man is suspect if he is
not corrupt."

Malone, his mouth full of crab and salad, said nothing. He
was ravenous, but he was doing his best not to look as if he
were shovelling the food into himself.

"I like to see a man eat." Madame Cholon bit delicately
at a grape as if it were a mango. "Men are always more honest about the sensual pleasures, do you not think so?"

Malone gulped, clearing his mouth. "I hadn't thought
about it. Are they like that where you come from? Where
do you come from?"

"Out East," said Madame Cholon, and Malone remarked
the evasiveness. He looked towards the doorway to see if
Jamaica was still watching them, but the American had disappeared.

"That covers a lot of territory, Out East."

"Yes, doesn't it?" said Madame Cholon, and smiled. She
ate another grape, spitting the seeds into her hand with
something of the peasant coarseness that occasionally showed
in her in the simpler bodily functions. She had seen this tall,
socially awkward man arrive with the Australian High Commissioner and she wondered if he would be returning to
Belgrave Square when Quentin returned there. Pallain,
Pham Chinh and Truong Tho would want as few witnesses
as possible when they killed Quentin.

"Do you gamble, Mr. Malone?"

Malone looked at her in surprise: he was finding it a little
difficult to keep up with this woman. All the girls he had
known had been straightforward, the sort that a confirmed

[56]

bachelor preferred: you knew where you stood with them. "Once or twice a year I might have a quid on a horse."

Betting on race horses: that was for peasants, like fantan and dice. "No, I mean chemin de fer or baccarat."

"Those games are illegal where I come from."

This was going to be harder than she had thought. Australia was beginning to sound like a country run by missionaries. "Don't you ever do anything illegal?"

"Not if I can help it," he said, and knew he must sound priggish. He waited for her to tell him so, but she was politer than Leeds had been. "Anyhow, what gambler ever finishes up in front?"

"Some of us do," she said, and her smile was secretive. "You should try your luck some time."

"Not at baccarat." He could see the headlines in Sydney *Truth:* COP DOES DOUGH AT BACCARAT. That would mean an early retirement, all right.

"I once met an Australian. He said Australians were great gamblers, they had very little respect for your law. He said your national hero was some sort of outlaw. Ed—Kelly?"

"Ned Kelly." *I'll shoot the next bastard that repeats that lousy joke.* He looked at Madame Cholon over a heaped fork and wondered at her interest in gambling. If she was Chinese, that would explain it; but somehow she didn't look Chinese. "He was what we call a bushranger."

"And you are not a bushranger?" Malone shook his head, his mouth full. "What are you, Mr. Malone? Are you on Mr. Quentin's staff?"

Malone turned his face away from the light while he looked at her out of the corners of his eyes. Was every newcomer to a High Commission or an embassy queried as he had been? Or was Quentin so important that anyone connected with him became important? If so, it was a distinction Malone did not want. "Let's just say I'm attached to him."

"Too attached to be allowed a night off?" This man was

[57]

not so stupid, after all. If he was a security officer, some sort of bodyguard for Quentin, then she did not want him on hand when the attempt was made to assassinate Quentin. She did not know how forward women were in this country of cold men, but she had to take a risk. She smiled, employing all the subtle charm she had acquired professionally over the last twenty years. "I want to go gambling, Mr. Malone. There is a club in Mayfair, but ladies are not allowed in unescorted. It is very English."

Malone put down his plate on the stone balustrade of the terrace and picked up his glass of champagne. This was Millionaires' Row and he was an intruder, a beggar whose bank book would have been laughed at as a worthless visa in this territory.

"Better try someone else, Madame Cholon. I'm not in the Mayfair class. With my salary they'd probably restrict me to the one-armed bandits."

"What is your salary, Mr. Malone?"

He raised his eyebrows. He had once read that the Asians had very different ideas on privacy from those of the Europeans, but he had never been asked a question as blunt as this before, not even by the Chinese opium smugglers he had met before he had gone on to the Murder Squad. "I get just over two thousand a year, Australian. Sixteen hundred sterling."

"It is not much, is it?" Diamonds winked derisively at him as she raised a hand to the pearls at her throat.

"I was happy enough with it back home." Which was the truth: He had never dreamed of riches and so had been incorruptible. He had never been smug about his incorruptibility. He knew that every man had his price: he had just never found out what his was.

"But you are not now?"

Malone looked back into the big main room, at the silk walls, the frozen explosion of the huge chandelier, the beautiful women in gowns that would have cost him a month's salary. "I came here tonight in a Rolls-Royce, the first time I've ever been in one, maybe the last. I'm not likely to lose my head over something I'll only taste once."

"What sort of car do you have back home?"

"A secondhand Holden."

"A Holden? What is that?"

"It's something you don't drive up to expensive gambling clubs in. Better get someone else, Madame Cholon." Then he saw Jamaica standing in the doorway watching them, and he nodded. "Ask that bloke. He's an American. They're richer than anyone else."

Madame Cholon looked towards Jamaica. "But he is coloured!"

Malone was not surprised at her reaction. He had heard a Chinese girl in Campbell Street back home in Sydney call an aborigine a dirty black bastard: colour prejudice could run right through the spectrum. All at once he did not like this tiny beautiful woman who seemed so curiously interested in him. He put down his glass on the balustrade and took random aim at her: "You Vietnamese have never belly-ached about the colour of American money."

He knew he had guessed right: she *was* Vietnamese. She stared at him for a moment, then she said something that was foreign to him but which he well understood: as a policeman he had been sworn at enough to catch the intent if not the words.

"And the same to you," he said, and walked away from her. He passed Jamaica as he went through the open doors into the main room. The American looked directly at him and he stopped. "Who's that woman I've just left?"

Jamaica looked after Madame Cholon as she went quickly along the terrace and through a doorway into another room. "I was wondering that myself."

[59]

He's lying, Malone thought. "Let me know if you find out."

"She's quite a dish, isn't she?"

"That's what she said about you," said Malone, who then left him and went on into the room.

Sheila Quentin came towards him. Two hours of diplomatic ping-pong hadn't touched her; she looked as cool, poised and unmarked as when she had arrived. "We are leaving, Mr. Malone. My husband is feeling very tired. Perhaps you would like to stay on?"

"No, I'm tired, too."

They began to move across the room. Men flashed quick smiles at Sheila Quentin; the women's smiles were a little slower. But her own response was warm and quick to everyone: it was a diplomatic smile, but somehow she made it appear sincere.

"Did you bring some bad news for my husband, Mr. Malone?" she said, inclining her head to a huge Nigerian woman, extravagant as an African sunset in her native dress.

"Why?"

"He was quite cheerful when he came home this evening. Confident the conference was going the right way. But now—" She looked up at him. "What sort of message did you bring him from Canberra?"

They were interrupted by two women, a Canadian and a German: Malone stood aside while the three women made arrangements for a committee to clothe the underprivileged of Stepney. Then he and Sheila Quentin moved on. "I think you'd better ask him."

"It's as secret as that, is it?"

"I'm afraid so."

"And bad?" He hesitated, then nodded. She bit her lip and for a moment there was a hint of strain in her face. "Damn! And everything was going so beautifully."

[60]

"I'm sorry," he said, and was surprised at the depth of sincerity he felt.

"Do you always bring bad news?"

Again he hesitated, then he nodded. "Too often. They think I have the right personality for it."

"I hate you, Mr. Malone." She smiled, and he warmed towards her. "But it's not your fault."

No, he thought, it's not my fault. He wondered whom she would hate when she found out whose fault it really was. Then they had reached Quentin and Lisa Pretorious, standing waiting for them just outside the entrance to the main room. Quentin did look tired, a man who had run a long race and had suddenly collapsed at the end of it. The two women looked at him with concern, but he managed a smile.

"It's nothing. Conferences are like marathon races—you have to wait for your second wind. A spoonful of Horlicks in a glass of Scotch and I'll be fine."

The women grimaced and smiled at him, but Malone saw that they were still not reassured. Quentin glanced at him. "Do you ever have need of a second wind, Mr. Malone?"

"The time's coming up now," said Malone, and underlined his next words: "I'll be glad to get home."

As the Quentins and Lisa went ahead of him out of the big entrance hall Malone looked back. On the other side of the big room Madame Cholon stood by the terrace door watching him, her gaze as cold and steady as that of a marksman taking aim. Jamaica was moving towards her: his face, too, had the look of a hunter.

2

Pallain sat in the rented black Ford Zephyr. He had learned the advantages of having several passports and driving licences, and the car had been rented in the name of Pierre Martin. He had never liked the risk of using a stolen

[61]

car on a job; it was always best to stay within the law as much as possible; in a stolen car you always stood the risk of being picked up by a too-observant *flic*. The Zephyr would be abandoned after they had made their getaway and it could never be traced to Jean-Pierre Pallain. The deposit would be lost, but Madame Cholon was paying for that and fifteen pounds was nothing against the stakes she was playing for.

Pham Chinh, sitting beside him, went to light a cigarette, but Pallain slapped the book of matches from his hand. "Save it," he said in French. "You can have one later."

Pham Chinh rubbed a nervous finger down his youthful cheek. He was thirty years old, but he had looked the same age for the past fifteen years: only the eyes had always been old, old and cunning and mean. "It is getting late. Don't these diplomats ever come home?"

"At least we're waiting in comfort. Pity poor Tho over there in the gardens."

He nodded across the square to the dark island of trees and shrubs in its center. Truong Tho was there, the rifle with the telescopic sight cradled in his arms like a wood-and-metal doll, the guerrilla in the London jungle. Pallain had bought the gun in a shop off Bond Street, where the salesman could not have been anything less than a duke.

"What did you plan to shoot, sir?"

An ambassador: Pallain was sure the man would have approved of the social status of the target. "Deer."

"With a telescopic sight, sir?" The man pursed his lips.

"Something wrong?"

"Oh no, sir. But it is hardly—er—sporting, is it?"

Pallain had paid in cash, another thing that had not impressed the salesman; and now Truong Tho was waiting there in the shadows to commit a deed that the English would probably condemn as also not sporting.

"He mustn't miss." Pham Chinh was glad he was not the one who had to do the shooting; he knew he would have been

[62]

too nervous to aim straight. "There won't be a chance for a second shot."

Pallain said nothing, but glanced at his watch. The square was deserted but for the occasional passing car or taxi. The tall pale houses gave an impression of being no more than empty shells, despite the lighted windows that showed in one or two of them. The car was parked at the end of Chesham Place where it entered the square; behind them was the German Embassy and across from them was the white portico of the Spanish Embassy. The sound of music came softly from across the road, Segovia in nostalgic mood: someone was homesick for Andalusia. There was the mutter of German voices and two men in white raincoats went by without glancing at the car. London is made up of foreigners, Pallain thought; but there would be one less before the night was out. But then an Australian might not be considered a foreigner; he had never really understood how the Commonwealth worked. Whatever Quentin was, he would be dead tonight, eligible only for the citizenship of the grave.

Then the big black Rolls-Royce, AUS-1, went past, slowing to turn left into Belgrave Square and follow the one-way route round to the Australian High Commissioner's house on the south side of the square.

CHAPTER FOUR

1

As the big limousine turned left into the square Malone, sitting beside Lisa in one of the jump-seats, glanced casually out at the car parked close to the corner. He saw the two men in the front seat of the car turn their faces away, but not before he had caught a glimpse of the man behind the wheel, a fleeting impression like the subliminal images he had once seen tried out on television. His brows puckered, the policeman in him at work. Why should two men, sitting in a parked car late at night, wish to avoid being seen? Then he shook his head and grinned. Leave it to the London bobbies: it was no concern of his.

"Something amusing you?" Lisa asked.

"Just thinking what my old mum would say if she could see me now. She's Irish, been in Australia for over fifty years, but she's still back in the bogs. Her idea of luxury transport is still a trap with two ponies."

"What did she say when she knew you were coming to London?" Sheila Quentin liked this almost naïvely frank man. Too many of the visitors from Canberra brought frankness with them as some sort of primitive weapon designed to bludgeon the crafty, too-superior swindlers of Whitehall. They bored her and irritated her with their rough approach, an approach she knew they worked on from the moment they left Australia, as if determined to prove they were one with the aborigines, an image they were convinced Whitehall held of them. But this new man seemed to use frankness as part of an unwitting charm.

"Told me to buy a bomb and throw it," said Malone, and confirmed Sheila's opinion of him. "She still thinks of herself as an auxilary to the I.R.A."

The two women laughed, but Quentin sat quietly in the corner of the back seat, his eyes closed. Sheila glanced at him, then put her hand on his. He opened his eyes, blinking a little despite the dimness of the car's interior, then smiled wearily.

"Miss something?" he asked.

"Nothing, darling. We're almost home."

The Rolls circled the square, then glided into the curb. The chauffeur, a middle-aged man with the build of a middle-weight wrestler and a voice to match, switched off the engine, got out and came round to open the door. Malone got out first, stopped and looked back along to where the parked car had now switched on its high-beam lights. The Rolls and the people getting out of it stood in a cone of light that threw them into relief against the darkness of the square.

"Hold it a moment," Malone said, and he would never know what prompted the premonition that something was about to happen. He put a hand against Lisa's arm to stop her getting out. "Ferguson, get back in and switch on your lights. High-beam."

Ferguson hesitated at being given orders by this newcomer, then grunted, went back round the car, got in and switched on the headlights. The beam blazed down towards Chesham Place; a taxi coming out of the street honked in furious protest. The two cones of light, from the Rolls and the Zephyr, met in silent assault.

Across the road Truong Tho stood among the thick shrubs, his rifle resting on the heavy wire-netting fence. His eyes had become accustomed to the darkness, and when Pallain had switched on his car's lights as planned he wondered if they were really necessary. He raised the telescopic sight to his eye and in it saw the chauffeur go round and open the door of the big black car. A tall man in evening dress got out, stopped and looked towards Pallain's car. Then the chauffeur came back round, got in and switched on the Rolls-Royce's lights. Truong Tho felt his hands begin to sweat and he blinked his eyes, trying to focus them into the unexpected blaze of light. Something had gone wrong, but he did not have time to consider it. Hazily, like figures behind frosted glass, he saw two women and another man alight. He aimed at the second man and squeezed the trigger.

Malone heard the bullet ping off the top of the Rolls. He yelled at Quentin and the women to duck; then he was running swiftly across the road towards the dark island of garden. He saw the car down at the corner switch off its lights, then its engine roared and with a squeal of tires it swung into the square and went speeding round the other side of the garden. Malone didn't see the wire fence. Brought up in a city where all the gardens were public, he plunged towards what he thought was a break in the shrubbery; made too trusting by egality, he was brought up short by privacy rights. He hit the fence and bounced back, sprawling on the pavement. He swore, picked himself up and ran towards the eastern curve of the garden. He heard a screech of brakes on the far side of the square; then he came round the curve of the garden. The Zephyr was gathering speed again, disappearing into one of the streets that came in on the north side of the square. He pulled up, knowing the gunman was now in the car and was gone.

He made his way back towards the house, limping a little as he became aware of pain in his shin. He heard the thud-thud of heavy boots and as he crossed the road a uniformed policeman came running up to the entrance of the house. The two women had gone inside, but Quentin and the chauffeur stood beside the car, on the lee side from the garden.

"I heard a shot—" Then the policeman turned with Quentin and Ferguson as Malone limped up to them.

"The bastards got away. That car down there must have been waiting for him. And spot-lighting us into the bargain." He felt blood trickling down his chin and he put up his hand to the cut there.

"Did he nick you?" Quentin stepped forward, his face full of concern.

"I ran into some wire. The bloke with the gun was over there among the trees."

"I'll phone the Yard, sir." The policeman made a gesture towards the front door. "May I use your phone?"

Quentin nodded and the policeman went into the house past Sheila and Lisa, who now stood in the doorway. Then Quentin looked at Ferguson. "That will be all for tonight, Tom. And don't broadcast what has happened. I don't want this to be in the newspapers. Same time tomorrow morning. Good night."

Ferguson kneaded the rock-cake of his face, went to say something, thought better of it and touched his cap. "Night, sir. I'm glad they missed."

"So am I." Quentin smiled wryly; he seemed undisturbed by the attempt on his life. "Let's hope their aim next time —if there is a next time—is just as bad. And don't forget—not a word to anyone."

The Rolls eased away and Quentin looked at Malone. "We'd better see to that cut on your face. Oh, and thanks."

[67]

He gestured towards the other side of the road; a taxi went by, slowed, thinking he had hailed it, then went on. "You didn't have to chase that chap—"

"It was instinctive."

"Reflex action? Never let a murderer get away?" Then he shook his head and passed a hand across his eyes. "Sorry, Malone. I didn't mean that."

Malone put up a hand and patted Quentin on the back; then dropped the hand in surprise and embarrassment. The two men stared at each other for a moment, snared by the gift of sympathy and the need for it. Christ Almighty, Malone thought, here I go again, everybody's friend. Then Quentin nodded in acknowledgment of the gesture, saving Malone further embarrassment by saying nothing, and turned and led the way into the house.

"You're all right, darling?" Sheila Quentin grasped her husband's arm. They stood together oblivious of the others in the hall, like lovers meeting after a long separation. Malone saw the anguish on Sheila's face and felt sick. This woman was going to die when she finally learned what Quentin had done, that she was going to lose him.

Then Lisa came forward. "You've been hurt, Mr. Malone!"

The next few minutes was a confusion of Joseph, the butler, being sent for hot water and sticking plaster, of both women ushering Malone into the living room with such solicitude that he felt he should have at least lost an arm, of Quentin bringing him a Scotch.

"Without Horlicks." The two men grinned at each other and the women smiled; they could have been a foursome returned from a joyful night out.

Then the policeman knocked on the door. "Someone is coming from Special Branch, sir." He was a young man with a large jaw and a slight lisp; he had an educated accent, appropriate to the diplomatic beat. "They shouldn't be long.

[68]

In the meantime I'll go across and have a look around the garden, just in case he dropped the gun."

You're wasting your time, mate, Malone thought; those boys weren't the sort to leave anything behind. But he said nothing; he had to keep reminding himself that this was not his territory. The policeman saluted and retired as Joseph, seething with good grace at having to play nurse to a man below his own social station, returned with a bowl of hot water, a bottle of antiseptic and a tin of Band-Aids.

"Shall I attend to the gentleman, madame?" he asked Sheila, his tone suggesting he had other and better things to do. He looked completely unperturbed by what had happened outside in the street. Malone wondered if all butlers were so imperturbable. Then he remembered that Joseph was a Hungarian and he wondered how many shootings in the street he had experienced.

"I'll do it," said Lisa, and began to bathe the cut on Malone's chin. He could smell the perfume she wore, sharpened by the heat of her fear and excitement of a few minutes ago, and he was uncomfortably aware of her bare shoulders and breast as she leaned close to him. He looked beyond her, focussing his gaze on the room around them. He recognized the two paintings on the walls: a Dobell and a Drysdale: Christmas cards had made him an expert in the more famous Australian artists. The furnishings here were richer than in the other two rooms of the house that Malone had seen. He lay back on the Thai silk cushions of the lounge where he sat; he was being trapped in a quicksand of luxury. He sat up quickly, his cheek bumping against Lisa's arm, and looked over her shoulder at Quentin.

"Have you any idea who might have taken that shot at you?"

Quentin shook his head. He looked worried, but somehow Malone knew that it was not worry for himself: it was almost as if he thought of the assassination as something im-

[69]

personal. He was not a career man, but he had already become poisoned by the foreign service officer's resignation:
nothing that happened to you must be judged in personal
terms. Insult, overwork, attempted murder: it was little to
ask for in return for a K.B.E. Policemen, Malone mused,
were asked for the same things; but policemen were never
made Knights of the British Empire. Quentin's reward was
probably to have been the Prime Ministership, but he had
said good-bye to that earlier this evening. If the bullet had
struck home, it might have solved the personal problem.
But it hadn't.

"The important thing is, I don't think anyone should be
allowed to make political capital out of it. If this should
have anything to do with the conference—well, that's why
I want it kept out of the papers." He looked steadily
at Malone. "I should imagine you'd want it kept quiet, too."

"What's going on between you two?" Sheila looked curiously from one man to the other.

"Nothing, darling—"

"Don't tell me *nothing!* Mr. Malone arrives out of nowhere, none of us knows he's even coming—" She looked at
Malone. "It was almost as if you didn't expect yourself to
come here. Where's your luggage?"

Malone was held dumb by Lisa's fingers as she pressed
the Band-Aid on his chin. Quentin answered for him:
"Sheila, we'll talk about it later—"

"Darling." She had calmed down again; she put a hand on
his arm. "You might have been killed tonight. Do you blame
me for asking what's going on? Why should something like
this happen the very night the—forgive me"—she looked
again at Malone—"the mysterious Mr. Malone arrives? I
don't want to pry into government affairs, but why are you
two so secretive?"

Malone, still aware of the closeness of Lisa, his nostrils
clogged with a mixture of antiseptic and her perfume, sat

quiet, waiting for Quentin to answer his wife's question. Quentin, as if he were avoiding Malone's stare, looked down into his Scotch and said, "Mr. Malone is a security man. That's all I can tell you."

"Secret Service?" Sheila sounded a little incredulous, almost amused.

Lisa, her medical aid done, stepped back, looked at Malone and smiled. "Somehow one never thinks of Australians as spies."

Malone stood up. He opened his mouth to tell the truth, get it over and done with; then saw the look (of warning? or of pleading?) on Quentin's face. He took a sip from his glass and said almost lamely, "I'm not a spy. All I have to do is look after your husband, Mrs. Quentin."

"You mean you were expecting something like tonight to happen?" Sheila's poise began to crack again; something like hysteria bubbled just below the surface of her. She had looked so intact, so self-possessed, that it was now like looking at another person, a relative with a family resemblance. "God, I can't believe it! Why should anyone want to kill my husband?"

In the end everything is personal to a woman, Malone thought. Viewed from her angle it meant nothing that her husband was his country's ambassador, that he was the influential man at a conference which, one way or another, was bound to have influence on the future of world peace. She could only see him as her husband: a wife had no diplomacy when she saw her marriage endangered. Malone looked at Quentin, a doomed man: Flannery waiting for him in Sydney, someone outside in the London dark with a gun.

"I'll do my best to see it doesn't happen, Mrs. Quentin," he said, and felt like a man promising to stop a landslide with a shovel.

Then Joseph knocked on the door, "There is a phone call from Sydney, sir, for Mr. Malone."

[71]

"We'll take it in the study." Quentin put down his glass. He looked like a man who had reached the end of his endurance: he was being shot at from near and far, they had got his range.

"Tell them you need more protection," Sheila said, then gestured helplessly. "Or ask them to recall you. Anything."

Quentin nodded and patted her arm reassuringly. Then he smiled slightly at Malone as he stood aside to let the latter go ahead out of the room. They went into the study, closing the door after them, and Quentin said, "Do you have to tell the Commissioner about tonight?"

Malone put his hand over the phone. "Scotland Yard will tell him as soon as they learn who I am. You shouldn't have told your wife I was a security man."

"What else could I say in front of Lisa?"

Malone stared at him for a moment, having no answer; then he took his hand away from the phone and answered the operator. How much simpler the world must have been before Alexander Graham Bell, he thought.

Leeds came on the line, his voice shredded by static. "Scobie? I've seen our friend. He wasn't happy, but he's agreed. On patriotic grounds." Despite the static the sarcasm came through loud and clear. "When will the conference finish?"

"It almost finished tonight," said Malone, and told Leeds what had happened. The line was silent for a while but for the interference; Malone began to imagine that he was listening to the grinding of teeth. "Are you there, sir?"

Something like a sigh came from ten thousand miles away. "My first reaction is to say bring him home at once. But what comes first? Justice or patriotism?"

This has probably never happened before and will never happen again, Malone thought: the Commissioner asking a detective-sergeant for advice. Malone looked across at Quentin standing in front of the fireplace. Behind the older man

[72]

the ormolu clock ticked quietly, like a slow teletype: time was running out, was the message. He looked disengaged, already resigned to the fates, a man already in the dock. Christ Almighty, Malone thought, I've just been elected to the jury. Don't get involved, Leeds had advised; and now had tossed him the rope that could bind him to Quentin.

"I think we should stay on here, sir," he said, and committed himself to Quentin. He cursed the Commissioner, cursed Flannery, thought of the simplicity of a murder in Bexley North: that had been his last case, the arresting of a garage mechanic who had killed a man with a tire lever for sleeping with the mechanic's wife. An open and shut case, with no involvement at all: the mechanic, struck dumb by grief or hate, had never opened his mouth, never even looked at Malone for help or sympathy.

"Good luck," said Leeds, safe on the other side of the world. "And be careful. I don't want someone taking potshots at *you*."

Malone hung up and looked at Quentin. "He left it up to me."

"I gathered that. I'm getting more and more in your debt."

"I'm a tough creditor," said Malone, trying not to sound like a liar. "Don't ask for too much more."

2

When they went back into the living room Lisa had gone, but two men were there with Sheila Quentin.

"Superintendent Denzil and Sergeant Coburn." Sheila had regained her composure; she had learned her lessons well as a diplomat's wife. "From Scotland Yard."

"Special Branch," said Denzil, and gave a purple tone to the word *Special*: he was not a *hoi polloi* policeman. He was a squarish man running a little to weight; every so often he seemed to become conscious of his belly and would tuck it

[73]

in, like a man trying to hide the error of an indulged life. Bright blue eyes in his red face gave him a false impression of cheeriness; the wide, thin-lipped mouth told the truth. He'd arrest his own mother, Malone thought, if it meant promotion. Despite the warm evening he was dressed in a tweed suit; a regimental tie, with stripes that went ill with his red face, hung on his broad chest. He had a gruff fruity voice, full of a false bonhomie that could trick an unwary prisoner. "Someone took a shot at you, sir. We'll have to put a stop to that."

"I'd appreciate it," said Quentin, and Denzil looked at him as if not certain whether the High Commissioner was being ironic or not.

"The constable tells me he found nothing over in the gardens. But Sergeant Coburn is going over just to double-check."

I bet the uniformed boys love working with you, Malone thought.

Coburn nodded and went out of the room. He was a young man, tall and thin, his face all bone and dark, intense stare. He looked as if he might never laugh, but that might be because he was always with Denzil. He had one eyebrow that sat much higher than the other, and Malone suspected he would never get far in the Force: he would always look quizzical of his superiors.

When the door closed behind Coburn, Denzil said, "Mrs. Quentin tells me you are from Australian Security, Mr. Malone. Have you been in touch with anyone else at Special Branch?"

"Mr. Malone only arrived tonight from Australia," Quentin said quickly.

Denzil nodded as if that were no excuse at all. "Did you have any suspicions that something like this might happen to His Excellency? Was that why you were sent over, Mr. Malone?" He smiled mechanically, big white teeth appear-

[74]

ing between the thin lips like a blank illuminated sign. "I'm looking for some sort of lead, you understand."

Malone looked at Quentin. "I think I'd better have a few words alone with the Superintendent, sir."

Quentin stared at him; for a moment Malone expected to see the pleading look again, and suddenly felt resentful. *Don't ask any more favours; you've had your lot.* Then Quentin took his wife's arm.

"We'll be in the study."

The Quentins went out of the room, but they took none of the tension that Malone felt with them. He moved to the door, made sure it was closed, then turned back to Denzil. Why do I have to reveal everything to this bastard? Why couldn't they have sent a man with some charity?

"I'm not a security man," he said flatly, and wondered what Quentin was saying to his wife in the room next door. "I am a detective-sergeant in the New South Wales Police Force. I'm here to arrest the High Commissioner on a charge of murder."

Denzil didn't even blink. "That's rather awkward."

The bloody British understatement: who does he think he is, Noel Coward? "Yes, it is, rather."

"Care to tell me more about it?"

Malone thought he heard a cry from the room next door; or perhaps it was his imagination. If there had been a cry Denzil gave no sign that he had heard it. The ormolu clock struck the half-hour and he turned his head and looked at it reproachfully. Then he looked back at Malone.

"Will you be asking for a court warrant?"

Malone shook his head. "He's coming quietly. Without a fuss."

"There'll be a fuss if tonight's affair gets into the newspapers."

"He doesn't want it in the papers."

"For personal reasons?"

[75]

Malone kept his temper. He was all at once utterly weary, drained empty by the long day and the unexpected climax of the night. He had been saddled all evening with the un-accustomed burden of secrecy and deception, and that too had exhausted him. He was in no mood to humour a Scot-land Yard man who seemed so full of himself as to be care-less of other people's reactions to what had happened. Steady, Malone, don't start any intra-Commonwealth in-cidents.

"There's a conference on. You must have known that?" The sarcasm was thick, real Australian scorn, but he didn't care.

Denzil gazed at him steadily, then nodded. He put a finger to his ear, screwed the wax in, and said, "What's the murder charge?"

Malone told him. Denzil sucked on his bottom lip, turn-ing his face away so that he looked sideways at Malone; the angle at which he held his head gave him an expression of disbelief, and Malone felt the temper rise in him again. "We've got all the facts, Superintendent—"

"I'm not disbelieving you, Sergeant. I'm just wonder-ing—"

"When I'm taking him back?" Malone backed down, put-ting himself in the other policeman's place. Then he told Denzil about Quentin's request and Leeds' agreement to it. "I've just got off the phone to my Commissioner—"

"It's highly irregular, I must say."

Malone took a chance. "I should think that in Special Branch you'd be used to a lot of stuff that's highly ir-regular."

For the first time Denzil really smiled, a genuine grin that was so unexpected Malone at first didn't believe it: Denzil had borrowed it from someone else, had tacked it on like a false moustache. Malone was reminded of Flannery's warm sincere grin, and knew how spurious that had been.

But Denzil's smile did seem genuine; and just as unexpectedly he put out his hand. "We'll keep it quiet, Sergeant."

Malone shook the firm beefy hand. "Nobody knows about this except you, me and him. Unless he's just told his wife—" He glanced towards the wall that separated the living room from the study. What emotions were boiling there? There was no sound from the next room. Christ, it's like being next door to a crypt! He looked back at Denzil, who had stopped smiling now: the man was not entirely insensitive. "Do you have to tell anyone else?"

Denzil hesitated only a moment. "Murder isn't my job. Unless it's a political murder. I don't think I have to tell any-one, Sergeant. Not for a few days, anyway."

"We'll be gone by the end of the week. After that you can tell anyone you want—just give me time to get him back to Sydney."

"And then the wolves get at him?" Malone nodded. There was a tap on the door and Denzil moved towards it. Before he opened it he stopped, looked back and smiled again, still a genuine grin. "I *did* know there was a conference on."

"Sorry," said Malone.

Denzil waved a hand, then turned and opened the door. Sergeant Coburn stood there and just behind him was Quentin. "Nothing over in the gardens, sir."

"I'm afraid this will mean having a man with you all the time now, sir," Denzil said.

"In addition to Mr. Malone?" Quentin said.

"We're responsible for you—at least while this conference is going on. Mr. Malone has explained the nature of his duty with you." He paused a moment, and Quentin nodded. "But I'm afraid Sergeant Coburn will still have to stay with you."

Quentin glanced at Malone, almost as if looking for the latter's approval, then shrugged. "If you say so. But I don't want a word of this to get out—"

"I understand," Denzil said. The bonhomie had gone

[77]

from the fruity voice. "I think we can keep *everything* quiet, sir."

"Thank you," said Quentin, but looked anxious rather than gratified. The publicity had begun: tonight to the policeman, tomorrow to the world. He pulled nervously at his moustache, as if wanting to tear off part of the disguise he had worn for so long. In a way, Malone thought, he'll probably be glad to get back to his own identity.

Five minutes later Denzil had gone and with him Coburn, who would be back again first thing in the morning. The uniformed policeman had taken up his post outside the front door. Joseph had locked the doors and windows, like someone shutting up the house before going away on a long holiday, and had retired to his room in the basement of the house. No one other than the policeman outside seemed to have heard the shot, or if they had they were diplomatically minding their own business. Or perhaps they had just thought it was a passing car backfiring. Whatever had been their reactions, no one had come out into the square to enquire what was going on. This was embassy territory and all the embassies were playing the diplomatic game: always remain neutral till you find out who is holding the gun.

Quentin and Malone stood in the living room; their exhaustion was mutual, they were like men who had escaped from a shipwreck. Only one of them had hope and he tried to share it with the other, like a stale crust: "They won't try again," Malone said. "Not now. They'll know Scotland Yard will be on the lookout for them—"

"I told my wife." Quentin poured himself a drink with hands that shook. He looked at Malone, who shook his head in puzzlement. "It was like committing a second murder. I feel like Bluebeard."

Malone was tired. He had to shift the focus of his attention; he was like a man with double vision. "The murder? Oh yes." He made a gesture that was meaningless; he was so weary he could hardly control his hands. "I *had* to tell Denzil—"

"You don't have to excuse yourself—what's your first name?"

"Scobie."

"I once read a book by a Russian. It said that after a while your gaoler becomes a sort of relation. So you won't mind if I call you Scobie when we're alone?"

"Call me anything you like if it relieves the strain."

"Nothing is going to relieve the strain, Scobie, believe me. Nothing at all. Least of all this." He looked at his glass, then drained it in one gulp. He coughed, shook his head and managed a smile that was like a scratch on his face. "I'll never take to drink. Even if there were time."

Then Lisa came to the door. "Mr. Malone, Joseph has lent you a pair of Mr. Quentin's pajamas, and I've put some books beside your bed in case you want to read. There's also a new toothbrush. We'll pick up your things from your hotel tomorrow."

"Miss Efficiency," said Quentin. "One day I'm going to find a flaw in you, Lisa. Not to gloat over. Just so that I won't feel so damned inefficient myself."

Lisa smiled. "I'm full of flaws. Women, if they want to, can hide them better, that's all."

"You should teach us men the trick," said Malone, and wondered why he had spoken, not for himself, but for Quentin.

Lisa looked at Quentin. "You're quite worn out. Is there anything I can get you?"

Quentin shook his head. "Has my wife gone to bed?"

"I think what happened tonight has upset her. I said good night to her, but she didn't seem to hear me." Traces of exhaustion, like faint smudge marks, showed on her own face; the night had bruised them all, but in different ways. And suddenly Malone was grudgingly thankful for the assassination attempt. It would provide an excuse for the atmosphere that would surely be here in the house tomorrow. "I hope you both feel better in the morning."

"Thank you, Lisa," said Quentin, and he was too tired to keep the irony from his voice. Malone looked quickly at Lisa, but she too was tired: she missed it.

Quentin said good night to them both and trudged up the winding staircase out of the hall. Lisa stared after him, a thin crease between her brows suddenly spoiling the cool beauty of her face. Is she in love with him? Malone wondered; and hoped not. Quentin could not go on killing women, physically or emotionally: no man had that amount of destruction in him. But even as he thought it Malone knew he was wrong: there was no limit to the destruction in any man.

"What's happened to him, Scobie?" Malone had told her his name earlier in the evening, but this was the first time she had used it. I'm becoming one of the family, he thought. I've got to get back to Sydney before they start mixing their blood with mine. "All of a sudden he looks so worn out."

"That conference is a load on his back." Malone was an experienced liar. Sometimes as a policeman you had to lie more than the criminal; it was often the only way to the truth. "And being shot at doesn't always raise the adrenalin."

She looked at him, the crease disappearing from her brow. "I think there is more buried in you than you allow to show."

"Flaws?"

"No. Well, maybe. But something else. Whatever it is, you hide it very well."

"It's environment. The—" His tired, careless tongue almost said *The Police Force;* he caught it just in time. "The Public Service is no place for an extrovert."

"A pity. It could do with some life in it." She smiled at him, accepting him now. "One doesn't think of a security

[80]

agent being a public servant. Or a civil servant, as they call them here. Do you have a number like James Bond?"

He shook his head. He would like to know her better, but not tonight; he was wishing she would go. "My boss has no head for figures."

She sensed his tiredness, began to walk up the staircase ahead of him. "I'll see you at breakfast. Are you talkative at breakfast?"

"Not usually," said Malone, and wondered who would be talkative at all tomorrow.

In his room a pair of blue silk pajamas had been laid out on the bed. He picked them up, rubbing the smooth material against his rough palms. He had never paid more than thirty shillings for a pair of pajamas in his life; what was the point of spending money on what you wore in bed? When he had someone in bed with him, someone to impress, he wore nothing at all: as far as he knew, silk had never improved a man's virility. Maybe I'm too crude and simple, he thought. I should have tried some of this luxury long ago.

He felt the sheets; they too were much better quality than he was accustomed to. He cleaned his teeth with the new brush that stood in the glass on the basin in one corner of the room. He noticed that Lisa, or Joseph, had provided toothpaste, shaving brush and razor, after-shave lotion, tissues. He picked up the after-shave lotion, something he had never used, and smelled it. He grinned at himself in the mirror: if Lisa or Joseph had decided that this was his smell, he liked it. Simple and sharp: they had decided he was not the sophisticated, languorous type.

He got undressed, put on the pajamas and got into bed. He lay back exhausted, lying in more luxury than he had ever experienced in his life before, yet knowing sleep was not going to come easy. He looked at the books Lisa had put on the bedside table: *The Art and Practice of Diplo-*

macy, a novel by Patrick White, a detective story by Ross Macdonald. She was taking no chances on his taste; or was she subtly poking fun at him? It didn't matter anyway; even as he looked at the titles the words blurred before his gritty eyes. He put the books back on the table and turned out the light.

The room was completely dark; the thick curtains made a night blacker than anything outside. Somewhere a car growled, then its exhaust coned off like a bray of triumph: some lover going home after an unexpected conquest. A plane went overhead, whistling like an exhausted beast: people looked down on the diamond-patterned city, began to prepare for the reunion, for the first step into a new life. In another room in the house Quentin and his wife lay in each other's arms; but they were deaf to the world outside, blind to the darkness. Nothing was as black as their own small world.

Malone rolled restlessly on his back, feeling the silk of the pajamas against his skin like a woman's touch. Why had he accepted this job? Why hadn't he found some excuse that would have kept him at home? What was going to be achieved by taking back Quentin for a murder that everyone but a malicious old man had forgotten? Well, not forgotten; but didn't care about any more. Freda Corliss had been dead a long time, would be no more than bones now; and bones by themselves never asked for revenge. And if they could speak, what would they say? Leave him where he is, he is of more use to the world in London than mouldering in Bathurst gaol for the rest of his life. Would the dead Freda say that? Maybe not. She had been German Jewish, and both the Germans and the Jews had long memories when it came to deeds against themselves.

Malone had never had any sense of vocation as a policeman. It was a job: he could have been a salesman, a bus driver, even a bookmaker just as easily: the fulfillment of justice had never been one of his ambitions. He had always respected the law; that perhaps had been a reaction against the revolutionary sermons of his Irish father. Con Malone had never got over the disgrace of his son's joining the police force; even when Scobie had gone from uniform into plainclothes, Con Malone had not wanted to be seen with him in certain company. Scobie's father had always been on the side of the underdog; he had always refused to believe that some underdogs might also be criminals. Sure, there were bad boys; but who had made them bad? The law —or, more specifically, the police. Con Malone had believed in the essential goodness of man—and with Irish logic had contrived to ignore the fact that a policeman was also a man. Including his own son.

So justice, respect for the law, the need for a certain conformity in society, had never been subjects for discussion in the Malone house. Eventually Scobie had left home, gone to live in a flat at King's Cross, where nonconformity was the way of life but where a man, no matter how poor or how much an underdog, had the luxury of privacy. Could build his own ethics, shape his own ambition, decide whether there was a God and how he wanted to meet Him when the time came. His mother came once a week, like a social worker, cleaned the flat, sprinkled holy water on the floor just inside the front door, and went away leaving a new holy picture, like a visiting card, each week on the dressing table. Once he had left his handcuffs at home and she had propped the holy picture up against them, as if to exorcise him from the evil that possessed him.

Con and Brigid Malone would say to leave Quentin where he was. There would be no lack of sympathy for his dead first wife, even though she was German and Jewish: their xenophobia and bigotry never extended to the dead. Nor would they deny that he had committed a mortal sin in killing her. But at times the Irish, the most impractical of people, could be more practical than anyone but the most primitive savage. But then again it was an Irishman, with an Irishman's long memory for revenge (one with the Germans and the Jews: his mother and father wouldn't like that), who had reopened this case and wanted it brought to its right, legal conclusion. And bound by the law, there was no escape for Malone, just as there was no escape for Quentin.

All at once, more like an actual pain in his head than a thought, Malone wished the assassin's bullet had found Quentin tonight. There was a horror that he could wish for another man's death; but Quentin, consciously or unconsciously, was beginning to make too much demand on him. The cord of the pajamas tightened round his middle, like a lasso; again he was reminded of a woman's touch by the silk, the touch of Sheila Quentin's hand. Abruptly he got out of bed, took off the pajamas and got back naked between the sheets.

He fell asleep and dreamed of Quentin and himself handcuffed together in the dock. The judge was Flannery, smiling his warm, sincere grin at both of them.

3

In the apartment in Exhibition Road Madame Cholon said, "We shall just have to try again."

"It's going to be more difficult from now on." Pallain's beard was dark on his face now; it made a sound like sandpaper as he rubbed his palm against it. "They'll have a guard with him all the time. Why not try someone else? One of the Africans?"

"Which one? There isn't an African at the conference who doesn't have enemies at home. It could be blamed on them, brushed off as having nothing to do with the conference. They would send another delegate and the conference would

[84]

go on. Africans are too readily expendable. The imperialists have proved that."

She borrows from everyone, Pallain thought, even the Communists. She is the complete amoral politician.

"No, no one else at the conference has Quentin's influence. The other delegates just make noises. They will vote when the time comes, but they do not want to go on record as having put forward any motions. Some do not want to offend China, the others do not want to offend America. One does not spit in the eye of the country that is paying one's bills. At least, not when abroad. At home it is a different thing."

"How much longer then do we have?"

"Not long at all. Two, three days at the most. The man who was with Quentin last night, the one you said seemed suspicious of your car—I think I met him at the reception. I wonder what he is."

"He seemed a little more adventurous than the usual junior diplomat. They are generally very intent on self-preservation, so they can survive and be promoted to ambassadors. Do you think he might be a security man?"

"Perhaps you had better find out. Are you covering the conference tomorrow?"

"I have to make a show of being a journalist." Pallain stood up, straightening his tie, shooting his cuffs. He had pretensions to being a dandy, but his face was too rugged, his body too thick: the effect was of a brick in Fortnum and Mason's wrapping. "When this is over, I hope I can retire."

"You should be able to." Madame Cholon led the way to the door. She showed a hint of gratitude, obliquely, as if it were a weakness: "I hope you will be paid enough."

Pallain looked around the apartment. "I'd like to live in something like this, but overlooking the Seine."

"Perhaps I shall visit you when I come to Paris," she smiled, having no intention of it.

[85]

He looked at her, at the slim figure under the *ao dais* that had learned all the professional tricks of love and was now going to waste. This was the first time he had been alone with her since they had arrived in London. Truong Tho had been dropped at the small flat where he and Pham Chinh were staying in Notting Hill, then Pham Chinh had taken the Zephyr south of the river to dump it. Pallain himself had come here to Madame Cholon's apartment by taxi. The night was still young by his timing:

"This is a big apartment for one woman—"

The smile went, the eyes turned to black glass. "I never sleep with the help, Jean-Pierre. You are being well paid for what you are doing. There will be no bonuses."

He pursed his lips, then shrugged. "It's my father in me. He always did have an eye for the native women."

He went out quickly, slamming the door behind him. He knew he had just nominated himself to be another victim on Madame Cholon's list. Damn his French tongue: always looking for the biting exit line.

CHAPTER FIVE

1

When Malone came downstairs in the morning Joseph was waiting for him in the hall. He looked with a sickened eye at Malone's suit, then said, "This way, sir. What would you like for breakfast?"

"What is there?"

"The cook is at your service, sir. You only have to ask for what you want."

"I like a good breakfast. How about a steak with an egg?"

Joseph was well trained: he managed not to throw up. "Medium or well done, sir?"

"The steak or the egg?" I'm at war with this bastard, Malone thought.

"The steak, sir."

"Medium. And the egg runny."

He followed Joseph into a dining room and out on to a small patio where Sheila Quentin, in a green silk housecoat, sat at a glass-topped wrought-iron table. Beyond was a small garden surrounded by high walls; London and the world were shut out, but for how long? Malone sat down and Joseph, the messenger of heresy, went back to the kitchen to order steak and *egg* for the barbarian's breakfast. Sheila nodded towards a large jug of orange juice on the table.

"Are you expecting a big day, Mr. Malone? I heard you ordering a real bush breakfast."

"Did I do the wrong thing?"

"Not at all. I like to see a man eat."

Where had he heard that before? His head was full of echoes; the nightmare of the night had still been with him when he woke up. He was unaccustomed to dreaming and it had only added to his exhaustion. But he would need his wits about him today and for the next four or five days.

"How's your face?"

He felt the small scab on his chin. He had taken off the Band-Aid; he knew from experience that cuts healed quickly on him. He had no doubts that physically he would be able to stand up to anything that might face him in the next few days; it was his emotions that might prove vulnerable. "I'll survive. Has Mr. Quentin gone?"

"I made him have breakfast in bed this morning. It was a long time before we both got to sleep last night." She looked old in the morning light; or anyway middle-aged. Her hair had been brushed and she was wearing lipstick, but she had on no other make-up; the morning sun, bouncing off the whitewashed walls of the garden, was cruel to her, exposing the lines that he hadn't seen last night. She smiled, a sad smile that only added to the look of age in her face. "Usually we both sleep very well."

"I'm sorry, Mrs. Quentin. I mean, about—" He flapped his hand, another meaningless gesture but which she understood. With the Irish in him he had never before been at a loss for words, but since entering this house he was becoming almost inarticulate. But dumb gestures were the real *lingua franca* of tragedy; only actors and playwrights made calamity ring.

"You have to do your job." She sipped her coffee, staring into the distance. How far, he could only guess: back to when she had first met Quentin? "He's a good man, you know.

[88]

Not just good in his job—he's excellent at that—but also good in himself."

"Did he tell you why he killed—his first wife?"

She smiled again, dryly this time. "A wife doesn't have to give evidence against her husband, Mr. Malone."

"I'm sorry. I didn't mean it like that."

"I know you didn't. Drink your orange juice." She spread butter thinly on a piece of toast. "Do you think they will try to kill my husband again?"

"Who? Oh, *them.* I don't know." He looked about him, at the garden neat as a stage set. Dwarf trees grew out of pots that looked as if they had been delivered only that morning; the creeper on the wall looked as if it had been tacked there only an hour ago. Everything looked un-real, like the outdoor garden sets in the old movies you saw on television; he looked up at the sky to make sure it wasn't just painted canvas. He looked back at Sheila Quentin, the shade of a beautiful and happy woman remembered from last night: she, too, was unreal. "I'm out of my depth here. I can't tell you how glad I'll be to step on that plane for home."

"With my husband? You're not very tactful, are you?"

"I just told you—I'm out of my depth here."

She stared at him for a long moment, then smiled, taking the sting out of her last remark. "I'm sorry, Mr. Malone. But now I'm the one who's going to be untactful. Are you going to the conference today with my husband?"

"That's the idea."

"Then you had better change into another suit. Do you have a dark one?"

"Only this one. And a sports jacket. I didn't expect a long stay."

"You'll be too conspicuous in that among the striped pants and black jackets. You'd better wear something of my hus-band's."

[89]

"I'm not getting into striped pants," he said emphatically, then grinned. "I can hear the call of duty just so far. After that I get stone deaf."

She returned his grin. "I like you, Mr. Malone. Why did *you* have to be sent to arrest my husband?"

"I've asked myself that several times." His face sobered.

"Why?"

He avoided the question. "I'll go and buy myself a dark suit. I could do with one, anyway."

"There'll be no need. You can wear one of my husband's." The toast crackled in her mouth; her voice came out harsh and dry. "He won't be needing them much longer. What colour do they wear now in gaol, Mr. Malone?"

"Don't," he said, and leaned across the table to put his hand on hers as she bowed her head and began to weep silently.

She kept her head lowered for almost a minute while he sat leaning towards her in the attitude of sympathy. Then she looked up, took a handkerchief from the pocket of her housecoat and wiped her eyes. The glare from the white walls was increasing as the sun climbed higher; she picked up a pair of sunglasses and put them on. They were a double defense: she retreated behind them. "A politician's wife trains herself for a lot of situations. Disappointments, abuse, requests that tear the heart out of you but that you have to refuse. Oh, I don't mean the wife personally. But any politician's wife who is worth her salt suffers everything that her husband does. So you train yourself." She bit her lip. "But never for anything like this. How are my eyes?"

"The glasses hide them. No one will notice."

"Joseph will. He notices everything. I'll go and repair them before he brings you your steak and egg." She stood up, pausing for a moment with her hand on the back of her chair. There was a natural grace to all her movements that not even her emotions of the moment could make awkward; he wondered whether she had trained herself to be like this, or whether she was naturally graceful. What had she been like when Quentin had first met her? "You're a kind man, aren't you?"

He shrugged, embarrassed. "I don't know. A man doesn't measure his own capacity for kindness—that's only for philanthropists who want a tax rebate."

An eyebrow came up above the sunglasses. "You're full of surprises."

"I surprise myself sometimes. It's unnerving." He looked up at her. "I may be kind, or I may just have a sense of guilt. Don't ask me, Mrs. Quentin. I'm busting a gut not to get too involved with you and your husband."

She stared at him for a long time; he could see himself reflected in the sunglasses, a tiny fragile figure. Then she nodded, and he disappeared from the dark mirrors. "You're right, Mr. Malone. Unfortunately for some of us, involvement is part of human nature. Especially when your nature is a good and honest one."

Then she turned and went into the house, leaving Malone wondering if she had been speaking about him, someone else or no one in particular. He had heard her cry of pain, and, by some osmosis he didn't understand, pain had woken in himself. A cop with too much imagination: he was asking for trouble.

Then Lisa, cool and beautiful in a mushroom linen suit, came out and sat down at the table. "I've had breakfast, but Mrs. Quentin thought you might like company. She's still upset about last night, isn't she?"

He nodded, saved from saying anything by the arrival of Joseph.

"Your steak and egg, sir," said the butler, and made it sound as if he were serving the head of John the Baptist.

"My apologies to the cook," said Malone, his appetite suddenly gone, "but I've changed my mind. I think I'll just have toast and marmalade. Am I being difficult, Joseph?"

"No, sir. Just wise, if I may be permitted the comment. Will there be anything further?"

Lisa was watching the fencing between the two men with a smile. She enjoyed observing the relationships between men, a spectator sport that too few women indulged in. She would like to see this almost gauche Australian put the suave Joseph in his place, but she would not bet on him. Joseph had been the uncrowned king of this household too long.

"I have to go out and buy a suit, a dark one. I'm a standard size, so I can buy one off the peg. Where would you recommend, Joseph?"

"Madame has already asked me to lay out one of His Excellency's suits for you—"

Malone shook his head, remembering the constriction of Quentin's pajamas last night. Keep this up and in no time he'd be wearing Quentin's skin. Again he cursed his imagination: it was like a virus in the brain. "No, I was going to buy one, anyway." He turned to Lisa. "Has Sergeant Coburn arrived yet?"

"He's out in the hall. There are also the two men from the External Affairs Department at Australia House. They come here every morning and ride in with Mr. Quentin. They're part of the advisory team at the conference."

"He'll be safe enough then," he said, and was instantly sorry. He saw the shadow cross her face and noticed her hand tighten on the coffeepot she had just picked up. He stared at her, trying to express his regret with his eyes; then he looked up at Joseph, whose face was as impassive as the white wall of the garden behind him. "Would you call me a cab? I'll be ready in ten minutes."

"Sir, perhaps you would care to have me come with you?"

Malone suddenly grinned and looked at Lisa. "You think it might be a good idea?"

"Joseph knows exactly what the well-dressed man should wear."

"Point taken," said Malone, still grinning, and nodded to Joseph. "Okay, Joseph. You and I mightn't pass for Jeeves and Bertie Wooster, but we'll give it a go. Ten minutes."

The butler went away, taking the steak and egg with him, relieved that disaster had been averted and the aborigines hadn't yet taken over Belgravia. Malone chewed on toast and marmalade and sipped the coffee Lisa had poured for him. They eyed each other with disguised glances, like strangers in some foreign hotel wondering if they dared risk getting to know each other better. Then Lisa said, "You did a very brave thing last night, chasing that man with the gun."

He swallowed toast and embarrassment: he had never been a man who could accept a compliment easily. "It was just a reflex action. I could just as easily have run the other way."

"Perhaps. But you didn't." She looked down at the cup of coffee she had poured for herself. She was confident and competent when handling the approaches made to her by men; she could not remember when it was last the other way round. She wanted to know this man Malone better, but she feared if it was left to him she would learn nothing. "When are you going back?"

"Four or five days." What was she getting at? Had she learned the real reason for his being here?

"Are you going to look around London?"

"I won't have time."

"Your first time here and you're not going to try and see it? This is the most interesting city in the world, don't you know that? There is a surprise round every corner. There is only one other city that has that quality of surprise—Paris."

[93]

"I don't know about Paris, but you're certainly right about London: it has its surprises. Such as gunmen in its gardens."

"All other cities are predictable. Even Rome and New York."

"You've been around," he said, and suddenly felt envious of her. He had never really thought much about travelling and now all at once he knew he had missed something. "What about Berlin? Have you been there?"

"The Germans are always predictable," she said, her voice abruptly harsh. He remembered something he had read, that the Dutch, more than anyone else in Europe, hated the Nazis for what they had done. She looked upon Australia as home, but she had inherited European resentments.

"What about the Asians?" Fashions in enemies changed. The Germans were yesterday's enemies; who would be tomorrow's? "The Chinese? The North Vietnamese or the South Vietnamese? Do you predict they might make another attempt to kill your boss?"

"We don't know it was any of those." Her Dutch caution showed.

"No. But that's where I'll lay my money if I have to."

"I'd like to know the form better," she said, picking up his metaphor. "I don't know the Asians at all."

"That's our trouble," he said, calling her an Australian now. "We've lived next door to them for almost a hundred and eighty years and never even tried to get to know them."

"We're trying to remedy that now, Mr. Malone."

Quentin stood in the doorway, dressed in dark jacket and striped trousers, a Homburg hat in one hand and a black briefcase in the other. Behind him were Sergeant Coburn and two other men.

"Mr. Larter and Mr. Edgar." Quentin introduced the two strangers, not in an offhand way but with due regard to each of them. He had all the small qualities that in sum would

[94]

induce loyalty. Next week, Malone thought, there is going to be an awful lot of people with shattered illusions. This was not going to be just one man's tragedy. "Each of them has spent several years in Asia. What did you want to know about it?"

"I was asking Miss Pretorious how predictable they might be."

"Not predictable at all." Larter was a short, slim man with horn-rimmed glasses and an Antipodean face: narrow cheekbones, bony jaw, wide thin-lipped mouth and eyes that had retreated beneath brows that seemed always on the verge of frowning: the Australian sun and climate were beating out a new image. "Mr. Quentin told us what happened last night. I don't think we can be too careful. What do you think, Sam?"

Edgar had been smiling at Lisa, only half-attentive to what was being said. Unlike Larter, a dedicated type, he would look for fringe benefits to his job; admiring beautiful women would be one of them. He was a large dark man who would run to fat easily; he lived under the strain of dieting, playing squash twice a week, doing his 5BX exercises every morning; he had already begun to age in the face with the effort of staying young. He turned away from Lisa reluctantly.

"If they were game enough to try it once, they'll be game enough to try it again. The Eastern Asians, the ones with some Chinese blood in them, they don't give up easily. The Chinese invented patience."

"You think the Chinese might have been responsible for this?" Despite what Sheila had said about his restless night, Quentin looked calm and in control of himself. There was just a hint of tiredness about his eyes, but that was the caste-mark of a diplomat, something he shared with the successful in all other professions. The greyness of last night had gone from his face and this morning he looked handsome, distin-

[95]

guished and a man to be trusted with one of the world's major problems. Christ, thought Malone, our country hasn't turned out many statesmen; why has this one got to be wasted?

"They're the ones I'd lay my money on," said Edgar, being more specific with his bet than Malone had been.

"Don't lay any money on anyone, Sam," said Quentin. "The field is wide open. Sometimes I think we are a generation too late, that things must have been much simpler in the Thirties. Dictators have their advantages. At least you know whom you're dealing with."

"We don't want another Hitler," said Larter. "Least of all an Asian one."

"We'll get one eventually, Phil. You can be sure of that. Dictators are like volcanoes. They keep recurring and no one has yet found a way of stopping them. Maybe not in our time, but some day there'll be another Hitler. I'm sorry to be so pessimistic so early in the morning and on such a beautiful day." He looked up at the sky, bright and cloudless; a high-flying plane glittered like a tossed gem. "In the meantime shall we go and try and preserve peace a little longer?'

"If things go as they did yesterday, we may do just that." Larter was all dedication, full of a nervous energy. But looking at him, Malone had the feeling that Larter would enjoy an unsuccessful conference just as much; all he wanted was the opportunity to bargain and argue. "Preserve peace, I mean."

Quentin looked at Malone. "Joseph tells me he's taking you shopping. I hope I haven't been the cause of you spending more than you'd intended."

You have, thought Malone; but said, "No, sir. I just don't want to be too conspicuous. I make too good a target."

Larter said incredulously, "You're expecting them to shoot at *you?*"

Malone saw Quentin smile; somehow it took away the

irritation he had felt at Larter's question. "No. But a security man should never be obvious. Back home—" He gestured at the suit; then wondered how conspicuous he had been back there. It had never worried him before: somehow policemen in Sydney, even the plainclothes men, expected to be recognized. Australians, it was said, had a sharper nose than anyone else for coppers. He just hoped that out of his environment he was not so recognizable. He looked back at Quentin. "I'll be at Lancaster House in an hour. I'm sure Sergeant Coburn will see you're all right."

Coburn nodded, still serious and intense even though he was out from under the shadow of Denzil this morning. Then Quentin turned and led the way back into the house. Lisa went with the men, Edgar sticking close by her elbow; and Malone was left to himself. He picked up the newspapers that lay on one of the wrought-iron chairs. The headlines were the usual miserable chant that seemed to-day's litany: war, floods, drought, accidents; it seemed there might be a certain avoidance of woe in illiteracy. He found the stories on Vietnam: men had died in a Viet Cong raid while a delegate at the conference was quoted as being "hopeful." He turned to the back pages, the refuge of those who couldn't face the disasters of the front pages. But they were no more encouraging. The tennis correspondent dole-fully complained that another Australian was expected to win Wimbledon; the cricket correspondent demanded to know why England had no fast bowlers; the boxing corre-spondent reported that yet another British heavyweight had been yet another gallant loser. Everyone had his problems. Including himself.

"Do you always look so worried when you're on a case?"

He folded the newspapers and put them back on the chair as Sheila Quentin came out on to the patio. "Often."

"Why are you a policeman?"

"My dad used to ask me that. But he used to be venomous

[97]

about it. I was never able to give him a satisfactory answer. I don't think I could give you one. It's a job, it pays me enough, and, well, it's interesting."

"And soul-destroying?"

"Sometimes."

She stared at him for a while, as if debating whether to query him further. Then she looked down towards the small garden and the dwarf trees. "I wish we had a real tree here. In our garden in Canberra we had some beautiful trees. I've always loved trees, even since I was a child. We lived in the country and I had a favourite tree, a coolibah, that I used to sit under and dream about what I'd do when I grew up."

"I didn't think coolibahs grew in the bush down around Perth. They're a tree from the eastern States."

She still wore the sunglasses, but he knew that her eyes had looked sharply at him from behind the dark panes. "Where did you learn about trees?"

"When you're a policeman you pick up lots of useless information."

"How did you know I came from the West?"

"I took it for granted. There wasn't much on you in the file on your husband, just that he'd married you in Perth."

"You have a file on him?"

"That thick." He measured with his fingers.

"Would I be allowed to read it?"

He shook his head. "It wouldn't help any. And it might make you feel worse. In any case, it's officially secret." But he wanted to know more about her: "*Are* you from New South Wales? Or over that way?"

"No, I'm from the West. This coolibah was brought over by my grandfather. I suppose he was like me, sentimental about trees."

He stood up. He wondered what would happen to her when Quentin was finally taken from her. There was an intensity about her that sometimes showed through the calm

[98]

exterior, a passion that might be a weakness as much as a strength. The sort of passion that could lead to despair, to suicide by hanging from a tree. Christ, I'm getting morbid, he thought.

He was relieved when Joseph, dressed for the street, as debonair and distinguished-looking as an ambassador, came to the door. "The taxi is waiting, sir."

"Well, here goes." He felt inside his jacket to make sure he had his travellers' cheques. "I didn't expect to come all this way to be camouflaged."

"You might enjoy it. It's fun sometimes." Then Sheila Quentin bit her lip: all the years of camouflage could not have been much fun for her husband.

Malone excused himself and went out to buy a suit that would not make him so conspicuous. Flannery had pledged him to secrecy; he wondered if the dark suit could be charged to expenses on that account. He wondered, too, how you charged the expenditure of yourself. Involvement was not something you entered under petty cash.

2

At the bottom of St. James's Street the newspaper poster announced in a jagged scrawl: *Saigon Bomb Kills Dozens*. Beside it the vendor did a little jig, glad to be alive on such a beautiful day and with something going for him in the 2:30 at Kempton Park. In Cleveland Place the raincoated tourists, suspicious of the London weather, and the red-coated Guardsmen, suspicious of the tourists, eyed each other like shy children at a party; a tourist raised his camera and a Guardsman almost imperceptibly stiffened, as if he feared he was going to be asked to dance. A Foreign Office man went by, umbrella at the trail, the gay carnation in his buttonhole contrasting oddly with the grave, grey mask he wore as a face. Malone looked out of the taxi at it all, drinking in London like a teetotaller suddenly addicted.

Stable Yard in front of Lancaster House was busy with the coming and going of black limousines as the taxi drove into it. A huge Austin Princess swept by like a Victorian dowager on her way to a funeral; the taxi skipped out of its way like an urchin. A Mercedes 600 pulled away, bearing an African who was a long way from home: he didn't have to worry what the taxpayers thought. A Labour Cabinet Minister went by in a Vauxhall: he didn't want the boys back at Transport House to think he had got big in the head. A rank of Rolls-Royces was parked along one side of the yard, their radiator grilles as ascetic and aloof as the faces of the more intellectual bishops. The taxi crept along the front of them, pulled in under the thick-pillared portico and Malone got out. He looked at the meter, felt in his pocket and pulled out the exact fare.

The driver stared at it. "Gawd help the Vietnamese. They'll never get any flaming aid from you, will they, mate?" And he drove off furiously, making a Rolls shy back into its pew as it prepared to pull out.

Malone went up the steps, showed his pass to the attendant on the door and moved on into the crowded vestibule. Quentin had obtained the pass and it had been delivered to Malone just before he had left the house with Joseph. He was marked on the pass as a *Special Assistant,* but Quentin had warned him it would admit him only to the outer halls of Lancaster House and not to the conference room itself. That had satisfied Malone: if Quentin was not safe in the conference room, safe from assassination and safely in custody, then he was not secure anywhere.

The first man he saw above the bubbling of heads was Quentin himself, coming down the broad stairs that faced the entrance. Edgar, Larter and a couple of other men were with him, but Quentin gave the impression of being completely alone: not only alone but lonely. He walked down the stairs with certain tread, but he was blind and deaf to everything in the high-ceilinged hall. His face was closed to the lively, gossiping world about him. He looks like a man in shock, Malone thought, one all ready for execution.

Then Quentin looked across the heads of the crowd and saw Malone. For a moment the eyes seemed to flinch; then the whole handsome face opened in a smile. He came down the last of the steps, losing Edgar and the others, and pushed through the crowd to Malone.

"I hardly recognized you." He looked at the dark blue wool-and-mohair suit, the blue silk knitted tie, the cream silk shirt, the black town brogues. "You've been throwing your money away, Scobie. All on account of me, too."

Malone shook his head. "It won't be wasted. I'm always being asked to be best man at other fellers' weddings."

"It'll go well at funerals, too," said Quentin, then shut his mouth as if he could have bitten off his tongue. Then he shrugged. "I'm getting morbid."

"I can't help you," said Malone with real regret. Then he glanced about the big high-ceilinged Staircase Hall, at the coloured imitation marble walls, the rich red carpeted stairs running up to the balconies with their tall grey columns, the intricately patterned ceiling itself. "They certainly knew how to live in those days. It would make a great Police Headquarters. I must tell Flannery when we get back."

Quentin screwed up his face at the mention of Flannery, but he made no comment on him. Instead he said, "I sometimes wonder if it's an appropriate place to debate the fate of men dying in paddy-fields. Marble halls and foxholes somehow don't complement each other." He nodded at a white marble bust just by him. "I don't think the old Duke of York here approves. Every morning I come in here that smile of his seems to get more disapproving."

Malone looked around at the chattering crowd: white, black, brown and yellow faces swam in a moving abstract pattern. "For all we know, there's a killer or two here. I don't think you're any safer than those fellers out in the paddy-fields."

"My fate's already decided, isn't it?" Quentin said; and turned away as Larter came up behind him. "How long do we have, Phil?"

Larter looked at him with concern. "Are you all right this morning, sir?" Quentin gave him a curious stare. "I mean, you don't seem to be concentrating too well. It was you who suggested the fifteen-minute break."

Quentin bit his lip. "Have I been that obvious this morning?"

Larter hesitated, then nodded. "You mentioned Indonesian history twice, when you meant Indo-Chinese history. I'm wondering, sir—perhaps we *should* tell them what happened last night?"

"Why?"

"Well, it might explain—" Larter took off his glasses and suddenly looked remarkably young, an undergraduate who had no confidence that he would ever get his degree. He fumbled with his glasses, then put them on again slightly askew; he straightened them, his thin angular face half-hidden behind his nervous hand. He was a junior diplomat, but he had not yet learned how to be diplomatic with his boss. "I mean, sir, you were not exactly in command of the conference this morning, not like the other days. If the other delegates were told what happened, they'd understand why you were—" He gestured, a flapping motion that suggested he had lost the bones in his wrist. He'll never make a top diplomat, Malone thought; he might know a hell of a lot about nations and history but he knows nothing about people. "I mean, they were looking to you yesterday—"

Quentin did not take offense at Larter's awkward criticism of him. The man has almost too much charity, Malone thought; and once again found himself wondering about Quentin as a murderer. "I'll do my best to win back their confidence, Phil. In the meantime, what happened last night is still classified."

Larter hesitated, then nodded. "Yes, sir." He turned to Malone. "We expect to break for lunch at one o'clock."

"I'll be here," said Malone, recognizing that Larter was trying to salvage some of his lost dignity by acting authoritatively. He felt a spark of resentment, but doused it at once. He was already involved enough here in London; he did not want further complications by battling with Larter. He smiled, taking the other man by surprise: Larter still had a lot to learn about the small arms of diplomacy. "Sergeant Coburn and I will see that His Excellency gets back for the afternoon session."

He had just seen Coburn standing at the foot of the stairs, staring intently at everyone who passed within ten feet of Quentin. He excused himself from Quentin and pushed his way through the crowd towards the Special Branch man. He was some yards short of Coburn when a hand gripped his arm and pulled him up short. He swung quickly on one foot, his fist balled to hit the assassin; and Jamaica said, "You're a touchy sort of guy. Are you always so aggressive?"

Malone looked down at the dark hand still clutching his arm. "You've got a pretty hefty grip there. Where did you get it? Shaking hands for the State Department? Or putting the squeeze on non-cooperative countries?"

Jamaica's face stiffened and his grip tightened; then he dropped his hand and smiled. Negroes' smiles are a trap, Malone thought: they always look twice as bright and friendly as those of anyone else. "Like they say, if you want honest criticism, always ask your friends."

"Are we friends?"

"Maybe not on a personal level. But our countries are supposed to be."

"What can I do for you then—on an international level?"

"You're a snotty bastard, aren't you?" Malone shrugged,

and Jamaica stared at him hard. "Have you got something against me because I'm coloured?"

"Now you're being personal."

"You don't blame me for asking, do you? You Australians have an official government complex about colour."

"I don't go along with everything our government does or thinks. I once got drunk with a West Indian cricketer. He was much darker than you. But he had better manners."

Jamaica smiled again. "I think I'd have liked to meet you ten years ago. In the ring, with or without gloves."

"Why not now? We could find a gym somewhere."

"I'm too soft. I've been living the white man's life too long."

Malone looked at him curiously. "Who's being critical of America now?"

Jamaica smiled wryly, nodding his head; something that could have been pain dulled his dark eyes. "A slip of the tongue. Don't tell the President."

Malone himself was guilty of the gift of too much charity. Too often in the past he had stopped himself just in time from being burdened with a prisoner's confidences because he had suddenly felt sorry for the man. Now all at once he forgot his antagonism towards Jamaica and said, "Look, Jamaica, what can I do for you?"

Jamaica recognized the change of tone in Malone's voice. He seemed to relax; his eyes came alive again. "I saw you talking to Madame Cholon last night at the reception. What do you know about her?"

"Nothing at all. She latched on to me, not the other way around."

Jamaica raised an eyebrow. "She seemed to know a lot about you."

Malone grinned. "All the girls like to boast that."

Jamaica did not return the grin. "I'd be careful, Malone."

[104]

"You said that last night. What's going on? What do *you* know about her?"

Jamaica said nothing for a moment, his dark face stiff as if he were debating with himself; then he shrugged and appeared to relax. "Nothing, nothing at all." He nodded across the room towards Quentin, now turning to go back up the stairs with Larter, Edgar and his other advisers. "How's it going in the conference room?"

"The High Commissioner doesn't confide in me."

"He's the top boy here, the one with all the influence. If anything happened to him, where would we be?"

Malone tried to sound casual. "What's likely to happen to him?"

"Who knows?" Jamaica smiled. "I heard one of the Africans say he wasn't on his best form this morning. He doesn't look well, does he?"

"Is there such a thing as conference virus? If there is, he's probably got it."

"You don't give much away, do you, Malone? You never hear much about Australian security. Are you all that good?"

"Isn't that the ideal security set-up, the one you never hear about? That's more than can be said about your C.I.A."

Jamaica nodded sadly. "Touché. Advertising is a national disease with us."

"Anyway, who told you I was a security man?"

It was Jamaica's turn to grin. "Madame Cholon. I told you, she seemed to know a lot about you."

The crowd had begun to move towards the stairs, like a tide flowing uphill. Africans and Indians in their native dress mingled with the black jackets and striped trousers; Malone wondered if his light grey suit would have been so conspicuous after all. Anyone could be lost in this crowd, even an assassin.

Phrases bubbled to the surface, the educational snippets

[105]

gained from the conference: "Revolutionaries, of course, can never acknowledge the honesty of counter-revolutionaries."

"Speaking of honesty, till I came to this conference I hadn't realized honest men could be such excellent liars."

Two small thin Indians went by, dark Puritans, their faces showing their disgust at the cynicism of the so-called privileged races. A Chinese brushed against Malone, murmured an apology and went on up the stairs, deliberately avoiding looking at the opulence that surrounded him as if afraid of being contaminated by it. But he was followed by the huge African Ambassador Malone had met last night. He stood on the landing of the stairs for a moment and gazed around with all the sensual satisfaction of a Nubian king; he smiled widely in enjoyment of what he saw, then moved on up the stairs, a man in whom the simple and the sophisticated had been perfectly blended, leaving him with no prejudices. Malone gazed after him admiringly.

Then Jamaica said, "I'd stay away from Madame Cholon if I were you."

He turned and walked away, disappearing out the front door. Malone started to follow him, then stopped. Up on one of the balconies Quentin had stopped to talk to a man whose face was vaguely familiar. Malone stared hard, trying to remember where he had seen the swarthy Oriental-looking face before. Then he remembered: the man had been sitting in the car parked in the street off Belgrave Square last night. He started towards the stairs, feeling the sweat already breaking on him. But his way was blocked by three Indians who all turned towards him and said, "Yes?" in three different keys as he excused himself to brush past them. By the time he had got over the international courtesies and had made the first landing of the stairs, he saw that Quentin was still alive, had gone on into the conference room. The swarthy man said something to Edgar, standing beside him, then turned and walked back along the balcony.

"What's the matter?" Coburn, suddenly alert, no longer unhappy-looking, came up on to the landing beside Malone.

"Find out who that bloke is." Malone nodded up towards the man now about to descend the flight of stairs on the west side of the hall. "Keep an eye on him till I come down."

Then hurrying, but trying not to attract too much attention to himself, he went up the east flight of stairs and along the balcony, just in time to intercept Edgar as the latter was about to enter the tall doorway of the conference room. Edgar looked back in surprise as his arm was grabbed.

"Who was that bloke just spoke to His Excellency?"

Edgar shrugged. "Some newspaperman, I think."

"What did he want?"

"An interview, I suppose. He wanted to know if Quentin would be going back to Australia House at lunchtime. Look, I've got to go—" He nodded towards the doors, where an attendant stood waiting impatiently to close them.

Inside the big room, beneath the pale blaze of a huge chandelier, Malone could see men seated round a long oval table, all staring curiously and with polite annoyance at him. He saw Larter stand up and begin to move towards him, his glasses flashing like twin heliographs: *Get out of here, you're holding up something of real importance.*

"Tell Mr. Quentin not to move out of here without Sergeant Coburn," he said to Edgar, and went back along the balcony and down the stairs at a run.

Coburn met him at the foot of the stairs. "I've checked on that cove. His name's Pallain. He's a correspondent, works for the East Asia News Agency."

"Is that a Communist agency?"

"I shouldn't think so. There's a list of all the newspapers and agencies covering the conference. The East Asia is based in Saigon, not Hanoi."

"Where's Pallain now?"

"He was in the press room making a phone call. There he is now!" Coburn jerked his head across towards one of the side galleries, then looked back at Malone. "What's going on?"

Malone watched Pallain move towards the front entrance. "I think he was in Belgrave Square last night. If Quentin goes back to Australia House at lunchtime, make sure you ride in the car with him. Even if you have to kick out Larter to get in." He grinned. "Kick him out anyway."

"Where are you going?"

Malone nodded after Pallain, now almost out the front door. "I'm going to stick with our mate for a while. I may just be heading up a blind alley, but it won't be the first time."

"We once caught a Russian agent in a blind alley." Coburn's eyes lit up for a moment, remembering some excitement; a Special Branch man could go for a year on dull routine stuff. "He couldn't get over the wall at the end. He was obliging enough to want to fight us. It was a real pleasure."

When Malone got out into the yard he saw Pallain just getting into a red Mini-Minor. He looked frantically about for a taxi, but there was none. As the red Mini moved out of the yard he saw Ferguson get out of the Rolls and look enquiringly towards him. Malone ran towards him.

"Get in quick!" He jumped into the front seat, slamming the door after him. "Follow that red Mini!"

Ferguson asked no questions. He swung the Rolls out of the yard into Cleveland Row. Ahead of them the Mini, a bright red moving target, was just turning up into St. James's Street.

"I haven't played this sort of lark in years," said Ferguson, his voice a growling chuckle. "Not since I used to stunt-drive in the old Ealing comedies."

[108]

"This isn't any comedy. That bloke up ahead might be one of those who nearly blew your block off last night."

"The bastard," rumbled Ferguson, and the Rolls seemed to surge forward like a luxury tank. Malone sat back, appreciating the comfort in which he lolled. He'd have to tell Leeds what sort of squad car he had used in London.

3

Truong Tho gingerly fitted the bomb into the black leather briefcase. He was experienced in bomb-making, but this, he knew, was a better job than anything he had ever been able to manufacture. The Englishman in Earls Court had been an artist; as he had told Truong Tho, he had worked for both I.C.I. and Omega and what better apprenticeship could a man have than that for making a time-bomb? He had not bothered to ask the Englishman why he should make bombs to blow up Western ambassadors; or maybe the Englishman hadn't known or cared who was to be the victim. He had sounded like the sort of artist who was interested only in his creation; who bought it or what it was used for didn't concern him. It had never been Truong Tho's habit to query why anyone did anything. He was not a revolutionary but a gangster. He felt neither pride nor shame at being described as such by Pallain: it was his trade. He knew of no other job that would pay him, a man from the paddy-fields of the Red River, so well.

He closed the top of the briefcase and turned the key in its lock. "You have to be sure none of Quentin's staff can open it," Pallain said.

"They can't open it without the key," Truong Tho said, and put the key in his pocket. He ran his hands over the bold initials above the lock: J.Q. "But you are sure they won't know the difference?"

"It's exactly the same as Quentin's case," Pallain said. "You can buy them in any store."

"Not *any* store," said Madame Cholon. "Mr. Quentin likes only the best."

Pallain smiled. "You're right. I was hoping I could have got it at Marks and Spencers, but I had to go to Harrods. A pity to waste so much money."

"It won't be wasted," said Madame Cholon. "One thing a gambler learns, one never wins high stakes with a small bet."

"I've checked on the time Quentin should be back at Australia House," Pallain said to Truong Tho. "One-fifteen at the latest. He eats lunch in his office, so he won't be moving about the building—he has his own washroom and toilet. When you see him arrive at Australia House, give him ten minutes before you go in. Just hand it to the porter, tell him Quentin left it at Lancaster House and that it should be taken up to him at once. If the porter asks who you are, you are from the South Vietnam delegation, a secretary."

Truong Tho nodded, but Madame Cholon said, "I wonder if we are taking enough precautions? What if the porter doesn't take it up at once? The fuse is set for one-thirty."

"We'll have to take that chance," said Pallain. "If Tho takes it up himself, he's likely to bump into that security man, Malone, or the Special Branch man who's with him."

Madame Cholon picked up some peanuts from a bowl on a marble table beneath the window and began to eat them, pushing them into her mouth peasant-fashion with the palm of her hand. "I should like shorter odds than this offers us. But what is there? What a pity Western ambassadors lead such dull, blameless lives! Blackmail would have been so much easier and cleaner."

"Blackmail leads to too many complications," said Pallain, who had tried several experiments in that direction.

Pham Chinh, who had been sitting quietly in one corner

[110]

of the room admiring the thin arrogant women in *Vogue,* now looked at his watch. "Time we were going."

"What sort of car did you hire?" Pallain asked.

"A black Hillman. Very anonymous."

Pallain nodded. "Drop Tho in Aldwych, just as you turn out of the Strand—it will be better if he walks from there. Drive on up Aldwych, down Fleet Street, then down Bouverie Street to the Embankment. Wait for Tho just opposite the ship moored there, the *Discovery.* If you see a policeman coming along to move you on, you'd better drive on, swing up into Temple Place and come back down again. The important thing is, you pick up Tho at the *Discovery.* Have you memorized all the streets?"

Pham Chinh smiled, his smooth youthful face turning into that of a smug schoolboy. "I've memorized every track in the Mekong Delta. This is nothing."

"They don't have traffic wardens in the Mekong Delta," said Madame Cholon. "Just watch you don't get booked."

"That would be funny." Pham Chinh wagged his head, chuckling to himself. He always enjoyed a job more when there was something to laugh about: it eased his nervousness. He closed *Vogue* on a beautiful skeleton in black underwear and stood up. "Do we come back here?"

"No!" Madame Cholon's voice was like the snap of a trap. "If the bomb does what we hope, I don't want to see you again. You have your tickets. Drive straight to the airport." She consulted a pad on the table by which she stood; everything had been planned like a military action. "You're on the Air France flight, AF819, for Paris at three o'clock. You know where to go in Paris. I'll phone you there this evening."

Truong Tho picked up the briefcase. He was wearing a black jacket, striped trousers and a Homburg; he had worn many disguises, but none in which he felt so uncomfortable. "If something goes wrong, what do we do?"

All three men looked at Madame Cholon. Even Pallain, the most imaginative of the men, had not contemplated how she would react if their mission proved a failure. The thought was too terrible; he would not be surprised if she tried to kill them all in her fury. She ate the last of the nuts in her hand, chewing slowly; she'd chew a man's bones with the same relish, Pallain thought. He had never met a woman like her, one who frightened him and excited him so much. No wonder Bay Vien had been such an admirer of her.

"We shall try again." Pallain wondered how the little-girl voice could have so much menace. Had she ever been innocent? "Jean-Pierre will phone you at the Air France desk at the airport. If the bomb hasn't worked, he will tell you where to go and wait for further orders. But do not come back here or try to get in touch with me. Understand?"

Truong Tho and Pham Chinh nodded, bowing their heads like servants. Madame Cholon looked at them with contempt; then abruptly she seemed to relent. She smiled and moved towards them, putting a hand on the arm of each. "Good luck. Soon you will be rich men."

Pham Chinh grinned and wagged his head again. "It will be like a dream. Me, in a Lincoln Continental. Who will believe it?"

"Come on," said Truong Tho, aware of the ticking bomb in his hand; only a fool dreamed when death was so close. Pham Chinh *was* a fool, and Truong Tho was surprised that Madame Cholon tolerated him.

They went out through the service door of the apartment. Madame Cholon never let them use the front door; they were still servants, even in this conspiracy to murder. Both men resented the distinction, especially since Pallain was allowed the privilege of the front door. But neither of them voiced their resentment, not even to each other: each of them knew what Madame Cholon was capable of. You did not insist on your democratic rights with a murderess.

[112]

They walked along a corridor, went down in the lift and out through the vestibule. Students were coming out of the college halls in Exhibition Road, all of them hurrying, as if time was too short for all that their education was fitting them for; they had to get on the bandwagon before it stopped rolling—fame and fortune no longer waited for the Englishman who took his time. You had to be with it, they said, hurrying past the two decorously walking assassins.

It was a warm cloudless day, reminiscent of days in Vietnam, and to Tho's stranger's eye the English seemed to have taken on new life. A gaggle of children went by headed for the park; the harassed young girl with them shone with perspiration and a new sparkle. Cars came down the road at full speed, every driver a Jim Clark, and Truong Tho and Pham Chinh had to skip nimbly to avoid them as they crossed to the black Hillman parked on the far side of the street. Tho held the briefcase carefully, remembering its maker's warning that, once the timing mechanism was set, it could go off ahead of time if it were subjected to a severe bump.

"I don't make crude jobs," he had said, wrapping up the bomb in a brown paper bag as if it were a loaf of bread. "I only make masterpieces. Delicate stuff. I'm the Fabergé of the explosives game. So watch yourself, matey. Take your time about setting it, and then don't go playing football with it."

Rather than work in the cramped confines of the car, where he might be seen by the inquisitive passer-by, Truong Tho had set the mechanism of the bomb before leaving the apartment. Now he got into the front seat beside Pham Chinh and carefully set the briefcase on his knees. He looked at his watch and clicked his teeth: the time was 12:50. Pham Chinh caught his nervousness and impatience, and without a word started up the car, swung it out from the red Mini-Minor parked in front of it, and pulled into the stream of

[113]

traffic. Intent now on losing no more time, neither of them had seen Malone come out of the entrance to the apartment building after them, swiftly cross the road and get into the waiting Rolls-Royce. Nor did they see the Rolls ease out from the curb and begin to follow them.

The lunchtime traffic was thick and their progress was slow. At the entrance to Hyde Park from Kensington Gore they were held up by the traffic lights. Both men stared at the red light, cursing it and willing it to turn green, and again they didn't notice what went on behind them: Malone jumped out of the Rolls and got into an empty taxi right behind the Hillman. When the light at last turned green the Hillman and the taxi moved off together, swinging right in the park and going down past the barracks and up towards Hyde Park Corner.

"We'll make it," said Pham Chinh, cheerful again now that they were on the move.

"We'd better," said Truong Tho, and looked out at the park, the great green bed of the dispossessed lovers of London. He had walked through here a few nights ago, shaking his head in wonder and disgust at what he had seen; he had always believed that the English were a cold, modest people, that love-making was only something they did to propagate their Empire. He was a puritanical man, one who had never even *kissed* a woman in public; even with the girls in the brothels in Saigon he had always insisted that the door be locked. He looked out now and saw a couple making love beneath a tree: their lunchtime break. A young Guardsman in red tunic and purple frustration stood outside the entrance to the barracks watching the lovers: in his plumage, his tight trousers that suggested his legs bent the wrong way, and his spurs, he reminded Truong Tho of a cock about to attack a successful rival.

Suddenly the lights ahead of them turned red and a car in front pulled up sharply. Pham Chinh slammed on the

[114]

brakes and Tho was flung forward. His body snapped shut over the briefcase and he felt his rib cage come down hard on the case. He held his breath, waiting to be blown to bits; then he relaxed, letting out his breath with a hiss. He looked at Pham Chinh, but the latter only shook his head.

"Not my fault. The English are terrible drivers."

Truong Tho said nothing, remembering the reckless exhibitionists of Saigon. The light turned green again and they went on up into the vortex of Hyde Park Corner, the taxi still following them like a double image of the black Hillman. A bus driver, driving by weight, challenged them on the left and again Pham Chinh had to brake quickly; the bus went by right above them, the passengers staring down with arrogant annoyance at the foreigners who were trying to take over British roads. Truong Tho stared back up at them for the moment the vehicles rode side by side, wanting to hurl the briefcase into their smug, superior faces. A woman from Maida Vale curled her lip at him, inviting murder; a small boy thumbed his nose at the funny-looking Chink in the hat that was too big for him. Then the bus and the car parted company.

The Hillman, still trailed by the taxi, was going down Constitution Hill, past the Palace, past the statue of Queen Victoria under her fluttering canopy of pigeons with their droppings of *lèse-majesté,* down the Mall, up round the exploding fountains of Trafalgar Square and into the chaos of the Strand. Truong Tho looked at his watch again: in the roar of the traffic he could hear both its ticking and that of the bomb. The time was 1:15. They were running late.

At last Pham Chinh pulled the Hillman into the curb in Aldwych. The car had stopped near a theater: posters proclaimed that a funny thing happened on the way to the Forum. Tho got out, holding the briefcase as if he expected it to shatter apart in his hand. He straightened his hat, wishing it didn't sit so far down on his ears, and did up all the buttons of his black jacket. He nodded to Pham Chinh, walked back down Aldwych, waited for the traffic to pass, then crossed the road and began to walk along the Strand towards Australia House. Walking carefully like a man in a minefield, the briefcase held primly away from his leg, he looked what he was supposed to be: a timid junior official from a foreign embassy. He glanced again at his watch: less than fifteen minutes before the bomb was due to go off.

He walked round the curve in front of Bush House, pulling up sharply and catching his breath as three young girls came hurtling out of a doorway in a skirmish of skirts. One of them brushed against the briefcase, flashed a smile of apology at him and went on, oblivious of how close she had come to death. He stopped, feeling the sweat break on him, and glanced back in the direction the girls had gone. And saw the Australian security man, the first man to get out of the Rolls-Royce last night, following him.

He blinked, blinded by sweat and shock. A file of street musicians went by, inching along the curb; they were playing a number he had heard American service bands play in Saigon: "When the Saints Go Marching In." He saw the name on the big drum carried by one of the men: The Happy Wanderers; and wondered what they had to be happy about. Passers-by were stopping to listen to the music, tapping their feet in time to the infectious beat. One of the musicians came towards Truong Tho, a box held out, a smile on his blunt, weatherbeaten face: "Good luck to you, sir." Tho stared at him, all terrified suspicion now: the file of musicians seemed to be closing in around him, their music getting louder and threatening.

Suddenly he lunged at the man with the box, pushing him aside. He felt the man clutch at him, but he had gone past him, knocking aside the man playing the trumpet: a note went sour in the middle like a wail of help. He ran across the road, dodging the shrieking, hooting traffic, the brief-

[116]

case still held primly in his hand. He made the opposite side of the road, flung a glance back over his shoulder and saw Malone running through the traffic after him.

He ran down a side street. Ahead of him he could see the river and the tall masts of a ship; he wondered if it was the *Discovery*, if Pham Chinh would be almost there yet. His hat fell off and a man shouted after him, but he kept running. The narrow pavement was busy with people coming up from the Embankment; he darted out between two parked cars and ran down the middle of the road. Somewhere he heard a clock strike and pigeons flew over the tops of the buildings like smoke from a blast. He was panting, the black jacket tight about his heaving chest, and he could feel the sweat running down his face. The briefcase was a great weight, almost breaking his wrist, but he daren't drop it. He was less than a hundred yards from the river; he would fling it far out into the water, let it explode harmlessly there. He darted another look back over his shoulder, saw that Malone was gaining on him, and increased his speed.

He ran down the middle of the street, between lines of gawking pedestrians, like a marathon runner at the end of his run; some youths urged him on, then yelled encouragement to Malone, the runner-up. It was a scene from a comedy film, all the spectators looked for the hidden cameras. But there were no cameras and the comedy was black.

Truong Tho swung right at the bottom of the street, down a sloping crescent. The ship on the other side of the Embankment *was* the *Discovery; Pham Chinh had* to be there! He hurtled down the slope, desperate now, the muscles in his arms already flexed for the throw that would get rid of the briefcase. He came out on to the Embankment, still on the run, was halfway across the busy road when he saw the black Hillman a hundred yards away coming towards him.

He drew in a sigh of relief at the moment the other car,

coming from the opposite direction, hit him. He felt the sharp pain in his back, then he went up in the air. He seemed to fall slowly, taking an age; he saw the briefcase still held in his hand below him, the gold initials, J.Q., flashing like the igniting spark of an explosion.

Then he hit the ground on top of the briefcase.

CHAPTER SIX

1

"They seem to be getting desperate." Quentin drummed his fingers nervously on the desk in front of him. "But who the hell are they? And why me? Why not one of the others?" Then he shook his head. "No, I shouldn't have said that. That's only wishing disaster on someone else."

Again the charity: Christ, Malone thought, does he always think of the other man first? Or was it guilt: was he making up for the one life he had taken years ago? But you couldn't ask a man that. "There was no way of identifying him. He was blown to smithereens. It was just sheer luck no one else was hurt."

"You were lucky you weren't closer." Quentin's fingers still drummed on the desk. "Don't get hurt on my account, Scobie. That's the prospect that worries me as much as any. You didn't come to London for that."

Malone grinned, trying to ease the atmosphere, to take some of the tension out of the other man. "I'm already hurt. These new shoes are killing me." He eased his feet out of them and wiggled his toes. "All right?"

Quentin nodded, then smiled, relaxing a little. "Do you have a lot of friends?"

Malone looked puzzled. "Quite a lot. Too many, maybe.

Then they become acquaintances more than friends. You spread yourself too thin, never spend enough time with one or two of them to get to know them properly."

"Do you regret that?"

"What? Not having one or two close mates? I think so. Maybe it's one of the penalties of being a copper."

"Are you getting to know me?"

"As a friend? Or as a prisoner?" Malone was cautious.

"I can't ask for the first. And I don't really want to know as the second. No, just as a man."

Malone paused before he shook his head. "No, you still puzzle me too much. I still don't understand—well, never mind."

"No, go on."

Again Malone paused a moment. "Well, I don't understand how you could have killed your wife. But don't quote me—I'm off duty, I'm not talking as a policeman."

"Would you believe me if I said it was an accident?"

Once more Malone hesitated. "I might. But I'll warn you—I don't think any jury would. Not after twenty-three years. They'd want to know why you waited all that time to make that sort of plea."

Quentin considered what Malone had said, then slowly nodded his head in agreement. He took another tack in the conversation: "I've never had a close friend. Before the war I was too—well, shy, I suppose. A real bushwhacker, thinking everyone in Sydney was out to take me down. Then after—after what happened to Freda—" He stopped and his eyes went blank; his face tightened as if he had suddenly been hit by migraine. I wonder how often he's thought of her? Malone wondered; and waited while the other man was racked by memory. Then the eyes cleared. "After Freda, I couldn't risk having friends."

"You didn't need them. You had Mrs. Quentin."

Quentin nodded. "But sometimes a man needs more than

a wife. I would have liked a son." He didn't say why he and his wife had had no children, but Malone hazarded a guess: the fewer people inherited the shame of his crime the better. It was as if he had been waiting all these years for the inevitable. But why had he gone into politics, taken the risk of public exposure? "But you can't have everything. Not many men have a wife like I have."

"You must have fallen for her quickly. How soon did you get to Perth after you'd left Sydney?"

Quentin was silent for a while, as if trying to retrace all the movements of so many years ago. "A week, maybe a little more. I went across by train. It was still possible then to travel from State to State without a permit. But you wouldn't remember all that, you'd have been too young. After the Japs came into the war, you had to prove your journey was necessary." He smiled: sardonically or with regret, it was hard to say. "My journey was necessary, all right."

"When did you meet Mrs. Quentin?"

Again it was as if he were trying to remember events that had followed what might have been a state of shock. "About a week after I arrived in Perth, I think it was."

"When did you think of marrying her?"

Quentin had been answering the questions as if he were only half-hearing them; but now his brows came down and he looked sharply at Malone. "Why?"

"I'm just trying to understand you, that's all. Why you murdered your wife, why you married a stranger only six months later, why you went into politics—you must have known that going into politics, sooner or later you were going to get your photo in the papers, especially in Federal politics. Were you shoving your neck out, hoping someone would recognize you and give you away?"

"Are you an amateur psychologist, too? You mean I hadn't the courage to give myself up, but I wanted to be caught?"

He shook his head. "If that was the intention, Scobie, it was all subconscious. No, I just drifted into politics. Then I guess ambition took over. First, I was asked to be a spokesman for ex-servicemen. Then I was asked to run for a State seat. A little while after that they spoke to me about Federal politics. I thought about the risks, but by then I'd begun to like public life. When you've been shy all your life and suddenly people start taking notice of you, listening to you and asking your advice, it—well, it goes to your head."

"What about Mrs. Quentin? She looks as if she enjoys public life now—did she then?"

"She has always liked it. Without her I wouldn't have got as far as this."

Quentin looked about him. They were in his office at Australia House. The big windows faced east and the late sun was reflected into the large room from the face of St. Clement Danes church opposite; the rich brown of the Tasmanian bean panelling was warm with the silver-gold light. The hum of traffic came up, but it was lulling more than disturbing. It was now seven o'clock and Malone and Quentin had come back here half an hour ago from the afternoon session at Lancaster House.

Malone waited for Quentin to go on; but the latter seemed to have decided that he had done enough confiding. So Malone said, "Why did you ask if I have a lot of friends?"

"You look as if you have a gift for friendship," Quentin said. "Or maybe it's a gift for charity."

Malone laughed, and Quentin looked at him curiously. "I was thinking the same thing about you. About charity, I mean."

Quentin smiled. "Thank you. We seem to be developing into a mutual admiration society." The smile faded. "We shouldn't. That could only be awkward for you."

Malone hesitated, then nodded. "The sooner we get home, the better."

Quentin nodded absently, staring at the wide desk in front of him. Then he picked up the newspaper that lay on it. "One thing we can be thankful for, the papers haven't connected the bomb with me. Not yet anyway."

"When the bomb went off and I saw there was nothing left of whoever he was, I made myself scarce. I got to a phone as fast as I could and rang Denzil at the Yard. He had a man along there within ten minutes." Malone nodded at the newspaper Quentin held. "You'll see there that one or two people said the bloke was being chased by another man, but none of them was able to describe me. It pays to be nondescript." He grinned, wiggling his toes. "And I thought I was the best-dressed man in London today."

"If Mrs. Quentin makes any comment on this, we know nothing." Quentin looked over the newspaper at Malone. "There's no connection with me, understand?"

"She'll make a guess or two. It's not that far from Australia House—"

"We'll still deny it. She has enough on her mind—"

There was a knock on the door and Lisa put her head round it. "Superintendent Denzil is here, sir."

Quentin stood up as Denzil and Coburn came in, their faces stiff and slightly distorted with strain. They were trained to expect and prevent assassinations, but this was their first experience of such an attempt. Lisa stood in the doorway, but Quentin shook his head at her and she went out, closing the door after her. Malone bent down, looking for his shoes; then decided against putting them on and stood up in his stockinged feet. Denzil looked at him, but said nothing: you knew he would let gangrene set in before he would remove his own shoes in front of an ambassador.

"We've made a little progress, sir," he said to Quentin. "We still don't know who the dead man was. But thanks to Mr. Malone's tip, we've picked up Pallain. We're holding him at the Yard now."

"What's he got to say?" Malone asked.

"He's all indignation and threats. He's half-French, half-Vietnamese, I gather, and we're getting the worst of both. It's like dealing with General de Gaulle and Ho Chi Minh on one of their worst days."

Quentin smiled, appreciating Denzil's imagination; it was obvious that he, as well as Malone, had made a mistake in his estimate of the superintendent. "I take it he knows nothing?"

Denzil shook his head. "Nothing at all."

"Who was he visiting at those flats?"

Malone's feet still hurt; he wiggled his toes again, and Denzil looked down, finding them a distraction. Behind him, something like a smile twisted Coburn's face. "I went into the foyer, but there was no porter there and more than half the flat numbers had no names against them on the board. I watched the lift indicator—he went up to the sixth floor. Then I saw it coming down again and I ducked to the back of the foyer. Then the two Asians came out."

"Why did you decide to follow them instead of waiting for Pallain to come down again?"

Malone shrugged. "I don't know. Instinct, I guess. It wasn't even a hunch. Maybe I was just trying to find out who else might be in this, where they belonged. It never entered my head they were heading this way with a bomb." He shivered, suddenly cold. "I'm just glad I never caught up with him! Christ, chasing a bloke to get yourself killed!"

Everyone was silent for a moment. Then Denzil said, "Well, we don't know who the dead man was, nor his mate. But Pallain was visiting someone named Madame Cholon."

Malone's eyebrows went up. "Cholon?"

"You know her?"

"Let's say I've met her." Malone went on to tell of his encounter last night with Madame Cholon. "She keeps crop-

[124]

ping up all the time. I was talking about her this morning with a feller named Jamaica."

"Who's he?"

"I don't know for sure. He's at the American Embassy."

"We'll check with him. He might know something about her."

"Why not check with her?" Quentin asked.

"She'd gone, sir, when we got back there. Baggage and all. She could be anywhere. In London or right out of the country. But we're having the Channel ports and the airport watched. We got a good description of her from the porter. He was back on duty when we got there. He hadn't seen her go. But he's a chap with an eye for the ladies and he described her in some detail. Seems she is quite a looker." He glanced at Malone.

"She's a dish, all right," Malone said. "But I don't know that I'd want to cuddle up too close to her."

Quentin went back and sat down behind his desk. He picked up the newspaper and looked at it again; the front-page story on the explosion was illustrated with a picture of the gaping hole in the middle of the Embankment roadway. "It's hard to believe—why would a woman want to kill me?"

"We don't know it's her, sir," Denzil said cautiously.

"I know that, Superintendent. I'm just including her in the list of possibilities, that's all." He put down the newspaper and sat back in his chair. "I'm just asking a rhetorical question, too, when I say why should she, or anyone else for that matter, want to kill me. I know why. It's not me personally they're after. It could have been anyone else who might have got the others listening to him at this conference. It just seems an extreme way of achieving whatever end they're after. Not only extreme, but crude. Have you any clue who this Madame Cholon is?"

"None at all, sir. The porter said he thought she looked

Chinese. But I'm afraid that to the ordinary Englishman in the street, anyone with slant eyes is Chinese."

"She's Vietnamese, I think," said Malone.

"Of course!" Quentin nodded his head emphatically. "It's probably not her real name. Cholon is the Chinese twin city of Saigon."

"It's an elementary suspicion," said Denzil, "but I tend to distrust people who change their names."

"Yes," said Quentin, and glanced at Malone, who chose that moment to bend down and begin to pull on his shoes.

Denzil appeared not to notice his gaffe, and went on: "I'd like Mr. Malone to come back to the Yard with me. Sergeant Coburn will escort you home, sir."

Malone stood up again, wincing as his shoes tightened on his feet. "You want me to have a look at Pallain?"

"If you can positively identify him as the man you saw in Belgrave Square last night, we can hold him a while longer. Perhaps till the conference finishes."

Malone looked at Quentin, who said, "We'll wait dinner for you. I'll tell my wife you've met an old friend and been delayed." He looked at Coburn. "We're keeping it from Mrs. Quentin that the bomb was intended for me. I'd appreciate it if you kept that in mind, Sergeant."

"I don't think you'll be troubled again, sir," Coburn said. "There's only a few more days till the conference ends, then you can relax."

"Yes," said Quentin, and this time Malone caught the ironical glance. This time Denzil also caught it and suddenly went red.

Malone, walking cat-footed in his pinching shoes, went out with Denzil. As they passed Lisa in the outer office she said, "Is His Excellency going home now, Mr. Malone? Mrs. Quentin has been on the phone. She sounds worried."

"What about?"

"She saw the news on television, about the bomb explosion down on the Embankment." She had been putting on her make-up when they had come out of Quentin's office; a new lip pressed down on an old lip, but it was also an expression of concern. "That had nothing to do with Mr. Quentin, did it?"

"Nothing at all," said Malone, and winced.

"What's the matter? Are you ill? Is there something wrong?" She didn't believe him. She's like all women, he thought: they're all pessimists. It didn't help that what she suspected was the truth.

He lifted one foot. "My shoes are killing me."

"Oh, is that all?" She looked relieved, smiled at both of them. "I'd just hate to have anything happen to—" She nodded towards the door of Quentin's office.

"We all should," said Denzil, and smiled reassuringly. He tucked in his belly. "We'll look after him."

The two men went on down out of the building. A black police car was drawn up by the curb, its uniformed driver reading the sports pages of the *Evening Standard*. He dropped the paper, jumped out and opened the door as Denzil and Malone approached.

"How are the scores?" Denzil asked.

"Our batsmen are in trouble, sir."

"They always are. We don't have the men we used to." Denzil gestured for Malone to get into the back seat, then got in beside him. "Are you interested in cricket?"

Malone nodded. "I played regularly up till a couple of years ago."

"Batsman or bowler?"

"I was a fast bowler. Or supposed to be."

Denzil nodded approvingly and looked at him with new interest. Anyone who played cricket must be a good type. "I used to be one myself. When I was out in Nairobi. Never got any first-class cricket there, unfortunately. I used to play for the M.C.C. when I was home on leave. Once bowled

Wally Hammond for a duck." He nodded his head, remembering his moment of glory; he had assured himself of his place in his own particular heaven. Malone had met the sort before: the Elysian Fields had a cricket pitch marked out in their middle, the pavilion bar was always open so the good and the just could go on talking about past matches for the rest of eternity. Denzil continued to muse for a while, then looked up and smiled the surprising smile. "My wife thinks it was the worst thing ever happened to me. Said it retarded my mental development by twenty years. Women never understand, do they?"

"That's what's kept me a bachelor."

Denzil looked sideways at him for a moment, the smile still in place; then abruptly it slid off his face and he said, "How long have you known the High Commissioner?"

Malone knew it was more than just an idle question; Denzil was not the sort who asked idle questions. "Why?"

"You seem to have an understanding with each other." He nodded down at Malone's feet. "I don't know any other ambassador who'd let his security man take off his shoes in front of him. Except some of these new coloured ones." His voice was edged with contempt. He had spent too long in Africa, seen an empire die: he longed for the good old days, when he had bowled Wally Hammond for a duck, when the Negroes knew their place.

"We met only yesterday."

"Um. I suppose it's that other business then—" He stopped, as if he had only just remembered the policeman in the front seat.

"I guess that's it," said Malone. "It does make a difference. Gives us a mutual interest. Just like you and me, with cricket."

His voice was bland. Denzil looked at him, trying to read something into it, but couldn't. Malone smiled back at him: in twenty-four hours he had become adept at using the hypocrite's mask. He wondered if it would come in handy back in Sydney when he would have to report to Flannery, the master of the game.

Denzil's room at Scotland Yard was not a big one; the Special Branch, Malone guessed, were the poor relations. It did have an outside view: trees, old men on the Embankment, a pleasure boat coming back from a day trip, its passengers singing "Knees Up, Mother Brown" as they passed the Mother of Parliaments. Denzil waved Malone to a chair, picked up a phone and asked for Pallain to be sent in.

"Oh, and have someone check with the American Embassy on one of their men. His name's Jamaica. Find out all you can about him. If he's there, ask him if he would mind coming over here. He might be able to help us with this chap Pallain."

By the time Pallain came in, Denzil had got his pipe going. He sat behind his desk, rock-solid, no nonsense: he wasn't going to let any threatening Frog half-caste get away with anything. But Pallain had got over his indignation or whatever had been exciting him. He came in, sat down and nodded amiably at both men.

Denzil ignored Pallain, looked at the plainclothes man who had brought him in. "Has he changed his tune, Sergeant?"

"Why not ask me?" Pallain said before the Sergeant could reply. "No, I haven't changed my tune. All I've done is to revise my opinion of British law and justice."

Malone had expected Denzil to bluster, instead of which the superintendent looked at Pallain and smiled. The man was a complicated sum of contradictions; Malone wondered if the real Denzil ever got to the surface. Perhaps the years in Africa had ruined him: prejudices had been laid over him like false skins.

"We're really not too bad, Mr. Pallain. I've heard the police in Saigon are much worse. Or is that just propaganda?"

[129]

It was Pallain's turn to smile. "I wouldn't know, Superintendent. I have never been picked up by the police in Saigon. Out there I'm accepted for what I am, a respectable newspaperman. I still haven't been told why I was brought here."

"We just want some information." Denzil was polite, patient. "We are investigating a bomb explosion. If you are a good reporter, you must have heard about it."

"I've been in custody most of the afternoon. How would I have heard about it? What happened—someone killed? And how do you connect me with it?" Pallain's voice rose just a little: it could have been indignation or fear, Malone wasn't sure.

Denzil ignored the flood of questions and put one of his own: "Why were you visiting Madame Cholon at lunchtime?"

"I've already told you. I wanted to interview her."

"Why? Who is she?"

"I was told she was a very rich woman from Singapore." Pallain's voice was calm again, almost bored. "I was just going to do a gossip piece on her."

"You leave an important diplomatic conference to go and write a gossip piece on a woman you know nothing about?" Denzil puffed out a cloud of smoke, then brushed it away with his hand: the gesture was also a dismissal of what Pallain was trying to tell him.

"I work for an agency, Superintendent," Pallain explained patiently. "An agency man does everything."

"What's so special about Madame Cholon, apart from her being rich?"

Pallain hesitated; for a moment it looked as if he might tell Denzil to go to hell. Then he said, "I might ask you the same question. Why are you so interested in her? Does she have something to do with this bomb explosion you spoke of?"

Denzil smiled again, cold as the wink of light on a dagger. "I'll ask the questions, Mr. Pallain. Where does Madame Cholon get her money?"

"I was told she had big business interests."

"What sort of interests?"

Pallain shrugged; then Malone said, "Gambling interests?"

Pallain's face showed nothing. He looked at Malone, then at Denzil. "Who is this man, Superintendent? He's not English, he doesn't have your accent. What's he doing here?"

"This is Mr. Malone. It doesn't matter who he is, he has a right to be here." Denzil then glanced at Malone. "Is this the man you saw last night in Belgrave Square?"

Before Malone could answer, Pallain said, "Saw me *where?*" He laughed, a cough of incredulity, of contempt; in Malone's ears it sounded like an echo of Flannery's laugh. "What the hell would I be doing there?"

"You were sitting in a car in Chesham Street, just off the square," said Denzil.

"I wasn't there, but even if I were, what's criminal about that? Aren't men allowed to sit with girls in cars in England?" He smiled, shaking his head. "You never have encouraged romance, have you?"

"You weren't romancing," said Denzil.

"No? What was I supposed to be doing then?"

Suddenly Malone knew they were trapped: they would have to let this man go. He looked at Denzil and said, "He's not the man, Superintendent."

Denzil almost bit off the stem of his pipe. He coughed on the smoke in his mouth; then he nodded at the plainclothes man. "Take him outside, Sergeant. But don't let him go just yet."

Pallain stood up. "This won't be the last of this. I have a French passport."

"Anglo-French relations have been cool for some time,

[131]

Mr. Pallain. Another small complaint won't be noticed. Now if General de Gaulle didn't say *non* so often—" Again there was the warm smile, almost breezy this time. *"Au revoir—* just in case we do see each other again."

Pallain recovered some of his poise; he bowed his head to Denzil and Malone. The best Frenchmen never lost their poise and dignity: he would have to remember that. "What if I said *non* to that?"

The smile widened. "We English can be very deaf at times."

As soon as the door closed on Pallain and the plainclothes man, Denzil dropped his smile as if it hurt and looked at Malone. "It was you, Sergeant, who suggested we pick him up. We don't like being made to look fools here at Special Branch."

Malone wanted to take off his shoes again, but he knew that would be a mistake. "If we had told him what we suspected him of doing last night, that he drove the car in which that bloke with the gun got away—we forgot he was a newspaperman, Superintendent. Suppose we hadn't been able to hold him, he'd have gone out and in tomorrow morning's papers the story would have been right across the front pages. That's what Quentin is trying to avoid."

Denzil's pipe had gone out. He didn't attempt to relight it, but laid it down on an ashtray made out of some hoof: something he had shot in Africa? Malone wondered. He glanced around the room while Denzil sat pondering. A pair of small horns, mounted on a board, hung on one wall; on either side of it were two wooden masks, the sightless eyes fixed on a photograph that hung on the opposite wall. Denzil, in white shirt and shorts and tropical helmet, was flanked by two native policemen: it was something from a bygone era, fly-specked and faded and dusty: the chars who came in to this office were not interested in the memories of someone else's past. Malone looked back at Denzil, suddenly feeling sorry for the man. Whatever you thought of the old British Empire, and Malone had been brought up in a household that equated it with Hades, it had been a way of life for this man across the desk, the *only* way of life.

"What are we trying to do? Save a man's life or save a conference?" Denzil rubbed a sandy eyebrow abstractedly. "That's the worst burden of this job, Sergeant. We're asked to be even more impersonal than the ordinary policeman. We're supposed to look beyond the man we're trying to protect—or trying to arrest—to the idea or the position he represents. It isn't easy." He tugged on his eyebrow and worked his thin lips over each other. He glanced up at the photograph on the wall: the younger Denzil had had a much easier job. Then he said, "When you take Quentin back to Sydney, if he's found guilty, will they hang him?"

"They don't have the death penalty in New South Wales. I don't know what his plea will be. He might even try pleading guilty to manslaughter and not guilty to murder. If they accepted that, he could get off with anything from seven to ten years."

"Whatever he gets, his life will still be over. The life that means something to him." Again he glanced at the photograph. "You know what we're trying to do, Sergeant? We're trying to keep a man alive for what may be far worse than a quick, painless death."

Malone said tonelessly, "What are you suggesting?"

"Nothing," said Denzil, and sounded weary. The phone rang and as he reached for it he said, "We'll keep him alive. That black chappie up there in the photo, the one on the right, he was gored by a rhino. I spent three days nursing him, but in the end he died. Then I got blind drunk for three days. I don't like to see a man die, Sergeant. Anyone at all." Then he picked up the phone. "Yes?"

Malone eased off his shoes; he knew now that Denzil wouldn't mind. He sat back in his chair, feeling as weary as

Denzil had sounded. Even his body felt spent, something that hadn't happened to him in a long time; he had always been a physical fitness addict, had been able to bowl all day at cricket or play flat out for the full eighty minutes of a rugby game. But now the exhaustion of his mind was seeping down into his muscles and bones, was weakening him like some creeping disease. He suddenly longed for the weekend and the plane for home. Fate was really piling it on Quentin: Malone wondered if he, too, was now longing for the plane back to Sydney.

Then Denzil put down the phone and said, "They know nothing about your man Jamaica at the American Embassy. They've never heard of him."

2

"Some walnut torte, sir?" asked Joseph.

"My husband has a very sweet tooth, Mr. Malone," said Sheila Quentin. "He is the despair of our cook. Every night she has to dream up something exotic for dessert."

Quentin said, "I hate diplomatic dinners. Except the Americans' and the Austrians', they have a sweet tooth, too. But the others always try to fob you off with some sort of ice. Especially the British. Their dinners taste like Blackpool Night Out." He opened his mouth for a forkful of torte, nodded appreciatively at the butler. "Cook's done it again. Joseph. Tell her I'll recommend her for an O.B.E."

Malone, enjoying the torte, watched Quentin covertly. The High Commissioner was as relaxed as if the conference were already over and a great success; it was as if he had nothing to worry about now but a holiday trip home, then a return here to another tour of duty. All through the meal he had been joking, keeping the conversation going like a television interviewer but with less banality, prompting the others themselves into jokes and repartee. There had been

[134]

no sign of strain, not even when Sheila had asked how today's session of the conference had gone.

"Not as well as yesterday," Quentin had said, then chewing with relish on stuffed chicken breast; whatever had happened today, it had not affected his appetite. "I don't know whether I'm telegraphing my punches or something, but one man there today, one of the Africans, had an immediate answer to everything I proposed. That hasn't happened before. All these delegates, maybe because they're inexperienced, I don't know, but they're great ones for saying nothing till the next day. As if they have to go home at night and get instructions. But not today. This chap was on the ball all day."

"Constructively?" Lisa asked.

"Anything but. It was a black face with a Chinese voice. He had all the answers I'd have expected from Peking. And he had them pat."

"More wine, sir?" Joseph had said to Malone, and Malone had nodded. He had not been a wine drinker back home, drinking a beer with his meals if he drank anything. Occasionally when he took a girl out to dinner he would order wine, but he had never really developed a taste for it. Now all at once his palate had changed. It would kill his old Irish mum, with her steak and kidney pie and rhubarb tart washed down with a nice cup of tea. He looked about the large dining room, at the green silk walls, the deep orange curtains, the Drysdale painting in which the orange of the curtains was repeated; then he looked at the table, at the silverware, the lace place mats, the glasses pastel-coloured with the wine they held. This was gracious living, something he had idly glanced at on the women's pages of newspapers back home; and he was surprised at how much he enjoyed it.

"What are you smiling at?" Lisa asked.

"Thinking of my old Irish mum again. She always suspects people who drink wine with their meals. Thinks it's a sinful foreign habit aimed at spoiling good plain cooking." He grinned, dropping the Irish brogue he had assumed. "Gracious living isn't up her street."

"She sounds like an aunt who brought me up—" said Quentin, and went on to describe something that had happened years ago. He's so relaxed, Malone marvelled, that he can now reminisce about something he must have tried to keep buried all these years. But how real would the people from the past be to him? Was John Corliss, as well as Freda Corliss, also dead? Malone had once read that everyone's life was a fiction, if not in full at least in part; and he had seen the proof of that so many times, had been aware of it even in himself. Which was the real man behind the handsome smiling face at the head of the table? Did even Quentin (or Corliss) himself know?

Then dinner was finished and Joseph said, "Shall I serve coffee in the drawing room, ma'am?"

Sheila nodded, but Quentin said, "I think Mr. Malone and I will have ours in here. Bring us a brandy, too, Joseph."

The two women rose; and Sheila, suddenly grave now after the enjoyment of the last hour, said, "What are you going to talk about?"

Quentin shook his head, smiling. "About something that I know would bore you and Lisa stiff. Cricket."

Lisa made a face and Sheila said, "Cricket? What on earth for?"

"When you ask a question like that, it shows we're doing the right thing staying in here on our own. I just want to forget the conference, that's all, for an hour or so. Talking about cricket with Mr. Malone might do that."

"How do you know Mr. Malone knows anything about cricket?"

"I know quite a lot about Mr. Malone. We've had our confidences, haven't we?" He winked at Malone and the latter nodded.

[136]

Sheila hesitated, staring at Quentin as if she were still not reassured, then followed Lisa out of the room. Quentin watched them go and as soon as their backs were turned on him the colour seemed to drain out of his face. Even as Malone watched him he aged visibly; he leant forward a little and by some trick of light his hair turned almost white; every year of the last twenty-three was sketched savagely on his dull, grey countenance. Malone felt he sat in the room with a stranger.

To break the suddenly awkward silence he said, "How did you know I was interested in cricket?"

Quentin didn't seem to hear. He sat staring down at his hands on the table, watching the trembling fingers. Then he made an effort to regain control of himself. He sat back, taking in a deep breath. "Sorry, Scobie. It's been a tough day."

"I think we ought to go out to the airport tonight and see if there's a plane for home."

"It would be the easiest way, wouldn't it?" Then he shook his head and said, "How did I know you were interested in cricket? I remembered seeing you play, oh, eight or ten years ago. You played for New South Wales, Sheffield Shield."

Malone grinned, wriggling his toes comfortably in his old brown shoes. "Just the once. They belted me all over the field."

"I never played cricket. Golf is my game—when I have the time."

"I know. That was where they traced the one photo of you that still existed, at Moor Park. You'd won some trophy."

Quentin smiled wryly: he had reached a depth of resignation where he could now be amused by his blunders of long ago. "I'd forgotten that one. I burned all the photos we had in the house. There weren't many—Freda and I weren't the sort for always standing in front of a camera."

[137]

"You were planning even then to go into smoke, take up a new identity?"

"Yes. Why?"

Malone shrugged. "You told me that killing of your wife was an accident. Then you do a systematic thing like that. Burning photos, getting rid of all the means of identifying you. That looks pretty much like premeditation. You'll have a hard job convincing a jury it wasn't."

"I'm just naturally systematic. Once it was done—"

"Once it was done, why didn't you call the police?"

"I—I told you last night. Basically I'm a coward. I just ran away."

"You're not a coward and I don't think you're systematic, either. That file I have upstairs on you, it's really thorough. The bloke missed your personality, your *personal* personality, I mean, but he took you apart politically. You don't come out of it as a man who plays it systematically. Some of your biggest successes were off the cuff. The compromise you worked out on that trade deal with Indonesia, for instance. I've only known you—" Malone paused, surprised. "Geez, it's only twenty-four hours! Well, anyway. That's all I've known you, but the last thing I'd say about you is that you're systematic. You're cool and you know what you're doing, but you're not the sort who goes in for systematic detail. Not like burning photos of yourself after you've accidentally killed your wife."

Quentin slapped his hand on the table. "Stop it! Who the hell are you—"

Malone sat silent, knowing he had gone too far. He looked about the room again, ill at ease now, suddenly longing for the cheerless but predictable comfort of his tiny flat in King's Cross: the roughly made bed, the television set (the bachelor's comforter), the rows of paperbacks in the small cheap bookcase, the view from the window of the rooftops of Rushcutters Bay and the six square inches of harbour water: home sweet bloody home.

Quentin breathed deeply, then said, "I'm sorry. Actually, I think you're trying to help me, aren't you?" Malone nodded slowly. Quentin sighed, almost a hiss of self-pity. "I should be grateful for any help I can get. Sorry," he repeated.

The door opened and Joseph came in with a tray. He poured coffee and brandy and set the cups and goblets before the two men. Then he said, "That bomb explosion today, sir. Did it have any connection with what happened last night?"

Malone looked up suspiciously, but Quentin just said, "Yes, Joseph. But don't mention it to Madame."

"No, sir. May I say I'm glad they didn't succeed in their purpose?"

"Thank you, Joseph." Quentin waited till the butler had gone, then looked at Malone. "Joseph suspects something."

"About me, you mean? I thought he'd accepted me now I've got out of my grey suit."

"You don't know what he was like before you came. Ice cold. He set the central heating back ten degrees every time he came into a room."

"What do you know about him? I mean, is there ever any check on blokes like him in a job like this?"

"I gather he was vetted by my predecessor. He'd worked for a couple of years for some lord before he came here. He's been in this job just over five years now. He's okay." Quentin sipped his coffee, then said, "How far did you get at Scotland Yard this evening?"

Malone told him. "The only thing we're sure of is that this Madame Cholon is mixed up in it somehow. But who's she working for?"

"And who's this chap, what's his name, Jamaica? Who's he working for?" Quentin sipped his brandy, but he might have

been sipping water: he showed no appreciation of it. "I expected some sort of shenanigans to go on during the conference. But nothing like this!"

"Has Mrs. Quentin said anything to you about the explosion?"

Quentin nodded. "I told her it had no connection with
me. She doesn't believe me, I know that, but I've got to keep
up the pretense." He took a deep swallow of the brandy.
"That's been the story of my life too long now. Keeping up
a pretense. I'm tired of it, Scobie. I think, selfishly, I'll almost welcome gaol when we get back home."

"Selfishly?"

"It will be over for me. But what about my wife? When
they shut the door on me, it won't be shut on her too. What
will she do? Change *her* name, go away somewhere and start
another life? Continue the cycle of pretense, of awful bloody
deception?" His voice cracked a little; he put a hand up to
his temple. Malone leaned forward, ready to catch him as he
collapsed; but Quentin closed his eyes and sat rock-steady in
his chair, and slowly the pain went out of his face. He
opened his eyes and looked at Malone. "It would solve a lot,
wouldn't it, if they did kill me here in London?"

Malone was silent for a moment. He looked across the
symbols of gracious living, the silverware, the fine lace, the
aromatic brandy in the goblets, at the man who talked of the
advantages of a violent death. "For you, maybe. But what
happened to everything you told me about last night? You
being the possible saviour of this conference, buying peace,
all that?"

Quentin didn't answer at once. Then his voice was mildly
sarcastic: "In my political career I've had a great many voices
of conscience. Opposition members, editorial writers, once
even the Archbishop of Melbourne got into the act. Now my
gaoler has his say." Malone put down his glass and went to

[140]

stand up, but Quentin raised a hand. "Sit down, Scobie. I apologize."

"I didn't ask for this job and I didn't ask to be taken into your confidence. If you want to talk to me, expect some answers back. That's the only way you and I are going to get on."

"I know that, Scobie, and my apology is sincere. I'm just not used to the situation. Oh, I don't mean being under arrest. I mean you and me. I'm the senior man and, if you don't mind my saying so, you're very junior—at least you would be if you had anything to do with Canberra."

"That's the beauty of States' rights," said Malone, unsmiling. "We still have some independence. You can't put me anywhere on the Canberra ladder."

"That's right. But I've been ten years either a minister or, in this job, an ambassador. How many juniors do you think I've had criticize me to my face in that time? Oh, behind my back, yes, scores of times. But not to my face, Scobie. You have a very special position. Have you noticed the look of disapproval Joseph wears?"

"I thought it was a natural look with him."

Quentin smiled. "It is, probably. It is with all butlers, I suppose. Butlers, floor walkers at Harrods, members of the staff at Buckingham Palace. The *real* British Establishment. But Joseph's disapproval has increased since you moved in. We've never had a junior public servant staying with us before, living as one of the family. Even Phil Larter and Sam Edgar were a bit surprised when they saw you having breakfast with us this morning. You and I have a very special relationship. The others are not the only ones who have to get used to it. So have I."

Malone relaxed, picked up his glass again. "Okay, it's my turn to apologize. But don't forget one thing—I was sent here to arrest you, to take you back home for murder. That's my job and that's my only job. Your position as High Commissioner and what you're doing at this conference is no real concern of mine. It's not what I'm paid for. It's the way our Constitution works, but the States don't reckon world peace is any of their business. I don't subscribe to the idea, and that's one of the reasons I took up your case with my boss last night. But I'll still get it in the neck if I lose you. The law is the law and it has first call on you because of what happened to your wife. Your first wife," he added, suddenly aware of the second wife sitting somewhere in the house, wounded by the shattering of her life. He swallowed a mouthful of brandy, then said, "So don't go making yourself an easy target for these killers. Or you'll find yourself whipped pretty bloody smartly on to the first plane back home."

Quentin had looked at him steadily all the while he had been speaking. "You're wasted in the police force."

"Nobody's wasted in the force. Not if he does his job properly." Then he gestured awkwardly. "That sounds pretty smug. But you know what I mean."

"Do you have any ambition to be Police Commissioner?"

Malone hesitated, then nodded. "Why not? Part of the rumour about you is you might eventually be Prime Minister. Is that your ambition?"

"You have your tenses wrong. Everything is subjunctive now. Or worse, past tense."

"Did you always have ambition—I mean before you killed your wife?"

Quentin was silent for a moment, trying to remember the emotions of a man he had long buried; then he shook his head. "None at all. I think Freda was the one with ambition. At least she wanted security, and the two things go together sometimes."

Malone raised an eyebrow. "People who think about security are usually the ones without ambition."

"Not Freda. After the time she'd had—she was Jewish, you know. German Jewish."

"I thought she'd come from Vienna?"

"You really know all the facts, don't you? Or nearly all." Quentin smiled dryly, without rancour; but the smile also held a hint of a secret. "Vienna was her last stop before she went out to Australia. But she came from Hildesheim in Germany. The Nazis, some Hitler Youth kids, stoned her parents to death in front of her. She landed in Sydney with two pounds in her purse and her mother's gold wedding ring. You understand now why security was such an ambition?"

Malone sat gazing at the pale, distorted reflection of his own face in the brandy goblet he held: this man across the table from him was also a distorted reflection. "Why did you kill her?" he asked quietly.

Pain darkened Quentin's eyes; then he blinked and looked quizzically at Malone. "You haven't warned me about anything I may say—"

"Forget it." Malone put down his goblet and straightened up in his chair. "I wasn't being a policeman then."

"What were you being?"

Malone chewed his bottom lip. "I don't know. I think maybe I was trying to be your friend. Does that annoy you?"

"On the contrary." He took a cigar from the humidor Joseph had brought in with the brandy, looked at it, then dropped it back into the container. "I've lost my taste. I'd be wasting a good cigar. I can't taste this—" He flicked a finger against the brandy goblet; Courvoisier had never been meant to compete against the taste of despair. "I didn't taste anything at dinner, not even the walnut torte. I ate that for Sheila's benefit. Was it any good?"

Malone grinned, but without much humour. "I don't have much taste myself right now."

Quentin nodded sympathetically. "What would you be doing back home now—I mean, if you hadn't been sent here to arrest me?"

Malone shrugged: the old life seemed years away. "Arresting someone else, I suppose."

"Does that thought ever worry you? Do you sometimes have doubts that you might have arrested the wrong man?"

"Am I arresting the wrong man now?"

Quentin shook his head quickly, almost too quickly, as if he wanted to reassure Malone and not offend him; he was like a lonely man who had suddenly found a new friend whom he didn't want to lose. "No, I'm your man."

Well, I have doubts about you, Malone thought, but didn't say it. Instead he said, "Well, I'll just have to make sure you're on that plane at the weekend."

Quentin realized the subject had been changed. He was silent for a moment, as if afraid that he *had* offended Malone; then he said, "What do you want me to do then? I mean about keeping out of range of these people, whoever they are."

"Don't move a yard without either Coburn or myself being right beside you. It would be a good idea if you could cancel all the functions you've been asked to."

"That may be difficult. It will raise awkward questions. And it's bound to cause offense to some people I'm trying to influence. Some of these new nations are like the *nouveau riche*—turn down an invitation from them and they think you're being snobbish."

"What about the bloke who had all the answers today?"

"He'd be one of the worst, I think. He'd like to belong to the West, but the Chinese have done some very smart buttering-up with him. Back home I believe he rides around in a Rolls-Royce bought with Chinese money."

"How do so many of these so-called uncommitted countries get into this act? What's Vietnam got to do with them?"

[144]

"They are supposed to balance the countries that are committed in Southeast Asia. When the conference was first mooted, they volunteered. Or one or two of them did, then the rest didn't want to be left out. Half a dozen of us could have settled something in two or three days. Now there are a couple of dozen and we're getting nowhere, or practically nowhere. There are too many witnesses if someone makes a mistake. So no one wants to risk going out on a limb."

"What about the Chinese?"

"In theory they are supposed to be only observers. The Americans wouldn't have them at the table as delegates. But though they just sit there, you can feel them pulling the strings. They've got their stooges working for them."

"Do you think Madame Cholon is working for them?"

Quentin mused a moment, then shook his head. "I'd be surprised if she is. The Chinese Reds are much cruder than we usually think Chinese are, but I don't think they are as crude as all that. But I'd like to know whom she *is* working for!"

"Well, you'd better play it as safe as you can."

Quentin nodded, took another sip at the brandy he couldn't taste: his whole life had lost its flavour forever. "The only thing I can't get out of is the reception at Lancaster House Friday night. If the conference runs to schedule, that's supposed to be the farewell party."

"Will the conference run to schedule?"

"If we haven't got some sort of terms by Friday, schedules aren't going to mean a thing. Everyone will go home and the war will drag on and we'll get the blame." He sighed and put his hand to his head again, as if he had a headache. "I don't think I'd mind dying very much if my death meant there was going to be some sort of peace. Oh, I'm not being a hero—" He looked at Malone, embarrassed by his own words. "All I'd be offering is a life that's over anyway. That's not much of a sacrifice. But if a man has to die by an assassin's bullet, he would like it to be in a good cause. Not so a war will be prolonged."

"How many assassins have killed in a good cause?"

"They might have been good causes in the killer's own mind. Who knows—" Then he stopped.

"Who knows what is in a killer's mind?" Malone said quietly; not cruelly but curiously. "Yes, I've often wondered."

Then there was a tap at the door and Lisa looked in. "Someone on the phone for you, Mr. Malone."

Malone turned, puzzled. "Me? Is it from Sydney?"

"I think it's a local call."

Malone looked at Quentin, who said, "Take it in my study."

Malone followed Lisa out of the dining room and down the hall to the study. He picked up the phone, waited till Lisa had gone out of the room, then said cautiously, "Malone here. Who's that?"

"Speaking on an international level, your friend and ally." Jamaica's voice was soft and hoarse over the wire; Malone had to strain to hear it. "I understand you're interested in Madame Cholon."

"Not just me. Scotland Yard are, too."

"You're working together, aren't you?"

"I guess so. But why call me and not them? It's their country."

"Put it down to shyness. I know you. Well, are you interested in the Cholon dame or not?"

Malone hesitated, but he had been a policeman too long: he couldn't deny an interest in any suspect. "Okay, where is she?"

"Right now, I don't know. But she's to meet me tonight at Fothergill's. She may or may not turn up. But you might reckon it's worth a try."

"Where's Fothergill's?" But Jamaica had hung up. Malone

[146]

put down the phone and stared with gloomy irritation at himself in the gilt-framed mirror above the fireplace. Why did he have to be so interested in Madame Cholon? Curiosity had killed too many coppers. This wasn't his beat; why couldn't he leave it to Denzil and the Special Branch? He reached for the phone, the door opened and Lisa came back in, and he heard himself say, "Do you know a place called Fothergill's?"

She looked at him with amused surprise. "So you're a gambling man after all? Remember I said you looked like a race-course tipster?"

"Am I some sort of escape valve for you?" he said irritably. All day people had been fretting his patience; he used her now as his own escape valve. "I mean, do you get fed up being diplomatically polite all day?"

Then it was his turn to be surprised, for she blushed: in that cool, slightly mocking face it was like a sudden rush of fever. "Sorry. Maybe I'm more Australian than I thought. Isn't it a national habit, always mocking the other fellow? It's part of the national inferiority complex."

He wasn't going to retreat too quickly. "The last thing you have is an inferiority complex. What's Fothergill's? Some sort of gambling club?"

"It's *the* gambling club. A sort of millionaires' Crockfords."

"How do you know about it?"

"I've been there a couple of times."

"On your salary?" It had been a long day: he was finding it hard to control his sarcasm.

"You're a bluntly inquisitive man, aren't you?"

"Another national habit."

She pursed her lips, then said "Are we going to fight all the time, Mr. Malone? I don't think we're in the right atmosphere for petty little spats. I mean—"

"I know what you mean," he said shortly. Christ, how insensitive did she think he was? Then he relented, relaxed a little and worked hard to smile at her: he wondered how it looked on his face, but the mirror was behind him. "Okay, let's declare an armistice. Now about Fothergill's—?"

Again she pursed her lips; it seemed a habit of hers before she put forward suggestions that she thought might not be accepted. "If you want to go there, would you like me to go with you? You have to be introduced."

He looked at her, brows creased in puzzlement. "I know I'm being bluntly inquisitive again, but how is it you're so welcome at this joint?"

"It's no joint, I assure you. As for your question—well, sometimes my duties here call for being more than just a secretary. Sometimes I have to stand in as a dinner partner. One night I was partner to an oil sheik—and afterwards he wanted to go to Fothergill's. I've been there a couple of times since—with a grazier from back home and with a Chinese businessman from Hong Kong. Fothergill's seem to think I brought them there. I'm just waiting for them to offer me commission."

"Your commission on me tonight won't break them."

"How do you bet?"

"When I do, it's usually two bob each way on a horse." He grinned. "I'm sort of reckless."

"They wouldn't know what a two-shilling piece is at Forthergill's. If you aren't rich enough to have your bank books cross-indexed, they don't want to know you."

Malone suddenly laughed, suddenly liking her. "Will you take me there?"

"Take you where?" Quentin stood in the doorway.

"I've just had a call from that feller Jamaica," Malone said. "He's expecting Madame Cholon at a club called Fothergill's tonight. I might need an introduction to get in."

"Lisa's not going with you," Quentin said firmly.

[148]

Lisa looked in puzzlement from one man to the other. "What is all this? Who's Madame Cholon?"

Each man hesitated, waiting on the other to reply. Finally it was Malone who said, "We think she might have had something to do with that bomb explosion this afternoon."

Lisa looked quickly at Quentin, her eyes opening wide in shock. "That bomb *was* meant for you!" Her composure cracked: she was being made confidante to more secrets than a private secretary expected. It was her job to intercept junior officers, newspapermen, unwanted visitors; but not assassins. It was almost as if she felt she had fallen down on her job. "Oh my God, they really do mean to kill you!"

Quentin looked over his shoulder, then came into the room, closing the door after him. "Please, Lisa." He patted her arm: one might have thought she was the one in danger. "I don't want my wife to know."

She looked up at him, said gently, "She does know. Oh, she hasn't said anything, but since dinner she's just been sitting in the drawing room, not saying anything—*she* knows. I should have known, too," she said, her voice rising, castigating herself. How much would she do for this man? Malone wondered. Then with surprise asked himself: how much am I going to do for him? Lisa turned to Malone. "Do you want me to take you to Fothergill's?"

"You're not to go near the place!"

"What I do in my own time is my own concern, Mr. Quentin." Lisa's voice was quiet; she spoke almost with love. "If I can help Mr. Malone find this Madame—Cholon?—I want to do it."

"I'm not going to let you risk yourself for my sake, Lisa." He looked at Malone, spoke with authority. "Call Superintendent Denzil. He can pick up this woman."

Malone hesitated, then picked up the phone. While he waited to be connected to Denzil's office he said, "I'm going there anyway. She's my pigeon as much as his. More, in fact.

[149]

She hasn't taken a shot at him yet." Then he spoke into the phone. "Not there? Could you give me his home number?"

He rang Denzil at his home in Bromley. Denzil sounded relaxed, as if he had his shoes off. "What can I do you for, Sergeant? Just been watching a television program. *The Fugitive.* All about an escaped murderer and a policeman who never gives up." Malone winced; how many black toes had Denzil trodden on in Africa? "Anything wrong?"

Malone told him. There was silence for a moment, a sigh, then: "I'll meet you there in half an hour. No, three-quarters. I'll have to come in my own car."

Malone hung up. "He'll meet us there. I'm going now."

"Then you'll need me. They won't let you inside the door without an introduction. I'll get my coat." Lisa brushed past Quentin and went quickly out of the room.

Quentin said, "I wish you'd stop her."

"How?" said Malone helplessly. "You should never have cultivated so much loyalty in her."

Quentin looked hurt, as if he had been accused of making advances to Lisa. "I didn't go out of my way to do that."

"No, maybe not. But you're stuck with it."

"But why are *you* going?" Quentin sounded cautious, even a little afraid: he did not want to be burdened with more loyalty.

Malone sensed the hidden question and avoided it. "Put it down to the copper in me. I don't like to see anyone get away."

"Either way, eh? Dead or alive?" The bitterness had at last come through; and he was ashamed of it. "Sorry, Scobie. Look after Lisa. I've harmed enough women."

Then he moved to one of the bookshelves and pulled on it; a section of the shelf of books swung out, revealing a wall safe. He opened the safe, took out some money from among the papers there, closed the safe and swung the books back into place.

"Now you know where the papers are kept. Just as well you're not a spy." His smile was no more than a twitch of the muscles; humour tasted like quinine, an antidote. He held out five five-pound notes. "You may have to spend some money at Fothergill's."

"There's no need—"

"Go on, take it. If you lose it, I'll put it down to expenses. If you win—" He tried to smile again, but the effort was too much. "But our luck hasn't been very good, has it?"

"You're still alive," said Malone, and tried not to sound unkind.

CHAPTER SEVEN

1

As they closed the front door behind them Lisa said, "We'll go in my car. It's parked over there."

They moved across the pavement and a uniformed policeman detached himself from the shadows and came towards them. Malone tensed, then relaxed: he could not remember ever being as edgy as this. The policeman, burly as a wool bale and with a chin that seemed to be trying to sap his helmet strap in two, saluted them.

"Oh, sorry, miss. Didn't recognize you at first. Evening, sir."

Malone had never been called *sir* before by a uniformed man: home was never like this. "Everything quiet?"

"Quiet as a church, sir. Belgravia isn't Chelsea."

"Sometimes I wish it were," said Lisa.

The policeman smiled; the helmet strap was stretched to breaking point. "I can't see the diplomats in Chelsea boots and long hair, miss. The Foreign Office would have a nervous breakdown."

The Foreign Office might have a nervous breakdown for another reason, Malone thought, and looked searchingly about the square. He and Lisa crossed the road to her car, an MG Midget with the top down. As they reached it a car came

round the curve of the garden, tires squealing, and went close
by them with engine roaring. Malone pushed Lisa against the
MG; then when the car had gone stood trembling. She
looked up at him, then gently freed her arm from the tight
vice of his hand.

"Is it as bad as that?"

He was looking after the car which had now disappeared
into Chesham Place. It had been an open E-type Jaguar and
he could see the four young people who had been squashed
into it waving back at him. He bit his lip, cursing himself for
his nervousness, then looked down at Lisa.

"I'm too expectant. Always waiting for the worst to happen. It's the Celt in me."

"I don't believe that," she said, but did not pursue the
subject any further. She opened the door of her car and got
in behind the wheel. "After riding in the Rolls all day, I like
to get the wind in my face occasionally. Do you mind women
drivers?"

When he had been on the Traffic Squad he had hated
them, but that was long, long ago. "I love 'em."

"Liar," she said, and took the car away from the curb with
a rush that jerked his head back. But she handled the car
well, weaving it through the late night traffic at Hyde Park
Corner with all the skill and cheek of a taxi driver.

"Do you want to tell me what this is all about?" she asked.

He told her about Jamaica, Pallain and Madame Cholon,
shouting to make himself heard above the rush of wind and
the whine and hum of the traffic; he flung secrets on to the
night air, but no one heard. Even Lisa had to lean close to
him several times to catch what he said.

There were no parking spaces in Park Lane and she turned
down into the underground garage beneath the park. "We'll
leave it here. Fothergill's is just down the street."

She parked the car in the vast grey cavern. They walked
back past the rows of other cars, through the subway and up

into Park Lane. "I don't know whether I'm glad or not that you've told me all this. Ignorance *is* bliss sometimes."

The days of bliss are over, love; there's worse yet to come. "Do you want to go back home?"

"No. Once I start something I like to finish it. That's the Dutch in me." She looked up at him and smiled. "We're friends now?"

"Mates," he said.

They came to a halt in front of a four-storied house with a patrician front and a doorman who had been chopped whole out of some quarry. A veneer of public school accent had been laid over the gravel in his voice, but Malone guessed he would be a fluent linguist in all the four-letter words.

He opened the heavy front door with its coat of arms and wished them luck. "Thanks," said Malone, and wondered if Madame Cholon was already inside.

He had thought the house in Belgrave Square was luxurious enough, but this made the High Commissioner's home look like a council house. "It belonged to a duke," said Lisa, noticing his roving eye. "One of the more hedonistic ones. He recognized the end of an era when he saw one, so he committed suicide. Shot himself with a silver pistol."

"I could have been a hedonist. But I got too set in my ways before I found out what the word meant."

"Would your old Irish mum go for this?"

Malone grinned at her and looked up at the huge crimson tapestry that hung on a panelled wall: hounds tore a stag to pieces while their master, still in his riding boots, made love to his mistress in the background. "As soon as she saw that she'd start hosing the place down with holy water."

The manager of the club squeezed himself out of a tiny office under the stairs. Everything in this mansion was designed for the comfort of the guests; the club management had the old duke's ideas about the proper place for staff. Lisa introduced Malone, and the manager, another man with

[154]

an accent that didn't belong to him, discreetly looked Malone up and down. His eyes rested for a moment on the old brown shoes with the dark blue suit, and Malone did his best to look like an eccentric millionaire.

"Mr. Malone is just over from Australia," said Lisa, recognizing the doubt in the manager's face. "He's here to buy cattle. And to enjoy himself. He lives a very lonely life on his cattle station. How big is it, Mr. Malone?"

"Just a manageable size. Three million acres. I sold off most of it last year." He looked at the manager. "Labour shortage. You probably have the same trouble."

"It's the same all over, sir," said the manager, leading them up the curving flight of stairs now. "I've often thought of going to Australia. Must be full of opportunities." His black eyes sparkled; he could see himself peeling money like bark off the suckers Down Under. "I understand Australians are great gamblers, but they don't have the right facilities."

Malone thought of the two-up schools in the clearing in French's Forest, in the various warehouses around Surry Hills. "The law's a bit old-fashioned," he said, and was glad he wouldn't be quoted to the Commissioner.

"The law is always behind the times." The manager handed out smiles like gambling chips to other guests as he led them into the main room on the first floor. "But at last our government has seen the light here."

He wished them luck, left them and Lisa said, "And now everyone can choose his own road to hell."

Malone looked at her in surprise. "I thought you were in favour of gambling?"

"Only in moderation. My socially conscious hackles stand on end when I see some of the money lost here. My oil sheik, for instance, lost eight thousand pounds the night I came here with him."

Malone patted the twenty-five pounds in his wallet, wondering how many minutes they would buy him at the tables.

He looked around the room. It was still too early for the serious gamblers and only a few players were at the tables. An aristocratic crone, face held together by make-up, her skeleton hidden in black lace, carefully placed chips as if they were the last moments of her life. Across from her a young boy, smooth, elegant and as expressionless as a store dummy, tossed chips onto the squares with the careless profligacy of someone with wealth and years to burn. No one seemed to be enjoying themselves, Malone noted; or if they were, they kept their enjoyment well disguised. The room was inhabited by clockwork corpses.

Lisa was also looking around. "Do you see your Madame Cholon?"

"She's not here yet," said Jamaica behind them, and Malone and Lisa turned round. He looked expressionlessly at Lisa and said, "You're Miss Pretorious, aren't you?"

"How did you know?"

"He seems to know everything," said Malone.

Jamaica smiled. "Not *everything*, Mr. Malone. It would make my job so much easier if I did."

"What is your job? You're not at the Embassy."

"Who said I was? You've been jumping to conclusions. You're too athletic in your prejudices, Malone."

Malone swallowed, keeping his temper in check. "What do you do, then?"

"I export Thai silk. From Bangkok. A harmless business, but profitable."

"Who do you sell to—diplomats? I didn't think blokes in the rag trade hung around embassies and international conferences."

"The rag trade?" Jamaica shook his head sadly. "Thai silk isn't rag."

"Mr. Malone is no fashion expert," said Lisa truthfully. "But if you were at Lancaster House this morning, it does

seem an odd place for you to be. I mean, you wouldn't expect Hardy Amies or Mary Quant to hang about the United
Nations in New York."

"What is your place in this set-up, Miss Pretorious?"

Lisa blinked when puzzled, a little girl's blink: for a moment it destroyed the poised woman-of-the-world image that
was her usual face. "Which set-up is that, Mr. Jamaica?"

They were both too polite for Malone's liking; impatiently he said, "What's *your* place, Jamaica? That's more to
the point."

The players and the croupiers at the tables were staring
at them with the discreet but fixed looks of thoroughbred
vultures: gaming clubs were not for gossiping. Jamaica
said, "We're making ourselves conspicuous. What are you
going to play? Baccarat, roulette, chemin de fer?"

"I'll take roulette," said Malone, acutely aware that he
would be playing with someone else's money. "I've got no
memory for cards."

Jamaica led the way into a side room where the fat horn-
rimmed cashier sat like a giant panda behind his cage.
"You're not a gambler?"

"No."

"Madame Cholon seemed disappointed in you. I think she
really wanted you to bring her here last night."

"Did you bring her?"

Jamica nodded. "Had a very disappointing night. How
much do you want to change?"

Malone took out the five five-pound notes. The cashier
looked pained and slid across five chips. "Is that all?" Malone
said.

"The minimum stake is five pounds, sir. We have plenty
more chips when you need them."

"Thanks," said Malone, hoping Madame Cholon would
make her appearance in the next two minutes.

Jamaica took fifty pounds' worth of chips and Lisa changed ten pounds. Malone looked warningly at her. "You don't have to go risking your money."

"I'm in this with you," said Lisa, leading the way to the roulette table. "Whatever it is."

"They play the French wheel here," Jamica said, his voice low now that they were by the table. "It's illegal in this country because it has the zero. But I gather the police never come into this club."

The croupier, a fleshless automaton with paper skin and marble eyes, waited for them to place their bets. Lisa put a chip on the red 8; Jamaica laid one on the black 9. Malone hesitated, aware of the icy patience of the croupier. He had no feeling that tonight would be lucky for him, but he had to buy as much time as he could with his five chips. He remembered an explanation of roulette given him by a member of the Gaming Squad back home. He placed a chip at the top of the table, linking zero with 1. Then he straightened up and waited, watching the door to the room as closely as he watched the spinning wheel.

The wheel spun its mesmerism, the silver centerpiece flashing a silent siren song, the black and red slots a blur that seemed to take the breath out of the watchers. Then the ivory ball began its slowly diminishing click-click: a hollow sound, thought Malone, that no mug ever takes as a warning.

The ball came to rest and Lisa said, "You've won! You get eight times your stake."

That buys me about another ten minutes, Malone thought.

"Your lucky night," said Jamaica.

Malone had four more bets and four more wins. Lisa won once and Jamaica lost all his five bets. He said, "Maybe I should follow you more, eh, Malone?"

I'm missing something here, Malone thought. There was something he was supposed to know; Jamaica had at last accepted him, but had forgotten to take him into his confidence. He looked at his watch. "What time were you expecting her?"

Jamaica shrugged. "She's from Vietnam. Time doesn't mean a thing to them. She mightn't even come at all."

"If she doesn't, I'd like a talk with you." Malone grinned. "As an international friend and ally."

Jamaica nodded absently. He was looking about the room, which had now begun to fill up as the serious gamblers began to arrive. There were people at all the tables, their faces turned into masks; anonymity was a form of leprosy, their faces would get blanker as the night wore on. An obscenely fat American sat next to an elderly over-painted Englishwoman, a pair of grotesques oblivious of each other; a Jewish diamond merchant sat across from a Syrian banker, each intent only on his number on the no man's land between them. Jamaica had seen the same blank countenances before: at Las Vegas, where even the slot machines had more expression, at Monte Carlo, in Macao in the old days. Nothing ever changed at the tables, he thought cynically and sadly. Madame Cholon was gambling on the one sure thing about human nature: its addiction to gambling. He looked about the room, then at the door. And saw the manager, the smile gashing his face like a white wound, come in. Beside him was Superintendent Denzil.

"I need some more chips," Jamaica said to Malone, and moved towards the side room.

"There's Denzil now," Malone said.

He gathered up his sixth winning bet and he and Lisa moved across to where Denzil and the manager stood looking as if they did not want to know each other.

"The gentleman says he is from Scotland Yard." The manager looked reproachfully at Malone and Lisa: this was a respectable club and he didn't want the tone lowered, least of all by the police. Malone knew the type, had met them back home in the dingy illegal clubs around King's Cross

[159]

and Woolloomooloo. They would have welcomed Hitler, Genghis Khan and Nero to their clubs if they had had money to gamble. A gambler only lost his respectability in the eyes of club managers when the police, like black sheep relatives, intruded from the outside world.

Malone smiled reassuringly. "It's just a social call. Superintendent Denzil and I are old friends. He used to be a stockman for my father on our station. A cowpuncher, as the Americans would call him." Malone was feeling a little lightheaded: he had three hundred and forty-five pounds' worth of chips, his luck was in tonight, Madame Cholon would walk in the door any minute.

The manager looked at Denzil. "I'm afraid I can't allow you to play, sir. It might look bad—for you and the club. You understand, of course?"

Denzil's smile was as painful as the manager's own. "I'll just watch. And I'll try not to look too much like a policeman." He glanced at Malone. "Or a cowpuncher."

The manager flinched the smile once more and went away. Then Denzil said, "We'll discuss the cowpuncher bit later. Is our lady friend here?"

"Not yet," said Malone. "But Jamaica is. Maybe you'd like a word with him?"

But Jamaica had gone. Malone went into the side room but there was no one there but the giant panda behind the bars. No, he hadn't seen the coloured gentleman. There was another door just there that led to the men's room . . . Malone didn't bother to go looking for Jamaica; he knew he would be already out of the building. He went back to Denzil and Lisa. "I just hope he doesn't get in touch with Madame Cholon and tell her not to come."

"Does he know where she is?" Denzil asked.

Malone shrugged. "I don't know. But if he does, why all the rigmarole of turning up without her and having us here to meet her? Why didn't he just tell us where to find her?"

"Perhaps he doesn't want her to know he's turned informer on her. If she had turned up here and we'd got on to her, he could have acted surprised. What's his game anyway?"

"That's a good question," said Lisa, and Denzil looked at her with surprise and a sort of amused tolerance. He belonged to a dying breed of Englishmen, the sort who called his wife "old gel" and treated her as one of the more privileged of the other ranks. Women were jolly good sorts in the right places, but they weren't expected to have opinions. "He says he's an exporter of Thai silk, has his business in Bangkok. I wonder how many successful Negro businessmen there are in the Far East."

"He could have been an ex-G.I.," Malone said. "Some of them stayed on around the Pacific after World War Two and the Korean show."

"I prefer to be suspicious of him," said Denzil. "He's up to no good. Just as I suspect this Madame Cholon is."

"What are you going to do if she does turn up?"

"Ask her along to the Yard for a little chat." Denzil grimaced. "But I never enjoy questioning women. That was one good thing about Kenya—very rarely had anything to do with women. No offense, Miss Pretorious."

"Women never enjoy being questioned," said Lisa. "Least of all by men. No offense, Superintendent."

Denzil looked at her out of the corner of his eye, but said nothing. He is not going to enjoy Madame Cholon, Malone thought; she will tear strips off him. Maybe we should enlist Lisa for the night as an interrogator.

They waited an hour for Madame Cholon, retiring to a small annex to nibble at the free caviar and smoked salmon: no patrons of this club would ever be allowed to collapse at the tables from starvation. The main room filled with people and smoke, one just a pattern in the other; personality and substance seemed to have been checked at the door with the

[161]

coats and wraps. But no Madame Cholon, the face Malone now knew he would recognize even in a stadium of Oriental faces, came in to break the pattern.

"She's not coming," Denzil said at last. "Either Jamaica got on to her or she never intended coming. At least not after this afternoon."

"How will you be able to prove she did have something to do with the bomb explosion?" Lisa asked.

"We won't be able to," Denzil said. "Our best witness against her went up with the bomb."

"There's the other bloke," Malone said. "The one who drove him to Aldwych."

"He's probably with Madame Cholon, halfway back to where she came from."

"If they are," said Lisa, "then our troubles are over, aren't they?"

"In Special Branch, Miss Pretorious, our troubles are never over. If it's not someone deadly serious like this crowd, it's a crank. The worst of it is that we have to treat them all as deadly serious until we prove otherwise."

Malone went away to cash his chips, then came back. "I won three hundred and twenty quid. The night hasn't been altogether unprofitable." He looked at Lisa. "Do you approve or are your moral hackles rising?"

"Chicken feed," said Lisa. "My social conscience doesn't stir under five thousand."

Malone whistled and grinned. "That's the world I'm after. Where poverty begins below five thousand quid."

"I wonder what stakes Madame Cholon plays for?" Denzil said. "Can I give you a lift back to Belgravia?"

Malone told him Lisa's car was over in the underground garage. When they were outside the house Malone took the keys from Lisa. "Would you stay here with her, Superintendent, while I get the car? We'd curse ourselves if Madame Cholon turned up just as we'd both left."

"My pleasure." Denzil did his best to look gallant, at one o'clock in the morning and after only five hours' sleep in the last forty-eight. "Do you like your job, Miss Pretorious?"

Malone, grinning, walked away. Lisa had said women never enjoyed being questioned, but Denzil had kept the conversation going by asking her the most boring question a woman would want to hear. But then, Malone told himself, Lisa *did* like her job. Or anyway the man she worked for; and for a lot of women, he guessed, that was their job. She hadn't come on this wild goose chase tonight just to get the wind in her face after a day in the Rolls and the office. She had come because Quentin meant something to her.

He went under Park Lane through the subway, deserted now but for the bearded derelict trudging with dead eyes towards a destination he had long forgotten. Poor bastard, Malone thought; and put out a hand and stopped the man. "Here," he said, and pushed five pounds into the grimy hand that came up in a frightened defensive gesture. "Just don't blow it all on plonk. Have a bath and a shave. You might find another man underneath all that dirt and hair."

But he knew the man wouldn't. The derelicts of the world were all alike: they wanted to forget, not rediscover. He watched the man shamble off along the subway; maybe the down-and-out was lucky. He had succeeded where Quentin had failed: he had buried his real self forever. Then Malone was angry with himself: why the hell do I worry so much over Quentin? And, like the derelict, didn't dig for the truth. Charity and justice, he had learned long ago, were often uncomfortable bedmates.

When he walked into the garage he was struck for the first time by its vastness. Two hours ago it had been almost full of cars; now it was virtually empty. The low-roofed cavern seemed to stretch for miles into shadows beyond the glow of the pale lights that were still switched on; the grey concrete pillars stood like long open ranks of headless pet-

[163]

rified men. He paid the attendant, who went back to his copy of *Playboy* and his dreams of the better life; he walked on down between the widely spaced pillars, his footsteps sounding like rhythmically tapped bones in the huge, low echo chamber. Lisa's car was parked at the far end of the garage beyond the shallow pools of light; he could see the dim white shape of it, like a calcified beast. He suddenly felt tired and he began to hurry towards it, wanting to get home to bed.

He heard the car start up somewhere over to one side of him, but he didn't look towards it: it was only a growling noise somewhere in the shadows. He heard it coming towards him, the driver shifting up into second gear; he turned his head casually, just to make sure that the driver could see him in the grey gloom. Then suddenly he was flooded in light and he heard the angry whine of the car as it accelerated. He stood for a moment blinded and stupefied; then he flung himself to one side as the car hurtled past. As he lurched up against a pillar he saw the car stand almost on its nose as the driver slammed on the brakes. It was a red Mini-Minor; and he remembered the car he had followed this morning from Lancaster House. It reversed, swung round and came speeding back at him; he ducked behind the pillar as it scraped past with a screech of metal. It went round in a tight circle, engine snarling, tires shrieking, and came back at him as he raced towards another pillar. The car went by as he tried to swerve away from it; it caught him a glancing blow and he went tumbling along the concrete floor. He hit a pillar with a sickening thud and lay there for a moment. Far away he could hear a voice yelling; it echoed and re-echoed in the vast empty space like a choir of furies. He heard the scream of tires again, the clashing of gears, the protest of the engine as it was revved too quickly; then he was flooded in light again. He got up on one knee,

[164]

crouching like a boxer who knows he can't beat the count, knowing he was about to die; he stared into the lights as they came towards him, trying to look beyond them into the face of his killer. He was aware of the pillar behind him and he got a swift peculiar satisfaction from it. When the car smashed him back against the pillar, the driver also was going to be hurt, might even be killed. If you had to die, it would be some negative compensation to take your murderer with you.

But the instinct to survive was too strong, in both himself and the driver of the car. As he flung himself to one side, rolling over and skidding along the floor in a pool of oil, the car went by on the other side of the pillar. It skidded and for a moment looked as if it were going to topple over; it scraped by another pillar and there was the sound of metal being crunched. The driver wrestled with it, steering it close by yet another of the concrete posts; then it was speeding down the garage, past the yelling attendant as he came running down from his office. Its sound died away and then there was only the light thump of the attendant's running feet.

Malone picked himself up and stood trembling. He wanted to curse, but he knew it would only sound like a whimper; relief and shock had turned him into jelly. He swayed, took two faltering steps and leaned against a pillar; the concrete hardness of it seemed to give him some strength, and he straightened up as the attendant came running up. He shook his head as the man, face as white as his overalls, incoherently asked what the bloody hell was going on.

"Some drunk showing off—" Malone was surprised at how calm his voice sounded. He had been involved in fights and brawls before and twice he had had to arrest a man at gunpoint; but no one had ever tried deliberately to kill him before. He was still sick and weak, his legs quivering like an old man's, but his voice was a stranger's, that of a good-humoured man who had tolerance towards drunken drivers. "Forget it."

"But how did he get in here? I've checked out everybody who's come in in the last hour. He must of been sitting in his car all night, just getting drunker— You sure you're all right? Cripes, he's made a mess of your clothes."

Malone looked down at the new blue suit, covered in oil and dirt and with a gaping hole in one knee. "I was due for a new one, anyway." How can I be so bloody easygoing, he wondered. He looked up and about at the huge emptiness. He wanted to scream abuse at the killer in the red Mini; but the garage was empty and silent. He looked back at the attendant. "Forget it, Jack. If ever I see him again, I'll thump him one and take the money off him for a new suit."

"Did you get a look at him?"

Malone shook his head; but he knew what Pallain looked like. "No, nor his number, either."

The attendant walked down with Malone to the MG. "You sure you don't want me to report this?"

"What's the use?" Don't be public-spirited, mate: go back to *Playboy* and the girls with big breasts.

The attendant shrugged. "Okay, if that's the way you want it. You're an Aussie, aren't you? Bet you wished you'd stayed home."

"Yes," said Malone, and got into the MG and drove it slowly and carefully out of the garage and up the ramp into Carriage Road. He paused at the top of the ramp, waiting to be ambushed; but the killer had gone home, the jungle was safe again. He eased the car out into the sparse traffic, drove up to the first turn-off and swung back down Park Lane. He had the feeling he was being watched, that he was still a target; but there was nothing he could do about it. His life, perhaps even his fate, was becoming more and more en-

twined with that of Quentin. He wondered why he should
no longer feel any resentment of the fact.

2

"I think we should wake up Mr. Quentin," Lisa said.

Malone shook his head and flinched as she bathed the
cut on his knee. His trouser leg was rolled up and he had
taken off his shoe and his bloodstained sock. There were
abrasions on both his elbows, the cut on his chin had been
opened again and he felt as if his body was one great bruise.
"Don't bother him. He'd stay awake the rest of the night.
He's got enough on his mind without worrying about me."

They were sitting in the big kitchen. A bowl of water
stood on the formica-topped table; beside it were the antiseptic bottle and the tin of Band-Aids. The fluorescent ceiling light added to the antiseptic atmosphere; they were in
their own small casualty room. "This is getting to be a habit,
mending your cuts and bruises."

"What's that perfume you wear?" She was leaning close
to him to wipe away the dried blood on his chin.

"Arpège. Why?"

"I like it, even mixed with Dettol."

She smiled, the sort of woman's smile that he had never
solved; women had always been a mystery to him, even his
simple old Irish mum. "Whom have you got back home to
miss you? I mean, if tonight—?"

"Just my mum and dad. And I suppose one or two mates."
How could you name who would regret your passing, measure someone else's regard for you?

"No girl?"

"No particular one." There were a dozen who might
grieve for him for a week or two, but none whose heart
would be broken. Christ, he thought, I've made no dent in
anyone. He had felt lonely before, but now suddenly for

[167]

the first time he felt *alone*. And that was much, much worse.

She pressed a Band-Aid on to his chin, then stepped back. "There. Let's hope this is the last time I have to play nurse to you."

She had driven the MG back from Fothergill's. She had not said much, as if shock had taken all the words from her; but by the time they had reached home she had got over her shock and become calm and efficient again. Denzil had been angry rather than shocked and had promised to have Pallain in custody by morning; instead of going home to Bromley he had gone back to the Yard and, for all Malone knew, was still there. Malone's own anger and shock had now drained out of him: he was too weary for either. He might feel different in the morning but for now he was content to sit here and be ministered to by Lisa.

"Why isn't a man like you married? Is it because of your job?"

He was about to say that most policemen married; then he remembered she did not know he was a policeman. In less than a week his life had become a masquerade; Quentin had endured such a situation for twenty-three years, but already he was tired and frustrated by it. He wanted to talk frankly to this girl, tell her about himself and ask her about herself, but he couldn't. In the shank of the night, the time for revealing secrets, he had to remain dumb. Suddenly, feeling selfish and personal, not Detective-Sergeant Malone, policeman, but Scobie Malone, human being, he hated Flannery, Leeds, even the sleeping man upstairs. He had become everybody else's property, sealed and classified as Top Secret.

"That's about it," he said. "But why isn't a girl like you married?"

"I just haven't met the right man. No, that's a lie. I did meet him, but he preferred someone else." She emptied the bowl of water into the sink, rinsed it and wiped it. She did it all with a brisk thoroughness, as if she were as much at home here in the kitchen as she was in an office, at an embassy reception or in an expensive gambling club. Malone remembered a fellow detective, who had married one, telling him that Dutch girls were among the best housewives in the world. Lisa put on some coffee, set out two cups and saucers, got out cream and sugar, then at last stood still and looked at Malone across the kitchen table. It was her time for telling secrets and the puzzlement at herself was sketched in her face; she blinked her little girl's blink. "I don't know why I told you that last bit. I've never told anyone else."

"Where did it happen? Here?" Was it Quentin, the man on whom all her concern was concentrated? He felt the stab of jealousy more than the wound in his knee. I'm weak and lightheaded, he thought: I'm not the sort who falls in love as quickly as this. I'm not looking for love; all I want is some comfort and sympathy, flavoured with Arpège and antiseptic. Thus does the cautious man try not to commit himself; and he knew it. He was already committed too much to this house.

"No, back in Australia," she said, and he was surprised at his own relief. "He was a lecturer at the university. Physics. He was looking for a girl he could read like a formula, someone he could solve and pigeonhole. I wasn't her." She smiled again, at herself as much as at him; he could sense there was still some pain left in her. "Do I sound bitchy?"

"It's permissible. I don't think being in love calls for any sort of honour. Afterwards, I mean."

"All's fair in love and war? I don't know if that's true." She poured the coffee and they sat down opposite each other. "I think if that were so, sooner or later there'd be a sour taste. Even for the winner."

"The other girl, the winner—were her tactics fair?" An hour ago someone tried to kill me and now ten thousand miles from home, at two-thirty in the morning, I am sitting

[169]

in another man's kitchen discussing love with a girl I hardly know. Whatever happened to Scobie Malone, the detective with the dull routine life?

"Oh, I think so. He was the one who wasn't fair. She didn't even know about me till he had made up his mind which one he wanted. Men can be rats, can't they?"

"I wouldn't know," he said, and wondered what she would think of Quentin who had killed the woman he did not want.

"I don't think you'd be a rat." She put down her cup and looked at him across the table. Her lips were wet from the coffee, glistening in the light, and suddenly he wanted to kiss her. He went to lean towards her and pressed his bruised ribs against the table; he caught his breath, but she didn't seem to notice. She looked at him soberly and without co-quetry; once again he cursed the fact that he could not read women. He did not want to read them like a formula, but it would be a help to have some inkling of what they meant when they said, "I'm glad you weren't hurt tonight."

CHAPTER EIGHT

1

"Three hundred and twenty, plus the twenty-five stake money you gave me." Malone laid the money on the glass table next to the Rice Bubbles and the marmalade. "It was your lucky night, if it wasn't mine."

Quentin took five five-pound notes and pushed the rest back to Malone. "It's yours, Scobie. No—" He held up a hand as Malone started to protest. "No argument, please. It's worker's compensation, if you like. You ruined a good suit last night."

"That wasn't all I ruined. I had a good set of nerves till I landed in this country." He held out a stiffened hand and exaggeratedly jerked it. "Ever seen nerves of quivering steel?"

Quentin didn't smile. "I didn't want you to go last night, you know that. If you'd left it to Denzil—" He broke off, began to butter some toast with the abstracted air of a man who had no intention of eating it; it was just something to do with his own nervous hands. "What did Denzil say when you told him what had happened?"

"Told me to go home by the first available plane."

"What about Lisa?"

Malone, too, began to butter some toast; but then he

[171]

chewed on it, manufacturing a long pause before he said, "She was pretty upset. For your sake more than mine, I think."

"That's not true. She'd have been concerned for you."

"Well, all right, she was." He did not want to reveal too much of what had passed between himself and Lisa last night, mainly because he was not sure if there had been any hint of committal on her part. "But I was incidental. You're her real worry. As you said last night, you—" Then he stopped. He had been about to accuse Quentin of ruining the lives of the women in his life. But even though Quentin had accused himself of the same thing last night, it was not Malone's place to add to the charge. Frankness could be taken too far. Whatever else he was, Quentin was still the ambassador. At least till the weekend.

"What did I say last night?"

"Nothing."

Quentin looked steadily at him for some moments as if debating whether to press the question. Then he said, "Scobie, promise me one thing. From now on leave this business to Denzil and his men. You stick to the job you came over for. Do that and nothing else."

"If I was to do that properly, you and I would be on our way to the airport now. Is that what you want?"

There was a swish of cloth and Sheila, auburn hair glowing above her green housecoat, came out on to the patio. "I've just seen Lisa! John, have you heard what happened last night?"

"Sit down, darling." Quentin pushed out a chair for Sheila and she sank down on to it. The mornings don't treat her kindly, Malone thought; she turned to look at him and he saw the cracks that had multiplied since yesterday. Quentin said, "Scobie thinks we should get on a plane right away for home. What do you think?"

"Scobie?" Sheila looked from one man to the other. Men always arrived at first-name terms ahead of women, especially Australian men, but this was an intimacy she obviously hadn't expected between her husband and his captor.

"We've become old friends," said Quentin. "A common enemy does that."

Sheila looked as if she were about to weep; then she sat up and poured herself a glass of orange juice. She was holding a small green bedside clock and she set it down on the table. "I'll have Joseph send this out." She looked at Malone. "I bought this for my husband on our first wedding anniversary. He never wears a wrist watch and I got tired of him waking me every morning to ask the time. It didn't go off this morning. For the first time in twenty-two years."

Everyone is telling me their secrets, Malone thought. Who else in this house wants to confide in me? Joseph, the cook, the daily help?

Sheila was regaining control of herself; somehow she even seemed to smooth some of the lines out of her face. She nodded at Malone's grey suit, even managed to smile. "Joseph must be disappointed in you, Scobie—may I call you Scobie?"

"If you like," Malone said, and wished she would not. When it came time to give evidence against Quentin he did not want to look around the court and have his objectivity upset by the sight of too many people who called him by his first name. "Joseph thinks I've reverted to type."

"You'd better wear one of my dark suits today," Quentin said.

"No, thanks—"

"I understand your feelings, Scobie," Quentin said, and Malone all at once realized that the other man did understand. "But it's not a question of tying in your identity too much with mine. I don't want you to put yourself in my shoes, figuratively or otherwise. It's a question of protection,

[173]

your protection. The less you stand out in that crowd at Lancaster House this morning, the better for you. And for me," he added unsmilingly.

Sheila had just noticed the money on the table. "What's all this?"

"Scobie's luck wasn't entirely out last night. He cleaned up at Fothergill's."

"This has been quite a trip for you, hasn't it?" Sheila said to Malone.

"Don't think I've enjoyed it." Then he looked from one to the other. "No offense."

Quentin smiled. "I'm beginning to wish I'd met you years ago."

Malone shook his head. "That wouldn't have done you any good. The best thing would have been not to have met me at all."

"If it hadn't been you, it would have been someone else," said Sheila, all the light dying out of her again. "The only consolation is that John has been able to make use of the time. Not just for himself, but for his country, too. But I think we knew it couldn't last."

Then Lisa came to the door. "Mr. Faber, from the American Embassy, is here. He's in the drawing room. And there's a phone call for you, Mr. Malone. From Sydney."

Quentin and Malone rose together. "Each to get his instructions," Quentin said with a dry smile.

"Are the Americans instructing you what to say?" Malone asked in surprise.

"They're trying. So are the British, the French, the South Vietnamese. Even the Chinese have had a go at me. All very polite, subtle and gentlemanly, though. Your friend Mr. Flannery should come over here for a couple of weeks. He might learn something."

"I don't think he'd be interested in politeness, subtlety

[174]

and being a gentleman. They've never been vote-catchers, not in Australian politics."

"He's talking about the Premier of New South Wales, Lisa." Quentin seemed to have forgotten that Lisa did not know Malone's real identity; she was his private secretary, privy to all his secrets. But now that he realized he and Malone had made a slip by talking about Flannery in front of her, he was not panicked into a fumbling cover-up. "But don't quote him in your memoirs."

Lisa looked at Malone with a warm sympathy that surprised and pleased him. The mood between them of last night still survived. "Mr. Malone got into enough trouble last night. I wouldn't want to make it worse for him."

Malone smiled his thanks and, still limping a little from his sore knee, followed Quentin into the house. A thin, balding man was waiting in the drawing room; Malone could see him through the wide-open doors. Larter was with him and both of them had the pinched look of pessimists who had not slept well. The conference had started to go badly and they had no confidence that it would go well today. Quentin went in to them, closing the doors: the man with no future at all, he was the one with the air of confidence.

Malone went on to the study, closing the door after him: his own conference *in camera* was about to begin. Leeds was on the line, sounding a little impatient. "Aren't you out of bed over there? How are things going?"

Malone was surprised to find himself hesitating. What was the matter with him? He had been about to lie, to tell Leeds there was nothing to worry about. Forcibly he reminded himself he was working for Leeds, not for the patriotic man in the next room. "Not too well—" he said, and told Leeds of the bomb explosion and the attempt on his own life.

He heard the curse on the other side of the world. "The

[175]

bomb explosion story is in all the morning papers here—but I didn't even connect you with it!" That's good, Malone thought; then perhaps no one else has. "Get on the first plane, Scobie! I don't care what happens to *him*—it might be better all round if he were assassinated. God forgive me for saying so—and don't you quote me to anyone!" There was silence for a moment, then in a much quieter voice Leeds said, "I don't want anything to happen to you."

Malone was glad the line was so clear; he could not have argued over ten thousand miles of static. "Believe me, Commissioner, I don't want anything to happen to me. But Mr. Quentin is the important one. If I put him on a plane today, the conference here would fold up tomorrow."

Again Leeds cursed: he sounded as if he were at the end of a long and frustrating day. He's lucky, Malone thought: I'm just beginning mine. "International politics aren't our concern. We've been handed a murder warrant and it's our job to see it's carried through."

Malone noticed he had used "we." He said, "I'm doing that, sir. He isn't making any attempt to get away from me— and I don't think he will. Once this conference is over, he'll come back with me. It just means a few days' delay, that's all. A week after twenty-three years isn't much, sir."

"Don't start sounding like a defense lawyer pleading for an adjournment." Leeds' voice was tart. "And what happens to our case if he doesn't last till the end of the conference?"

Malone took a risk, asked to be sent to a bush beat again. "You just said it, sir. If he is—assassinated—" He paused; he could hear the murmur of voices in the next room; Quentin laughed. "If he is assassinated, won't that solve everything?"

There was a long silence over the line, then Leeds said, "Scobie, are you getting too friendly with this man?"

Malone hesitated. "I could be, sir. But I'm doing my best to stay objective."

"You don't sound it."

[176]

Malone took another risk: "I'm not entirely convinced he did murder his wife."

"If you were back here, Sergeant, that would get you taken off the case right away! Damn it all, I hate the way this thing has been done, everything wrapped up and laid in our laps, but the facts are there, the facts are there! You checked and reported on them before you left here."

"I know that, sir. And the facts could still be right. But I'd like to double-check."

Leeds' voice was firm. "Sergeant, you have a warrant to bring him back for murder. See you do that—and let the jury decide whether he's guilty."

"Do we stay on, then, till the conference is ended?"

Leeds sighed, his voice no longer firm. "All right. But be careful. Of yourself, I mean."

Malone put down the phone. He could still hear the murmur of voices in the next room; someone sounded a little angry, but he couldn't tell whose voice it was. Out in the square there was a clamour of bells as a fire engine went by: disaster, he had learned long ago, was always just around the corner. But what would come to save Quentin? *I want him to be saved,* Malone told himself with some surprise. Not just from the assassins, but from Flannery, too. And that also surprised him: that Flannery should have replaced justice in his own mind. *Why am I so sure that he didn't kill his first wife?*

Then the door opened and Joseph came in. "Oh, I'm sorry, sir. I didn't—"

"It's okay, Joseph. It looks as if I'm going to have to borrow one of Mr. Quentin's suits today."

"Yes, sir. May I just wind the clock first?" He crossed to the mantelpiece, began to wind the ormolu clock. "I saw your dark suit in your room. I took the liberty of laying out one of Mr. Quentin's, just in case. You had an accident, sir?"

"In a way. I was almost knocked down by a car."

Joseph shook his head, tut-tutted. "London traffic, it is a stampede now. When I first came here, drivers were so polite. Even taxi drivers occasionally pulled up to allow one to cross the street."

"How long ago was that?"

"You mean when I first came here, sir? Nineteen fifty-six. I got out of Budapest during the rebellion."

"Were you a butler in Budapest?"

Joseph smiled, the first genuine look of humour Malone had seen on the bland, sallow face. "Butlers went out when the Communists came in. No, sir, I was only a waiter." Then his pride came to the surface: "But at one of the best hotels. The Duna. You wouldn't know Budapest, sir?"

"No, I'm afraid not." Malone grinned, unashamed of his small world. But he would have to buy an Atlas when he got back to Sydney. "Do you like it here?"

Joseph finished winding the clock, gently closed the glass face and looked about the room. "I like being among good things, sir. I was born poor, but I have aristocratic tastes. If one cannot be rich, the next best thing is to be a butler."

"A Hungarian saying?" Malone had met one or two Hungarian refugees in Sydney, cynical men who seemed to have had little faith in human nature.

Joseph smiled again. "I know what people say about Hungarians, sir. If you have an Hungarian for a friend, you don't need an enemy. All sorts of remarks like that. But most of the worst remarks about Hungarians were made by other Hungarians. It is a national sport."

"We have a version of it in Australia. It's called 'Always Knock the Aussie.' Have you ever thought of going out to Australia?"

Joseph was too good a butler to wrinkle his nose. "Not really, sir. It is so—remote, is that the word?"

Malone grinned. "It's good enough. I've heard worse."

He went out into the hall and Coburn, face stiffly set in

[178]

its on-duty mould, was standing in front of the big mirror adjusting the knot of his purple knit tie. Unexpectedly he grinned at Malone and said, "My girl is a very gear type. She bought this in Carnaby Street and insisted I wear it this morning. If the Super sees me in it, I'll be back on the Chelsea pub beat, chasing up the queers."

"Your girl's got taste. It goes with your eyes."

"You mean the bags under them? What with her and the Super, I never get enough sleep." Malone led the way up to his bedroom. Coburn, showing a capacity for relaxation that Malone had not suspected, sprawled in a chair, one leg hung over its arm. "They nearly did you last night? Denzil phoned me this morning at seven o'clock, gave me a run-down. You were lucky."

Malone nodded, slipping out of his grey trousers and pulling on Quentin's dark blue ones. "What about Pallain? Did Denzil say if they had checked on him?"

"He's staying in a hotel in Queen's Gate. We've had a tail on him ever since he left the Yard last night. He didn't move out of his hotel at all last night."

"I could have sworn that the car that tried to crumple me was the one he drove yesterday morning. A red Mini."

"There must be fifty thousand red Minis in Britain. It was probably a rented job. It'll never be returned and some time next year or the year after it'll be found in a quarry somewhere. By then this crowd will be out of the country. I don't understand why they tried to do you. Do you know something you shouldn't?"

Malone shrugged. He sat down on the bed and debated whether his old comfortable brown shoes would go with Quentin's suit, decided they wouldn't and reluctantly began to pull on the black ones he had bought yesterday. He would be crippled by this evening, but he would be a sartorially correct cripple. He longed for the old days when no one had cared how he was dressed, just so long as he *was* dressed. "I

[¹79]

don't know. I'm puzzled about this bloke Jamaica. Who's he working for?"

"We're still trying to check on him. So far we've got nothing other than what Denzil said he told you last night, that he exports Thai silk or something from Bangkok. The Old Man went back to the Yard last night after he left you and phoned our embassy in Bangkok. They checked for him. Jamaica has a registered business out there."

"Doesn't Denzil ever sleep?"

"Sometimes. He's a stiff-necked old sod, he should never have come home from his outpost of Empire, but he's a worker, all right. And he works *us*."

Malone stood up, pulled on Quentin's jacket. He shifted his shoulders uncomfortably: Quentin, not the suit, was beginning to fit too tightly. "We've all been working these last two days. But we haven't got very far. What about Madame Cholon?"

Coburn stood up, spreading his hands. "Thin air. But one thing worries me—what do we do with her when we do find her? This is supposed to be a free country, a democracy and all that. You can't deport foreign visitors because you *think* they might be up to something. If she has no record, if her visa is okay, now she's here there's nothing we can do about her."

"You can keep tabs on her, see she stays out of mischief."

Coburn shook his head. "You don't really think she's the one who's been taking potshots at you and Quentin. She might be running the show or mixed up in it somehow, but she's not the one doing the dirty work." He looked at his tie again in the mirror, shook his head doubtfully, then turned back to Malone. "Have you considered the possibility that Jamaica is working with her? He was the one who got you to go out last night. She didn't turn up, and I gather as soon as the Old Man put in an appearance Jamaica disappeared."

"He didn't know where we were going to park the car."

"You could have been followed from here. Maybe they hadn't intended going for you there in the garage—that could have been just an improvisation."

Malone smiled sourly. "I didn't think assassins went in for improvisation. But somehow I don't know about Jamaica —he strikes me as a loner. Next time I see him, if there is a next time, I might try a bit of strong-arm stuff on him."

Coburn grinned. "Don't try it in public. Nowadays you can knock down a white man and that's good clean British fun. Knock down a coloured bloke and it's racial prejudice. We'd have trouble getting the charge smothered."

"Do *you* have any racial prejudice?" He wondered how Coburn would have treated Jamaica.

Coburn shrugged. "I try to tell myself I haven't. But I find I get a bit tired of having to lean over backwards if a bloke *is* coloured. I know it's harder for him, but when he forgets he's coloured, then I'll forget it, too."

"Well, Jamaica's colour is incidental with me. I'd just like to know *who* he is and I wouldn't care if he was zebra-striped."

Coburn had been carrying a brown paper parcel. Now he unwrapped it and brought out a gun. "Do you have one of these?"

"No." Malone had left his pistol behind in Sydney because he had not wanted to explain to the British Customs why he was bringing a firearm into their country. And he had never expected to have any use for a gun in London.

"Denzil sent this. It's a Smith and Wesson .38 Special Airweight. We're not supposed to carry them, but on certain jobs they issue them to us. Here's a shoulder holster to go with it—the gun's held in by this spring."

Malone hesitated a moment before he put out a hand and took the gun and holster. The situation was serious enough with the attempts on his own and Quentin's life, but, divorced from his usual surroundings, he still had a feeling of

[181]

incredulousness, as if everything was not quite real. But now the gun, as guns always were, was a proof of reality. He took off Quentin's jacket, slipped on the holster, put the gun in it, and redonned the jacket. The fit was even tighter now.

"The gun is loaded," Coburn said, "and here's some extra ammo. If you have to use the gun, make sure you remember all the details. The Home Secretary will want a full report. In triplicate."

"I've never yet fired a gun in anger. I just hope I can when the time comes."

Coburn opened the door and Joseph was standing there, a pair of dark blue socks in his hand. "I forgot the socks, sir—"

Malone pulled up a dark blue trouser leg and showed a length of light brown sock. "I'll be okay, Joseph."

Joseph rocked slightly on his heels, but didn't fall over. "Perhaps if you didn't sit down, sir—?"

Malone grinned. "I'll stay on my feet all day. Don't worry, Joseph. I won't let the High Commissioner down."

He and Coburn went down the stairs. On the landing Coburn stopped for a moment and looked at his tie in a mirror. "Why did I have to fall for a bird who has to be always with it?"

"Better a bird than a butler," said Malone. "At least you get some return for your pains."

Quentin, Larter and Edgar were waiting for them in the hall. Malone looked around for the man from the American Embassy, but he had gone. "We're late," said Larter reproachfully; he was too aware of time ever to be a good diplomat. "It creates a bad impression if everyone has to wait on the chairman."

But Quentin's smile at Malone and Coburn brushed aside Larter's waspishness. "We'll try a little diplomatic immunity and get Ferguson to break the speed limit. That's a nice tie you're wearing, Sergeant."

Coburn's face crumpled in embarrassment. "I thought it might have been a bit bright, sir—"

"Nonsense. We can all do with some cheering up. I've been trying to persuade Mr. Larter and Mr. Edgar to wear carnations in their buttonholes."

"That'll be the day," said Edgar, and winked at Malone. "They'd have me investigated back in Canberra as a security risk. You might even be given the job, Mr. Malone."

"Eh?" Malone for a moment had forgotten his cover. "Oh yes. If ever I am, I'll give you a clearance."

"Shall we go?" said Larter: nobody would ever be investigating *him*.

There was a black Wolseley drawn up behind the Rolls-Royce at the curb outside. Coburn got into the police car beside the plainclothes man driving it, and Malone got into the front seat of the Rolls beside Ferguson. The two cars moved off, the policeman on the corner saluting the Rolls as it went past. It was a fine summer morning, the sky cloudless, the sun flashing like a silent barrage from the windows on the west side of the square. Three or four children played in the gardens where the assassin had waited the night before last: a small boy put a gun to his shoulder and a young girl screamed and fell dead. Pigeons fell like ripe grey plums from the trees, a shifting windfall on the green grass. Two nannies crossed the road, pushing prams ahead of them like portable thrones. The cars went round the square and joined the traffic going up Grosvenor Crescent towards Hyde Park Corner. Malone looked out, suspecting every vehicle that went past, moving his upper arm nervously against the hidden gun.

"Relax, sir. I don't think they'll have a go at him again in broad daylight." The glass partition behind Ferguson's head was closed; he and Malone rode in their own compartment. "But you were lucky yesterday, you know. I mean that you didn't catch up with that joker with the bomb."

[183]

Malone looked at him sharply. "How did you know I had anything to do with that?"

"Put two and two together. You were chasing a bloke when I dropped you off and you got into that taxi—twenty minutes later there was a bomb explosion not more than a quarter of a mile from Australia House—" He grinned, exposing false teeth that were too small and perfect for the rough frame of his face. "A chauffeur gets a lot of time for reading. I read half a dozen detective books a week."

"You said anything to anyone?"

"Not a word, sir. You don't hold these sorta jobs very long if you can't keep your trap shut, you know. If Mr. Quentin wants me to keep mum, then mum I'm gunna be."

"You have a lot of time for him, haven't you?"

"They don't come any better. He's a prince, you know?"

Malone glanced back into the rear of the car. The prince sat staring out the window, his grey handsome face slack and tired-looking: his princedom was at an end, he was about to be removed from the ladder of succession. He closed his eyes for a moment, as if he had felt a stab of pain; when he opened them he was looking straight at Malone. The two men stared at each other; then Malone turned back to gaze straight ahead as the car went down Constitution Hill past the Palace. Maybe the assassin's bullet would have been better after all: it was too cruel to see a man dying by degrees.

They pulled up in front of Lancaster House. Malone got out and a man came forward with a rush. Malone's hand went inside his jacket, clutched the gun; but the man was curious, not threatening. "Aren't you Scobie Malone? Detective-Sergeant Malone, from Sydney?"

Malone hesitated, withdrawing his hand. He nodded curtly, aware of Quentin and the others getting out of the car behind him. He moved away, drawing the man with him. "Who are you?"

[184]

"Jim Locke. I'm with the *Sydney Morning Herald.*" His thin dark face, disfigured by huge black eyebrows, was drawn tight by suspicion: he scented a story, one that should have been announced by the press officer at Australia House. "You're a bit off your beat, aren't you?"

Malone was saved from stammering when Quentin came up beside him. "Something wrong, Scobie?"

Locke's eyebrows went up. "Morning, sir. I was just asking Sergeant Malone why he's over here—"

"He's on holiday," said Quentin. "And while he's in London he's staying with me. We're old friends. I think he'd like to forget he's a policeman for a week or two. Isn't that right, Scobie? You forget it, too, Jim. Let him have a bit of peace."

Locke was persistent: "But when I saw him here—"

"We never get this sort of conference back home, you know that. He's just widening his education."

"It would make a nice little sideline story."

"Spare me," said Malone, recovered now. "The boys back on the squad would give me hell. Do me a favour and I might be able to do you one some day."

Locke shook his head. "I don't expect ever to be back on police rounds. That's dull stuff after this. Well—" He mumbled a few more words, then edged away.

Quentin watched him go. "You'll have to learn to think quicker on your feet, Scobie. That could have been awkward for both of us."

"Do you think he'll print anything?"

"If he intends to, he'll be back to pump you again. He's not a gossip writer. He's a journalistic snob, only interested in the big stuff. You heard what he said about police rounds being dull. If he only knew, eh?"

He went on into the big mansion, nodding affably to the photographers, a man in control of himself and any situation he might have to face. The exhausted, defeated man Malone had seen in the car only a few minutes ago had disappeared.

Larter and Edgar followed him, and Malone and Coburn brought up the rear.

"I saw you go for your gun when that cove came up to you," Coburn said. "You'll shoot in anger, all right. There's your mate!"

Malone looked back over his shoulder, expecting to be accosted by the newspaperman again. But Coburn pulled his arm. "No, over there. Just going into the press room."

Malone turned his head quickly, just in time to see Pallain turn back at the entrance to a side room and smile at him.

"The sod," said Coburn. "Sometimes I wish I was in the KGB instead of Special Branch."

"KGB?"

"The Russian secret police." Coburn looked at him curiously. "Don't you Aussie security coves know about them?"

For the second time in a couple of minutes Malone had to try and cover up. His brain was turning to blancmange; there had been a time when he *could* think quickly on his feet. "I think I must have cracked my head last night. I'm not too bright this morning. And initials always confuse me. I thought the KGB might have been some English government outfit. You're as bad as the Yanks now for initials."

"Ah yes, but then we make up some nursery name out of the initials. Like Neddy and Nicky. All our headline writers can't forget the influence of their nannies."

Malone grinned: Coburn was more of a rebel than he had expected. "Why do you wish you were in the KGB?"

"They don't have to worry about minor things like proof of guilt. Suspicion is good enough for them. Grab 'em and lock 'em up, that's their motto." Coburn glanced up at Quentin, Larter and Edgar on the main balcony; they were just about to enter the conference room. "Our boy is safe for the next couple of hours. Shall we go and bait your mate?"

Pallain, still standing in the doorway of the press room, smiled as they approached him. "Mr. Malone, how are you?

You don't look well this morning. It's the English climate. It doesn't agree with me, also."

Malone introduced Coburn, and the latter said, "I understand the climate in Saigon isn't too healthy just now."

Pallain's smile widened. His teeth were not good, uneven and slightly yellow, and the smile was not pleasant. "English policemen are becoming sardonic, more like the French. I noticed it with your Superintendent last night." He looked up at the doors of the conference room which were just being closed. "Well, there they go. The optimists."

"You don't think they'll get anywhere?" Malone said.

"Do you?"

"Anything is worth a try. Or do you find war easier to write about?"

"Don't misunderstand me, Mr. Malone. I am all in favour of peace. But talk rarely achieves it. Only force. That's a nasty cut on your chin."

"I'd like a little talk with the bloke who did it," said Malone. "A little forceful talk."

"I'm afraid I couldn't help you." Pallain looked from one to the other. "I can't get out of my hotel for policemen watching me. They should watch you instead of me."

He smiled again, bowed his head slightly and turned and went into the press room.

"I'd like to throttle that bastard," said Coburn. "With my purple tie. What's the matter?"

Malone had been looking about the now sparse crowd still in the vestibule and on the upper balconies. "I wonder where our mate Jamaica is this morning?"

2

"I am expecting Mr. Jamaica any minute," said Madame Cholon. "But you should not be calling from Lancaster House, Jean-Pierre. It is too risky."

[187]

"I have the press room to myself," said Pallain at the other end of the line. "And who's to know whom I'm calling?"

"The lines might be tapped."

"In Moscow or Washington, yes. But not here. The British would consider it too much trouble. They have enough bother getting their phones to work ordinarily." She heard him chuckle maliciously; he had inherited his French father's hatred of the English. "I have been talking to your Australian friend this morning. Mr. Malone. He doesn't look well. Pham Chinh must have upset him last night. Has the car been disposed of?"

"Yes. What about Quentin?"

"Worried-looking." There was a pause; then: "There isn't much time left. You must be worrying, too."

"Don't start analyzing me, Monsieur Pallain!" But she was worried; there wasn't much time left. She slammed down the phone. Her hands were trembling and she could hardly see for fury. Even as a child she had never taken kindly to criticism; she knew that when she had turned fourteen her mother had been only too relieved to let her go to the brothel in Cholon. There, in her first year, she had scratched the faces of several men who had complained of her lack of technique; by the end of her first year she had the best technique of any girl in the house, but some of the men were still afraid of her temper and chose more placid girls. In the twenty years since, she had improved her status and her fortune, had become sophisticated, had learned to command. But the fury of the child was still in her and it would always be her weakness. She knew it and hated it, but there was nothing she could do about it.

She walked to the window and looked out at the traffic passing up and down Avenue Road. She had rented this house in St. John's Wood at the same time as she had rented the apartment in Kensington. Bay Vien had taught her that a good general always had a second prepared position in case of retreat; she had also learned from the Viet Cong that a good guerrilla never operated from the same base all the time. She looked about the luxurious room in which she stood and smiled to herself: this was the sort of guerrilla war she enjoyed. The house belonged to a stockbroker who, she had discovered after taking the house, was currently summering in one of Her Majesty's prisons for misusing clients' funds. She had not been shocked by the discovery: corruption, like sex, was a commercial way of life with her. The man, whoever he was, was just a fool to have been caught.

She wandered restlessly about the room, impatient for Jamaica to arrive. She had learned to control herself, but she had never mastered the art of relaxing; the quality of repose was to her often no more than a resignation, the bowing of a woman to a man's domination. And no man, not even Bay Vien, had ever dominated her. She picked up several of the morning newspapers, with their stories and pictures of the bomb explosion yesterday. Each paper had its own approach to the story. The *Daily Express* didn't think it was part of the British way of life; the *Financial Times* said the effect of the explosion had not been felt on the Stock Exchange; the *Daily Telegraph* commented that nothing like this had happened in thirteen years of Tory government. She threw down the papers with a curse of anger. If it had not been for that interfering Australian security man, Quentin would now be dead and the conference would already be crumbling into ruins of suspicion, charges and countercharges. She had to do *something!* But what?

Pham Chinh opened the door, his flat brown face seemingly flattened further by shock. "There are two Chinese to see you," he said in French, his voice hissing a little. He was a superstitious man and he was beginning to be afraid: too much had gone wrong over the past two days. And now these unknown Chinese: "They won't give their names."

Madame Cholon hesitated. Curiosity was another of her

[189]

weaknesses, a peasant inheritance; her first reaction was to say she was not at home, but she knew she would not rest till she knew who the Chinese were and what they wanted. "Show them in."

Pham Chinh opened the door wider, jerked his head and stood aside to let the two Chinese, both of them short, one fat, the other thin, pass by him into the room. Then he came into the room behind them, to stand beside the door with his arms folded and his feet planted together. Madame Cholon hid a smile: Pham Chin always looked ridiculous, like a bad actor, when he tried to look tough.

She spoke to the Chinese in French. "What can I do for you gentlemen?"

The fat man said something in Chinese, but Madame Cholon shook her head. She spoke some Chinese, but she was not at home in the language and she did not want to miss any of the nuances that might be in the conversation.

"Do you speak English?" he then said, and she nodded. She did not ask them to sit nor did they look as if they were waiting to be offered chairs: this was not going to be a cozy chat. The fat man wore rimless glasses that seemed to make his smooth round face as blank as a plate; he appeared to speak without moving his lips. "Madame Cholon, whom are you working for?"

"Tell me first, whom are *you* working for?" Her voice was tart: she was going to let them know she was not accustomed to being questioned in her own house, even a rented one.

The two Chinese exchanged glances and the thin one smiled. He was young, hardly more than a boy, and in the lapel of his ill-fitting grey suit he wore a charity badge: St. Francis' Home for Disabled Dogs of Gentlefolk. The English had extracted toll from him: it was a small price for the jokes he would tell about them when he returned to Peking. "There is only one government that honorable Chinese work for," he said, and did not seem aware that he sounded like a parody of all the Chinese Madame Cholon had seen in American movies. "We trust you do not work for the Kuomintang?"

It was Madame Cholon's turn to smile. "No. I am working for no one."

"We do not choose to believe that." The fat man held his hat in front of his belly like a small grey felt shield; he would never trust anyone here in the West. "Why were you at the reception the night before last at—" He named the African embassy. "And why did you go after the reception to the gambling club with the American, Jamaica?"

Madame Cholon looked at Pham Chinh. "Would you show the gentlemen to the door?"

She turned her back, took two paces towards the window, then stopped. She heard Pham Chinh hiss, but she did not hear him move. She turned her head and saw the thin Chinese was holding a small pistol aimed directly at Pham Chinh's belly. She recognized the pistol, a Beretta; she had once had one herself and had twice used it on men. She had no feeling at all for Pham Chinh and would not miss nor even remember him when he was gone. But she did not want him dead just yet. A live employee, while he was still useful, was better than a dead one.

"Put the gun away," she said, and motioned to the thick-cushioned couch nearby. "Won't you sit down?"

Pham Chinh let out another hiss, then relaxed, leaning back now against the wall. Madame Cholon sat down in a chair, tensed inside but outwardly calm, and waited for the two Chinese to sit down. The fat man sat stiffly on the edge of the couch, his hat still held like a shield in front of him; but the thin man lounged back in the rich comfort of the cushions, one leg propped up on the other and the pistol held loosely in his lap. The chat was still not going to be cozy, but an understanding had been arrived at. This was Madame Cholon's house, but the Chinese held the mortgage.

"Why are you concerned about Mr. Jamaica?" Madame Cholon asked.

The two Chinese glanced at each other, then the fat man said, "What do you know about him?"

"Nothing very much. He says he is a silk exporter from Bangkok, but I suspect he is more than that."

"He works for the American Central Intelligence Agency," said the thin man, and smiled when he saw Madame Cholon bite her lip. He looked up at Pham Chinh, who had suddenly stiffened and straightened up. "You did not know that?"

"No," said Madame Cholon.

"I believe you are telling the truth." The thin man shook his head wonderingly at his companion, as if amazed at such ignorance on the part of Madame Cholon. Then his face tightened and he looked back at her. "If you are not working with the Americans, whom are you working with?"

"Do I have to be working with anyone? I am here on holiday. It is just coincidental that other people from our part of the world should also be here in London."

"We do not accept the coincidence, Madame." The fat man wore a stiff collar and a waistcoat and he was feeling the heat in the unventilated room. He took out a handkerchief and wiped his face and looked meaningly at the unopened windows, but Madame Cholon spitefully did not take the hint. "We know who you are, that you have not been to Europe for three years, that you have never been in London before. Such coincidences do not occur, Madame Cholon. We think you—we *know* you have had something to do with the attempts to kill the Australian High Commissioner."

Madame Cholon bit her lip again and glanced quickly at Pham Chinh. Shock and puzzlement had reduced him to an idiot stare; he was still leaning against the wall but limply now. He was really afraid, certain that all their luck had run out: the omens had been correct. Then he blinked and saw

[192]

the accusing look in Madame Cholon's hard eyes. He shook his head desperately, suddenly even more frightened.

"No, I've told no one! I don't *know* anyone—" He was babbling in his native tongue; fear made him dumb in French. "Someone else must have told them!"

"Who?" The fury was taking hold of her again. "Jean-Pierre?" Then she looked at the Chinese again. "Or was it Mr. Jamaica?"

The young thin Chinese shook his head and smiled. "If ever we were going to employ a double agent, Madame, we should not have an American. One cannot trust them. No, we have our source. It is no one you know."

"The conference is going the way we want it to go," said the fat man, wiping his face again. He took off his glasses and his whole face seemed to become featureless; words issued from a blank mask. "We are achieving what we want without your help." He wiped the glasses, put them back on again. "You are a nuisance."

"Why are you so interested in me?" Outwardly she was calm again, but she was still quivering inside; her voice grated, she coughed to clear it. "There are others with something to lose if the conference goes wrong."

"You are spoiling our plans, ones we have taken great care and trouble with! Your stupid, crude methods are ruining everything we have arranged! Shooting, bombing, trying to kill the security man with a car!" The fat man also was furious; his whole body quivered, his glasses flashed as his head bobbed. The young man looked at him and appeared to smile, but he said nothing. "You will have to stop, Madame Cholon!"

"You know what happened in the garage?" She could not contain her surprise: her small voice cracked like a schoolgirl's.

"We know," said the young Chinese, and looked at Pham

[193]

Chinh. "Was it you who drove the car? What made you try something as stupid as that? Don't you know that you could have killed *yourself?*" He shook his head again; he just could not believe that so much stupidity existed. Thank Mao the New China did not have morons like this working for it.

Pham Chinh looked to Madame Cholon to answer for him. She hesitated, but for the moment she was defeated: these Chinese seemed to hold all the cards. The gun did not frighten her, only their knowledge: till she found out exactly how much they knew and who was their informant, she could not plan her own next move. For the time being she had to buy cards of her own: "We hadn't *planned* to kill the security man."

"One should not kill a man without making plans," said the thin man, and Madame Cholon heard the echo of her own advice. Both Chinese shook their heads. "That was stupid, Madame. Really stupid." The young man spoke like an honours graduate in political assassination. "Murder should never be done on the spur of the moment. You should always allow for the consequences."

Madame Cholon stared hard at the men: if she had the gun that the young man held, she would kill them both and to hell with the consequences. "As you say, it was done on the spur of the moment. And perhaps that was stupid. But I thought the security man was proving dangerous, he kept getting in my way. And this was an excellent opportunity. Doesn't Mao Tse-tung in his excellent book on guerrilla warfare advocate some opportunism?"

The Chinese were not going to be caught out in criticism of their leader. "Go on, Madame. Tell us how you got yourself into this awkward situation."

She hesitated again; then she went on to describe what had happened last night. Pham Chinh had been driving her to Fothergill's in a rented Mini-Minor— "What's the matter?"

"A loss of face for you, wasn't it, Madame?" said the young man. "One can't see you in a Mini-Minor."

She was not going to be drawn by the bait: this young Chinese would dearly love to see her erupt into a storm of temper. He was her real enemy; she was beginning to forget the older, fat man. "One indulges oneself at times. In this country one can be ostentatious by being unostentatious."

"Strange people, the English," said the fat man.

"It was just sheer chance that I saw Malone, the security man, and the girl who works for the High Commissioner. They were in an open car and they passed us at Hyde Park Corner. That, too, was sheer chance. Pham Chinh missed the gambling club as we went down Park Lane and we had to go right down—it is one-way—and come back up round Hyde Park Corner."

"Luck seems to play a large part in your life, Madame. We hope you do not rely too much on it."

"I am a gambler," she said. "When luck presents itself, you don't turn your back on it."

"What happened when you saw Mr. Malone and the girl?"

"We followed them up to the garage. I stayed in the car while Chinh followed them on foot. He came back and told me they had gone to Fothergill's. I was to meet Mr. Jamaica there. I at once thought Jamaica had got in touch with Malone, was trying—how do they say?—to cook something up."

"And so you lost your temper and decided to kill one or both of them?" The young Chinese shook his head again; too many amateurs were at large.

Madame Cholon smiled thinly. "I am not as crude as all that. I got a taxi and came back here. I left Pham Chinh in the garage. He was only to kill Malone if he got him alone. I left the method up to him. As it happened, he chose the wrong one." She looked at Pham Chinh and he dropped

[195]

his eyes; he had already felt the lash of her tongue for the bungled job. "Next time I shall name the method."

"There won't be a next time." The young man looked at the fat man and both of them stood up. "We think you should catch the first plane back to Saigon, Madame. How soon can you be ready?"

"I shall be ready in my own time!" The fury began to come to the surface; he had scratched deeply. "I am not leaving here—"

The fat older man put his hat carefully on his head with both hands, as if crowning himself. The young man put his own hat on carelessly, but he was not careless about the way he held the gun. He brought it up and pointed it with emphasis at Madame Cholon. "We shall even pay your fare, Madame, yours and your servant's. Can you be ready to leave tomorrow?"

"No! I tell you I am not leaving here till—"

"Saturday then. In the meantime you will not go near the Australian High Commissioner, near his residence, Australia House nor Lancaster House. Neither you nor anyone you may hire, including this stupid man here." The young man hadn't raised or hardened his voice; he might have been arranging a holiday flight for Madame Cholon and Pham Chinh, a packaged tour for amateur assassins. "There is a Qantas plane leaving at half-past five Saturday afternoon. You can change at Singapore. Your tickets will be here at lunchtime today. First class for yourself and tourist class for your servant. Will that be all right?"

"You are making a mistake—"

"We make mistakes occasionally, Madame," the thin young man conceded. It was evident now that, though he was the younger of the two Chinese by almost thirty years, he was the one with the senior authority. The veterans had won the revolution, had slogged through the Long March, fought the Nationalists; but the young men, educated by

[196]

propaganda, injected with hatred, were taking over. Madame Cholon knew that was the frightening thing about China: the young people were even more fanatical than the old. "But we are not making a mistake in this case. You will be on Saturday's plane."

"And if I'm not?" For once she had no prepared retreat to fall back on; but she did not feel her defiance was hollow. Resignation had never been one of her weaknesses; fatalism was for fools. She would fight them, all seven hundred million of them.

"Then I am afraid something crude may happen to you," said the young Chinese. "The tickets will be here at lunchtime. Good morning, Madame."

They both bowed, raised their hats and backed out of the room, the young man still holding the gun in front of him like a badge of office. Madame Cholon heard the front door close, then she looked at Pham Chinh. "We don't have much time, Chinh."

"Do we catch the plane on Saturday?" Pham Chinh's voice was hopeful, relieved: other crimes, other murders, lay ahead for him, but in Saigon, where the climate was better and the chances of being caught were much, much slimmer.

"We shall be on the plane. But our work will be finished by then." She had no plans, but her confidence had begun to return. But first, certain obstructions had to be done away. "When Mr. Jamaica arrives, show him in."

"But if he is working for the Americans—?" Pham Chinh wanted no more mistakes. Let them play it safe, get on the plane and go home. He had already forgotten his ambition to be rich: a dead man could not drive a Lincoln Continental.

"Mr. Jamaica has finished working for the Americans. Or anyone else." The doorbell rang. "There he is now."

[197]

CHAPTER NINE

1

Malone lay on his bed. He had taken off his shoes and every now and again he would wriggle his toes, easing the soreness of them. He was still stiff from last night's bruising and the cut on his chin had begun to itch under its Band-Aid. But he was hardly aware of any of his discomfort except as irritations on the periphery of his mind. He was no stoic, nor had he ever been one to indulge himself in the contemplation of pain. He had discovered that it was best cured by being ignored; the system might not work with everyone but it did with him. And if the mind had its own pain, the body in any case was forgotten.

The curtains were open and the early evening sky outside the window was the colour of a kingfisher's breast: a high-flying jet pierced it like a tiny dart. There was a distant hum of traffic, the breathing, sighing, occasional shrieking of the city; but it was not disturbing. Dead silence would have been worse, would have made him more aware of the people in the house. One of whom had tried to open his briefcase in which was locked the file on Quentin and the warrant for his arrest.

It had been a long day and not a good one. The conference, he knew, had gone badly again. He had become concerned for its success, a little to his own surprise. He was not apolitical nor, like so many of his fellow countrymen, completely uninterested in what went on in the conference halls of the world. He knew that Australia, culturally and socially, was still isolated from the rest of the world; he had once helped arrest a drunken English actor who had described it as the arse-end of civilization, and he had stood by while his fellow officer, cut to his patriotic quick, had dreamed up other charges to lay against the offending actor. The slur on his country had not worried him, because he was well aware of the fact that he was not himself culturally and socially minded. But he had never ignored the fact that, politically, Australia was no longer isolated. No matter what eleven million white Australians thought, their country was now part of Asia. And what went on in Vietnam, Indonesia, China, in any country to the north of them, concerned them as much as the problems close at home, the traffic toll, the rising cost of living, the possible winner of the next Melbourne Cup. But while he had been back home in Australia, surrounded by an environment that looked upon an Asia-oriented foreign policy as some sort of treason, it had been easy to become one of the mob, one of those who buried their heads in the sand of Bondi beach and thought the price of beer more important than the price of freedom. He had been guilty of the same apathy.

But no longer. Now he was as concerned for the success of the conference as were Quentin, Larter and Edgar; he had become a silent, unacknowledged member of the delegation. He wanted the conference to succeed for its main purpose, to achieve some sort of peace, no matter how fragile, in Asia; he also wanted it to succeed for Quentin's sake. The man would want to take something with him into the dark years ahead in gaol.

At the afternoon break in the discussions Quentin had come out of the big main room and along to where Malone had stood by himself on one of the balconies. Other delegates went by in pairs and threes, heads drawn together in the one net of earnest discussion. Malone saw the American who had come to the house this morning; he passed by with two other men and as he did so he looked at Quentin with hurt eyes. Quentin missed the glance and the American passed on, looking even more hurt.

"Thinking of buying the place, Scobie?" Quentin said.

Malone had been gazing admiringly at the staircase and the big hall below him. "I'm going to find it tough going back to my flat in King's Cross. No marble walls and chandeliers there."

"The marble is imitation. Like the attitudes of some of the delegates here today."

Quentin sounded bitter and disappointed, but he managed a confident smile as a Malaysian delegate went by. Then he looked about the balconies, at the groups clustered together like salesmen in some gem market. That's what they are, Malone thought: salesmen selling their influence. The thought disgusted him; some ember of youthful idealism flared again for a moment. Then cynical realism prevailed. He was supposed, as a policeman, to be experienced in human nature. Everything today was based upon buying and selling: even love was a commodity and not just sold by prostitutes. Why should he expect men to make a gift of peace? Christ had tried it and they had nailed him to a cross for his pains.

Quentin said, "The man who designed this house also built the house where you were last night, Fothergill's. He built Crockford's, too. I wonder how he feels now? Three of his biggest commissions finishing up as gambling clubs."

"Three?"

"Wouldn't you call this a gambling club? The odds are longer here than at Crockford's or Fothergill's. Especially today."

"Things are getting worse?"

Quentin nodded, then looked over Malone's shoulder. "Mr. Chen, Mr. Pai. Enjoying yourselves?"

Malone was introduced to the two Chinese, one thin and young, the other fat and middle-aged. "Our stay has been enjoyable, but we are looking forward to going home," said the young man, Chen. "We do not make very good observers. We prefer to work."

"I thought you had been working all the time you were here." The look of sour depression had gone from Quentin's face; he smiled with frank good humour. "Winning friends and influencing people."

"Dale Carnegie is required reading in Peking. And Norman Vincent Peale and Godfrey Winn." Chen was not without a sense of humour; he had learned that outside China propaganda had to be more subtle than at home. "How else can we understand the West unless we read their philosophers?"

"You should not neglect Dorothy Dix."

"Women have never made good philosophers," said Chen, still smiling, and looked at the fat man. "We know that, don't we?"

"Too emotional," said Pai, taking off his glasses and polishing them with a handkerchief. He was a nervous man and Malone could imagine him taking off his glasses every few minutes, rubbing away at them till they splintered apart in his fingers. "We are fortunate there are no women here at the conference trying to influence decisions. Do you not think so, Mr. Quentin?"

Quentin looked at Malone, then back at the two Chinese. "Perhaps they are in the background. One never knows. Most of the delegates here are married men."

"Wives are not the women to be wary of," said Chen, still unmarried and still innocent. "Wives do not have ambitions for power, except perhaps over their husbands. At least I understand that it is like that in the West."

"I must ask my wife what power she has over me," said Quentin, still smiling.

"I did not mean to offend," said Chen: the revolution had not killed all politeness.

"I know that. I was only joking. But what about Lady Wu —wouldn't you say she had ambitions for power?"

"Lady Wu was a concubine, not a wife. Not as you Western men understand the term wife."

"Who was Lady Wu?" Malone asked.

"She lived in the seventh century," Quentin said. "She was about the most villainous bitch of all time. She made Catherine the Great and Lucrezia Borgia look like a couple of Girl Guides."

"An absolute reactionary," said Pai.

Quentin hid a smile, kept a straight face. "Yes, you could say she was that. She murdered hundreds of people, including some of her own sons. She lived to a ripe old age, ran a male harem till she was almost eighty. When she died she left a will saying that she forgave all those people who had made her kill them. They don't make women like her any more, do they, Mr. Chen?"

Chen shrugged. "One never knows. Perhaps the climate is not right any more. Could you see Lady Wu as a London hostess?"

"Perhaps not," conceded Quentin. "Wholesale disposal of corpses in London is difficult."

"You could stand them in queues at bus stops," said Malone. "No one would know the difference."

Chen and Pai looked at Malone as if seeing him for the first time. "Mr. Malone has a macabre sense of humour," said Chen. "One does not expect that of Australians, only the decadent Europeans."

[202]

"We're full of surprises," said Quentin.

Then Chen and Pai bowed their heads, excused themselves and went away. Quentin watched them moving round the balconies, their faces open in bland smiles, only closing up as they passed the American delegation and the Russian observers. The Americans and Russians had at last become allies of a sort: they had a common enemy.

"What do you make of those two?" Quentin said. "Do you think Madame Cholon would be working for them?"

"I doubt it. Those two blokes are real wowsers—" Malone used the Australian term for puritanical killjoys. "I only had about ten minutes with Madame Cholon, but she struck me as anything but a wowser. She'd be in every sort of sin going."

"I wonder if she has ever read the story of Lady Wu?"

"If I knew what her ambitions were, maybe I could tell you."

"It's a pity your friend Jamaica won't tell you what he seems to know about her. Have you seen him here today?"

Malone shook his head. "He seems to have blown through. Denzil is trying to find out what he can about him. I gather he's up at the American Embassy now making a nuisance of himself." Malone hesitated, then said, "Sergeant Coburn will see you home this evening."

"Where are you going?"

"Up to Qantas to book our seats for Saturday. There's a flight out at five-thirty in the afternoon. Shall I book Mrs. Quentin on it, too?"

Quentin drew a deep breath and his brows came down, as if he were trying to concentrate on a problem he had for the moment forgotten. He tugged at his moustache; Malone had begun to notice it was almost a reflex action when Quentin had to consider his other, real identity. He wondered how soon Quentin would shave off the moustache, would revert fully to being Corliss. Or would that ever be possible?

"Make it for the three of us. First class. I may as well have the comfort while I can. I'll pay the extra."

"There's no need. They authorized first class for you and me. But I'm afraid you'll have to pay for Mrs. Quentin."

"How did you come over?"

"Economy class."

Quentin grinned, with a little effort, and shook his head. "See how I make things so much better for you?"

"You don't, you know," said Malone; and was glad that at that moment Larter came up to say everyone was moving back into the conference room.

He had left Lancaster House late in the afternoon, when Coburn had come to relieve him, and gone up to the airline offices to book the seats for Saturday's flight. "Will it be crowded?"

"No, sir. So far there are only two other passengers in first class."

He did not know why he wanted to continue the protection of Quentin right till they arrived back in Sydney; once they boarded the plane in London everything for Quentin was finished. The curiosity of fellow passengers who might recognize him would be nothing to what he would have to face as soon as they arrived in Sydney.

He handed the girl two ticket vouchers. "For yourself and Mr. Corliss, is that right? And the name of the third person?"

"Mrs. John Corliss." The voucher for Quentin's ticket had been made out in the name that was on his warrant for arrest. Malone wondered how Sheila Quentin would react to bearing the name of another woman, a woman now dead. Perhaps he had made a mistake in giving that name, but it was too late now: the girl was already writing it down.

"And the address in case we want to get in touch with you?"

He gave the number of the house in Belgrave Square; the

girl did not seem to attach any significance to it. "That will be another three hundred and ninety pounds, sir."

He took out his traveller's cheques and the money he had won last night. He laid down the notes and wrote out cheques for the balance. "What time will we reach Sydney?"

"Seven-twenty Monday morning. Rather early, I'm afraid."

But not too early for the newsmen to be out there, their pencils sharpened for mayhem. He had always got on well with newspapermen, but now suddenly he hated them. They would only be doing their job, just as he was only doing his. But at seven-twenty Monday morning they would begin to drive the first nails into Quentin. It didn't help to know that he was playing Pilate.

"Enjoy your trip," said the girl, safe in the heart of Piccadilly.

Then he had come back to the house in Belgravia, come up to his room, taken off his jacket and shoes, picked up his briefcase and at once seen the scratches on the lock. Whoever had been in his room had not succeeded in opening the lock, but they had damaged it; it had taken him some time to open it and he had bent his key in the process. Now he lay on his bed wondering who had made the crude attempt to open the briefcase. Quentin himself? He had been home at least half an hour before Malone had returned. Sheila? She would have had all day. Or Joseph? Or even Lisa? But why would either of the latter two want to know what he had locked in the case? It looked like Quentin or his wife.

He reached for the case again and took out the file. He had not looked at it since his arrival in London; but he knew that he could now read between some of the lines. Quentin, on acquaintance, had been opened up a little more; he was down now to the bones of the man. But not to the heart, not yet. How long did that take? A month, a year? Or as long as the tide took to reach the heart of a rock? Justice was going to claim Quentin, the man who right now, somewhere in this house, was worrying himself sick trying to salvage some peace for a world that, involuntarily or otherwise, had begun to devalue the human condition. Was justice interested in the heart of a man? What was justice? Malone had once looked it up in a dictionary and got no satisfactory answer. It had not been an expensive dictionary, but one should not have to pay a lot of money to learn what justice was. The quality of being just, the book had said; from the entry above he had learned that to be just was to be lawful, upright, exact, regular and true. All the definitions had, in his mind, added up to smugness. There had been one other definition: retribution. Then, because he had been in doubt and doubt had engendered cynicism, others had occurred to him: revenge, compensation to the victim. And, sometimes, a sense of guilt: society blaming itself for what had happened and sentencing the man in the dock, its own representative, to punishment. Society could not be blamed for what Quentin had done. But how would it feel when it came to sentence him, especially if he should somehow drag the conference back to a successful conclusion? If he owed a debt to society, what of society's debt to him?

Malone's head ached; it was not accustomed to the exercises of philosophy. He opened the file, began to read it again from the beginning, skipping some of those pages that held only the opinions of the researcher. It now read like another story; or at least the story of another man . . .

". . . Corliss kept very much to himself while working for the Water Board. He seems to have been incapable of communicating with other people. He had no friends there and belonged to none of the social clubs. He played golf at Moore Park, which is a public course, and even there had no friends; he played either alone or would join a pick-up foursome. None of his workmates had ever met his wife or been invited to his home. Their neighbours in Coogee remember him as a shy, morose man who never did more than pass the time of day with them; the wife Freda was also shy but one or two women remember her as pleasant; she would not talk about her life before she came to Australia . . .

". . . Certain of Corliss' workmates remember thinking of him as unhappy. He appeared to be a man without ambition or interest, living only from day to day. Then, roughly three to four months before he disappeared, those working closely with him in survey parties noticed a change in him. He still did not join them out of work hours in any social functions. But he was gayer, seemed to be enjoying life more . . ."

Why? Malone asked himself. Had the relationship between Quentin (he could not bring himself to think of him as Corliss) and his wife Freda improved? But if so, why had he killed her so soon afterwards? Or had the killing, as Quentin had claimed, really been an accident?

". . . Two weeks before the murder Corliss took his annual holidays. He went away for a week. He did not take his wife with him nor is it known where he went. He returned to work on Monday, December 8, 1941. His workmates noticed that he seemed troubled and unhappy again, but put it down to the news about Pearl Harbor. He was asked if he was going to enlist. He made one of his few confidences of his private life; he said he would have to see how his wife felt. Up till then, he said, she had been against his joining up; she had lost her parents to the Nazis and she did not want to lose her husband. But now the Japanese were in the war, he said, things might be different. He left work early that afternoon . . ."

Where had Quentin gone for that week alone? Why had he not taken his wife? Had they had an argument on December 8 about his enlisting, an argument that had blown up into a fierce row, which had come to blows and in which she had been fatally stabbed?

". . . There is another gap in Corliss' movements. From leaving the head office of the Water Board at 3:30 P.M. on December 8, 1941, till he enlisted in the Royal Australian Navy at H.M.A.S. *Leeuwin,* the Navy depot in Perth, Western Australia, on May 12, 1942 . . ."

Where had he been for those five months? Had he been going through torture that was only to be assuaged when he met Sheila Redmond? Malone flipped through several more pages.

". . . On July 10, 1942, he married Sheila, daughter of Leslie and Elizabeth Cousins Redmond, at the Registry Office, Perth. Nothing can be traced of Sheila Redmond's history prior to her marriage. When Corliss (now Quentin) became Minister Without Portfolio, Mrs. Quentin was interviewed by several newspapers. But all the articles written about her are vague about her beginnings. All that emerges is that she grew up on a farm in northern Queensland . . ."

Malone sat up. Northern Queensland?

Then there was a knock at the door and Sheila Quentin said, "Mr. Malone? Would you care to join us for a drink before dinner? My husband has something he wants to discuss with you."

2

"Sherry? Whisky? Beer?" Sheila was pouring the drinks. "I don't know your taste, Mr. Malone."

"He's not a sherry man," said Quentin, and smiled at Malone. "That's one thing we have in common. Give him whisky. But where's Joseph?"

"It's his afternoon off." Sheila looked at Quentin, her eyes darkening with concern. "Have you lost track of the days? It's Thursday."

Quentin nodded his head sharply, as if annoyed with his

own abstraction. "Of course. He's lucky, having an afternoon off. Did he take that clock of mine to be mended?"

"He had it with him when he went out." Sheila handed Malone his drink. "How's that?"

Malone tasted the drink and coughed. He looked up at her, thinking how beautiful she looked even through the tears in his eyes, wondering what she had hoped to achieve by finding out what was in his briefcase. "Are you trying to knock me out?"

She smiled. "Whisky is supposed to be medicinal. I thought it might help you forget your bruises."

Which ones? he wanted to ask. The physical ones or the bruises to his trust. He had trusted her husband, gone much further than he should have as a policeman, and Quentin had rewarded him with lies. He looked at Quentin and said, "You wanted to see me about something?"

"How much do I owe you for Mrs. Quentin's air ticket? You got us on Saturday's plane?"

Malone nodded. "You owe me seventy pounds."

Both the Quentins looked at him curiously. "Seventy pounds for a first-class air ticket to Sydney?" Quentin smiled. He was relaxed, enjoying this free moment at the end of the day. It was almost as if his personal fate no longer concerned him; when he left here Saturday he would only be going away for a long weekend. A life's end, Malone thought; but Quentin was still smiling. "What is it, bargain week?"

"I already had three hundred and twenty pounds of your money." He remembered the fiver he had given to the derelict; he must have been really lightheaded last night. But that was going to be his last act of charity till he got back to Sydney. He had read somewhere that charity was the overflow of pity; you poured out your pity and experienced relief and a sort of sweet suffering. Well, he had suffered all right, but not sweetly.

"I told you that was *your* money!" Quentin had stopped smiling. His voice was sharp, irritable; he sounded like an ambassador speaking to a junior official with whom he was losing patience. Well, maybe that's the way it should be, Malone thought. But I'm beginning to lose my own patience, too. And don't forget it, mate: I'm the one with the real authority.

"Not any more," said Malone stubbornly, cutting bonds deliberately and with a quiet savagery.

Quentin stared at him, all at once sensing an antagonism that hadn't been in Malone before this. Something like hurt crossed his face, as if he had been betrayed. You shouldn't trust anyone so much, Malone said silently, almost with malice; I trusted you and I know exactly how you feel, except that I'm not hurt. But he was and he knew it, hurt deeply. He suddenly resented Quentin's look of having been betrayed.

"What's the matter, Mr. Malone?" Sheila stood behind Quentin's chair. She had turned round from the drink cabinet, naturally and without premeditation; but now it seemed to Malone that they were both arrayed against him, defenders drawn together against the enemy, him. "Something's troubling you."

He wanted to laugh at that, but he had never been able to manage the sound of sour humour: he knew he would only sound like a bad actor. He took another taste of his drink, coughed because he had drunk it too fast, then said, "Which one of you killed Freda?"

Then there was a knock at the door and Lisa opened it. "Superintendent Denzil and Sergeant Coburn are here, sir."

Quentin had been staring at Malone. There was no expression at all on his face now, it had turned to grey lava. Behind him Sheila had put out a hand and clutched his shoulder; Malone could see the bone of her knuckles, like white abscesses. They both looked suddenly old; and just as suddenly Malone was stricken with pity again for them. He turned away from them, unable to go on looking at them, and said to Lisa, "Did the Superintendent want to see me or Mr. Quentin?"

Lisa hadn't taken her eyes off the Quentins; the room held a triangle of fixed stares. Out in the hall Denzil coughed impatiently; he wasn't accustomed to being kept waiting, not even by High Commissioners. Malone stood up and moved towards Lisa; there was much more that he wanted to ask the Quentins, but it would have to wait. He remembered the simplicity of other murder cases: the long questioning without interruption, the non-involvement, the feeling of authority that came from working in your own environment. "You'd better bring them in," he said, and for the second time in this house sounded authoritative. The first time had also been with Lisa and she seemed to remember it. She looked at him with the beginning of resentment; then she smiled and nodded. She was still on his side, but he knew without doubt whose side she would be on when the truth came out. She was a woman; they were always prepared to excuse the betrayal of trust; they were used to it. She looked back once more at the stiff and silent Quentins, then she pushed the door wide open and looked into the hall.

"Would you come in, Superintendent?"

The first thing that Malone noticed was how tired Denzil looked. Most of the colour had faded from the red face and for the first time Malone remarked the scar above the sandy eyebrow. The thin lips were tensed and the beefy hands were pressed firmly into his jacket pockets, not casually but as if they were anchored there to prevent them from slashing nervously at the air. He took them out of his pockets as he said good evening to the Quentins, then shoved them back in again. Behind him Coburn, also tired, looked more quizzical than ever, as if he did not believe what Denzil was telling Malone and the others:

[211]

"We've found your Mr. Jamaica. His body was in a rented car outside the Chinese government's office in Portland Place. He'd been garrotted." Denzil realized his mistake and looked at the two women. "Sorry, ladies. I didn't mean to be so blunt."

"I think my wife and Miss Pretorious should be excused." Quentin had stood up when Denzil and Coburn had come into the room. He had regained his composure, had somehow even managed to force some colour back into his face; once again Malone was amazed at the man's resilience. He ushered the two women towards the door, gently pushing Sheila who said nothing but was reluctant to go. As she went out of the door Sheila looked at Malone, but he turned his face away. Why the hell do I feel *I'm* in the wrong? he thought. Pity was a virus; it weakened you. Quentin stood in the doorway looking after Sheila; she was out of Malone's sight, but he guessed that some glance of warning, despair, something, must have passed between them; he saw the reflection of it in Quentin's face, even though the man was in profile to him. Then Quentin, once more the High Commissioner, turned back into the room.

"Do the Chinese know about this?"

"If they do, sir, they haven't told us," said Denzil. "We were very lucky—the body was found by a uniformed man on the beat there. Sergeant Coburn went up there and took the car and the body back to the Yard."

"He kept falling into my lap every time I turned a corner," Coburn said to Malone; then saw Denzil's sharp look of disapproval. "Sorry, sir."

"Do you think the Chinese did it?" Quentin asked.

"Hardly, sir. Not right outside their own place. No, he was planted there. And I think you can guess by whom. Why, I don't know." He was tired enough to admit some ignorance: "I don't understand women too well at the best of

[212]

times. I'm afraid the working of an Oriental woman's mind is just beyond me."

"You're sure Madame Cholon's responsible?" Malone said.

"Do you have any other nominations?" Denzil sounded weary, not sarcastic. Malone hesitated, then shook his head. Denzil went on, "We haven't even been to see the Chinese yet, sir. I talked it over with the Assistant Commissioner, told him what you wanted, to keep everything out of the papers. He doesn't feel we can go on covering up things for too long—especially in a case of plain murder like this. We've put a D notice on it for the time being."

"What's that?" Malone asked.

"Defense security notice for the benefit of any newspapers if they get on to the story. It will hold them for a while, but once they're on to it they'll start asking awkward questions. And we'll have the Americans to consider. I suppose Jamaica was still an American citizen."

"Are the papers likely to get on to it?" Quentin said.

"Not right away, unless someone gives them a tip. But they'll be on to it in a day or two. We can't just dump Jamaica in the river and forget all about him." Denzil looked at the drink cabinet. "It would be nice if we could."

Quentin had recovered almost completely, enough to catch Denzil's hint. He looked at Malone, not telling him what to do but as if asking a favour. Malone poured two Scotches and handed them to Denzil and Coburn.

"We shouldn't," said Denzil, "but it's been a long day. Your health, sir."

"Thank you," said Quentin, and avoided Malone's eye. "Now about the Chinese. If they don't already know, do you have to tell them? I mean immediately?"

Denzil sipped his drink; he appreciated good whisky and the High Commissioner's stuff was better than one got in some embassies. "Strictly speaking, no. The body was found in the street, not on their property. If we speak to them at all, it will only be out of courtesy or curiosity. I think we can contain ourselves on those two counts for the time being, sir. How long do you want?"

"I'd like a year." Quentin smiled, a little embarrassedly, as if he had made a joke in bad taste. He was bankrupt of time, for himself and the cause of peace. "But twenty-four hours will do. The conference will be over tomorrow, Saturday morning at the latest."

"How's it going, sir?"

"Not too well, I'm afraid. But one keeps hoping—" But his voice was already that of a hopeless man: he was slowly turning blind to the future.

Denzil finished his drink, smacked his thin lips. "That is excellent whisky, sir."

"Compliment my butler. He knows where to get all the best stuff." Quentin had no illusions about Joseph's love of the sybaritic life. "He tells me I'm the only non-Scot in London who gets that particular whisky."

"Trust a Hungarian to have the best contacts," said Denzil. "Well, sir, we can keep this other matter quiet till Saturday, if you wish it. It might give us more time to find out who Jamaica really was. I wonder if I might borrow Mr. Malone for a while?"

Malone could see his own surprise reflected in Quentin's face, but he said nothing, left it to Quentin to reply: "Of course. I'm not going out tonight. I'm expecting one or two delegates to drop in to see me."

"Sergeant Coburn will stay here. Just in case."

"You think there might be another attempt on my"—Quentin seemed to stammer—"my life?"

"I think we have you pretty well sheltered now, sir. If you don't go out, other than going to the conference tomorrow, they'll have to get into the house to get at you. And there's no chance of that, short of them putting on a commando raid. You won't mind if Sergeant Coburn looks over your visitors tonight? Discreetly, of course." He looked at Coburn and managed a smile that, though weary, had some warmth in it. "He doesn't wear very discreet ties, but otherwise he's very circumspect."

Coburn fingered his purple tie and grinned. "I'll tell my girl she's subversive, sir."

Denzil continued to smile; the two men seemed to have found a new relationship. "Just see no one subversive gets in here tonight." He looked back at Quentin. "You'll be safe enough, sir. If the conference finishes tomorrow, that should be the finish of all our troubles, too."

Let's go before you put your foot in it again, Malone thought. He led the way out of the room into the hall, wondering why Denzil wanted to take him out of the house tonight. He glanced up and saw a movement of yellow at the top of the stairs: Sheila had been wearing a yellow dress. But when he stopped and looked steadily up at the landing he saw nothing; he could feel Sheila Quentin watching him, but he could not see her. It disturbed him, suddenly reduced her to an ordinary criminal level. He turned back, saw that Coburn was standing alone as Denzil had a last word with Quentin. He moved towards the sergeant.

"Keep an eye on Mrs. Quentin, too." He kept his voice low. "See she doesn't go out of the house. If she tries it, tell her you're acting on my orders."

Coburn was either tired or conditioned: he showed no surprise. "You think they might try getting at her?"

"They could. Everyone's a target now."

"What about the secretary?"

He might as well go the whole way with the interpretation Coburn had put on his words. "Yes, they might even try it with her. Keep 'em all in the house."

"What if Quentin wants to go out?"

[215]

"Tell him the same. He can't go out till I get back."

Coburn looked doubtful, fumbled with his tie again. "I'm not used to giving orders to High Commissioners. But if you say so—" He shrugged. "You Aussies are bloody informal, aren't you?"

"That's us," said Malone. "Jack's as good as his master every time."

"My name's Fred. Whoever heard of a master named Fred?"

"What about Fred the Great?"

"A German. Freds never get anywhere in England."

Malone had enjoyed the short nonsense with Coburn; he was smiling as he followed Denzil out of the house. There had been bloody little to smile at since he had arrived in London; any small joke now seemed to give double its value. A police car was parked by the curb and the uniformed policeman from the beat was talking to the driver. Denzil stopped on the steps of the house and looked at Malone.

"I had to get you out of the house. Didn't want to talk in front of Quentin. I'm afraid I had to spill your little secret to the Assistant Commissioner tonight. I mean why you're really here."

Malone stopped smiling. "What did he say?"

"Shocked, naturally. He's a bit old-fashioned," said Denzil, and Malone almost smiled again. "Said he wouldn't have been surprised if it had been a foreigner, but not a Commonwealth ambassador."

"I'm taking both of them, Quentin and his wife, out of here Saturday afternoon. We'll be back in Sydney Monday morning. Can the Assistant Commissioner control his shock till then?"

"Don't be rude about him, son," said Denzil. "We've been leaning over backwards for you two Aussies all the week. Allow us a few old-fashioned reactions." Malone apologized, and Denzil nodded, even raised a hand and patted Malone's shoulder. "I know it's been no easier for you. This is when I'm glad I haven't got long to retirement."

"You're lucky," said Malone, thinking for the first time ever of the pleasures of retirement. No responsibilities, no involvement, nothing; but all that was thirty years away. He brought himself back to the present. "What now?"

"I'm on my way up to the American Embassy. I may be barking up the wrong tree, but I think they may be able to help us about Jamaica. I thought you might be interested—"

He's not a bad old bastard, Malone thought. "Thanks, sir. I'd like to come." There were more questions he wanted to put to the Quentins, but suddenly he wanted more time. He wanted to be less abrupt, less the inquisitor: he wanted to know *why*, not *what*.

The uniformed policeman saluted as they got into the car. "Anything been happening?" Denzil asked.

"Nothing, thir." It was the young policeman who had been on duty two nights ago when the attempt to shoot Quentin had been made. He had caught a summer cold and it had accentuated his lisp. He sounds more like a Boy Scout than a copper, Malone thought. "Things are vewy quiet."

"There'll be some visitors tonight. Stay on this side of the square, check everyone who goes in. But be discreet."

"One always has to be discweet awound heah, thir. It isn't an easy beat."

Denzil nodded, got into the car after Malone and they started off. "I've never understood why so many educated Englishmen lisp. Even some of our generals do, and they sound like Boy Scouts." Malone smiled in the darkness of the car. "That young fellow back there is one of the toughest forwards in the police rugby team. You'd never think it to listen to him. Do you Scots ever lisp, Muir?"

"No, sir," said the driver. "I come from Edinburgh. We speak the best English in the British Isles."

Denzil looked at Malone. "Well, let's see what sort of Eng-

[217]

lish this American speaks. He's a new man, haven't met him yet. Just hope he isn't a Southerner. Can't understand them at all."

"Maybe he won't want to talk at all. Presuming, of course, that he knows something about Jamaica." Malone thought of the dark Southerner from Georgia who would never talk again. He felt nothing approaching sorrow or grief, but the old feeling was there again: death, even that of a stranger, always chipped something out of him.

"That's quite possible. That he won't talk, I mean. I'm afraid the Americans still don't trust anyone but themselves."

Don't let's mention the word *trust* again tonight, Malone thought. Somehow it had become obscene.

The car drew up outside the huge embassy in Grosvenor Square. Malone got out of the car and looked up at the block-long face of the building. It reminded him of a fort, one built for Cinerama; the Americans were entrenched behind it, waiting to be besieged by the perfidious English. Across the road in the gardens the bronze Roosevelt stood serene, impervious to the treachery of the British, the dung of the pigeons and the spittle of visiting Republicans. Big American cars stood at almost every parking meter, tanks from Detroit. Grosvenor Square was now American territory.

"The only place in London where I feel a foreigner," said Denzil. "Well, let's try our luck."

Most of the embassy staff had gone home, but the man Denzil wanted to see was still in his office. A porter checked them in, a Cockney as concerned for the security of the United States as for that of the Mile End Road; Denzil eyed him as if he were a traitor, but said nothing. A second porter led them through a maze of corridors till they came to a door that said: Investment Counsellor.

The man in the office was not a Southerner and spoke English that had only a faint transatlantic accent. "I'm Ed Royston," he said, rising to meet them. He had that courteous charm that Malone found so unexpectedly in so many Americans; people thought of Americans as brash and loud, but some of them had the best manners in the world. Royston was one of them. "I got your phone message, Superintendent. It's a pleasure to meet you."

Denzil came straight to the point. "I understand you are the new CIA man here, Mr. Royston."

Royston obviously thought that was not a very polite remark. He sat back in his chair, propping one leg up on the knee of the other. He was a man in his late thirties, with dark crew-cut hair, a nose that had been broken and eyes that could become as opaque as frosted glass. They were opaque now. "I'm afraid you're in the wrong office, sir. All I do is advise Americans where and how to invest their money in Europe."

"Is that still official government policy?" Denzil said, still sure of himself. "I thought President Johnson was trying to stop the dollar drain." He looked around the office, at the charts on the walls, the leather-bound books on the shelves, the stacks of the *Wall Street Journal* and the *Financial Times* on a tilted reading bench against one wall. "You have a neat cover here. Your predecessor was a telecommunications engineer. I had a little trouble communicating with him, too." He smiled and looked back at Royston. "Don't let's waste time, Mr. Royston. I'd like some information about a man named Jamaica, first name unknown."

Royston shook his head. "I'm afraid I've never heard of him."

"We have his body down at the morgue." Denzil was matter-of-fact and patient. "We found it in a car parked outside the Chinese, the *Red* Chinese, offices in Portland Place."

Royston stiffened only slightly, his bent knee flexing. He

[219]

picked up a ball-point pen and began to doodle on the blotter on his desk. He looked at Malone. "May I ask who you are, Mr. Malone?"

"I'm from the New South Wales Police Force," said Malone, inventing his own cover. "Attached to the Australian High Commissioner for special duty."

"Why are you so interested in Jamaica?" Royston addressed the question to both of them; then sat silent while Denzil told him everything they knew about the dead man. At last he said, "He didn't tell you much, did he?"

"Was he working for you?" Denzil asked.

Royston shook his head. He seemed no longer interested in keeping up the pretense of being an investment counsellor; his dark eyes took on some light. "We knew he was here, but he wasn't under our control. The Ambassador knew nothing about him and neither did the rest of the staff. That was why they told you they'd never heard of him when you checked on him last night. He was working direct with Washington."

"He told you nothing?"

Royston hesitated, then threw down the pen and sat forward. "I can't tell you much, Superintendent, because I don't have the authority. You'd have to get on to Washington for that. All I *can* tell you is what he told me about this Madame Cholon. He rang me this morning, made an appointment to see me tonight. That's why I'm here now, waiting for him." He sat back, glanced down at the doodling he had done on the blotter. He bit his lip, then moved a newspaper over the scratchings; but not before Malone had recognized them as rough drawings of what could have been tombstones. "How much do you know about this Cholon woman?"

"Nothing," said Denzil.

"Well, he got on to her about three months ago. She used

[220]

to be one of the favourites of Bay Vien—he had no proof that she was one of Bay's mistresses, but she knew him pretty well."

"Who was Bay Vien?" Malone asked.

Royston looked at him, his politeness dropping from him for a moment. "You Australians have never really been interested in Southeast Asia, have you?"

"I only work for the government." Malone's own manners had a rough edge to them. "I don't run it."

Royston said nothing for a moment, as if considering suggesting that the Australian security agency should follow the CIA's example and be its own government. But he thought better of it, smiled politely and went on to inform the ignorant Australian: "Bay Vien ran the Binh Xuyen sect in Saigon during the time of Bao Dai, the last Emperor. The Binh Xuyen had everything wrapped up in Saigon—the brothels, the dope traffic, the gambling, the lot. Bay Vien ran the police and no one could do anything in Saigon without his okay."

"How many were in the sect?"

"About half a million. But their influence spread much wider than that. Then Ngo Dinh Diem became President and he got to work on them. Whatever else he was and forgetting all about his brother and Madame Nhu, Diem was a moralist. He wasn't interested in any rake-off from the brothels or anything else that the Binh Xuyen ran. He set his troops on them and wiped them out."

"All half a million of them?"

Royston smiled without much humour and shook his head. "Not all of them. You can't find and kill half a million people, especially when they are out of uniform and look just like everyone else. You have to be Jewish to have that happen to you." Royston was not a Jewish name, but somewhere in his background there was a Jew; the dark opaque eyes had a sadness about them that held inherited memories of pogroms. "There are still a lot of the Binh Xuyen people around. Including Madame Cholon."

"There's a man named Pallain, too. What about him?"

"He knew Cholon in Vietnam, but Jamaica had no proof he was working for her."

"What does Cholon want here in London?" Malone asked.

"Jamaica was only guessing, but he thought she wanted to revive all the old rackets in Saigon. There's millions in it for anyone who could get them going again. But she couldn't do it if there is ever a stable government put in power. Either one backed by us or"— he smiled—"by the Communists."

"So if this conference reached a stalemate, was adjourned—" Denzil sucked his bottom lip. "She'd be in a position at least to get started."

"Not on a big scale, but enough to be profitable. And if things are allowed to drift, get worse out there, she'd be sitting pretty. Especially if she could get one or two of the local generals on her payroll. They're not all on our side, you know, even though we're paying them now. Some of them are only interested in Number One. They'd make deals with anyone who raised the ante high enough."

"What had Jamaica intended doing to stop Cholon?"

"I'm not sure, but I think he was going to turn her over to you when he knew exactly what she was up to. When he called this morning he said he had something important he wanted to talk about—maybe he'd finally gotten something on her. But he was very cagey with us here, told me a couple of times not to interfere." Again he smiled, the opacity now melting in his eyes. "You think we're very jealous about cooperating with you fellers, Superintendent. But we have our own little jealousies, too, right in the outfit."

Denzil nodded sympathetically. "You must come over to the Yard some time, Mr. Royston." He stood up. "Did Jamaica tell you where the Cholon woman could be found?"

Royston rubbed the bridge of his broken nose; Malone could imagine him doing it all the time, like a man trying to rub away a deformity. "I'm sorry. Like I said, these little jealousies—" He spread his hands. "She's in my territory. I really ought to have over-ridden him."

"You'll pardon me," said Denzil, and somehow managed not to sound pompous, "Madame Cholon is in *my* territory."

Royston admitted his error; he was not without grace. "Sorry. I've just spent three years on a desk in Washington. Your perspective gets a little blurred there." He stood up, shook hands with both of them. "I'll get on to Washington, find out if Jamaica had filed anything else on her."

"Who was Jamaica?" Malone was curious. Despite their antagonism, the man *had* tried to help him. You should not bury a friend and ally without knowing something about him. "Where did he come from?"

"He was from some small town in Georgia. He got out of the army right after Korea finished, never went back to the States. I gather he was pretty bitter then about conditions for Negroes down South, said he never wanted to go home again to being kicked around." Royston picked up the pen again, began to doodle. "He could have turned Communist, he had enough provocation, I guess. But he didn't."

"What happened?"

"He got this silk business going in Bangkok, did pretty well out of it. But though he didn't want to go home, he never stopped being an American. We approached him about three years ago. He refused at first, then one day he came to our control out there and said he'd work for us. He became one of our best men." He threw down the pen again. He had been drawing long conical shapes: they could have been Klan hoods. "His mother still lives in Georgia. I guess he's going to go home after all."

"Will you take care of his body?" Denzil said.

"We'll attend to it. How was he killed?"

"Garrotted."

"Better make it a heart attack. We'll accept that if you will."

"If we catch up with this Cholon woman, we might want to charge her with his murder."

"Do you have any evidence?"

"None at all." Denzil shrugged. He looked utterly weary, a fast bowler who had lost all his speed; he would have trouble tonight even remembering the day he had bowled Wally Hammond. "Righto, heart attack it is then. I'll get a death certificate for you and you can ship the body back to America as soon as you like. We'd appreciate it if you kept all this as quiet as possible."

"That's what we're here for," said Royston, and smiled again.

Outside on the embassy steps, watched through the big glass doors by the Indian scout from the Mile End Road, Denzil looked at Malone. "Well, now all we have to do is find her."

"What then?"

"I'll have her watched so closely she won't be able to turn round without our knowing it." They got into the waiting car and he flopped back against the seat. "Women! They're always the worst of the lot."

"I wouldn't know," said Malone, thinking not of Madame Cholon but of Sheila Quentin. "I've still got to find that out."

3

When Malone let himself into the house with the key he had been given, Edgar was standing in the hall examining his jowls in the big mirror. "I'm putting on weight. The harder I work and the more I worry, the fatter I get. What's new on the security front?"

Malone didn't feel in the mood for long expositions. "We're progressing. Where's Coburn?"

"In the library watching TV." Edgar slapped his jowls and turned away from the mirror. "The boss told us about the dead Negro outside the Chinese office. He's in there with some of the Yanks now." He nodded towards the closed door of the drawing room.

"Has he told them about Jamaica?"

"I don't know. He's got more on his mind right now than a dead Yank. He's got three very hot-tempered live ones in there." Malone could now hear the sound of angry voices behind the door; someone swore in undiplomatic language. "I got out, left it to the boss and Phil Larter. Sometimes it pays to be the junior."

"What's it all about?" Malone looked at himself in the mirror behind the broad bulk of Edgar. *He* wasn't putting on weight: work and worry were acting on him like diet pills. He wondered where Sheila Quentin was and hoped she had not gone to bed. He looked at his watch and was surprised to see it was only a quarter to eight. Then he remembered they had not yet had dinner and all at once he felt hungry.

Edgar cocked an ear to the voices, still sharp and awkward; then he looked at Malone and shrugged. "The Yanks—quite rightly, I think—are blowing their tops that everyone seems to know their business. They've been giving some of us inside information on what they're planning and now some of it is getting back to them. They want to know where the leak is."

"Where do you think it is?"

Edgar sat down on the narrow red plush settee beneath the mirror. The mirror reflected the back of his head, showed the white scalp beneath the thinning hair. Malone realized that, though Edgar was the junior man, he was probably at least ten years older than Larter. He would never make ambassador, would always be the man waiting in the hall outside. He sighed, put one arm along the back of the settee and let his belly relax. This is a night for everyone to suddenly look older, Malone thought; and looked at himself again in the mirror. If he did not look older, he certainly felt it.

"It could have been a dozen places. Someone from their own delegation got careless—though I doubt that. Someone from the British crowd—they've never trusted British security after the Burgess-Maclean business. It could be a leak in the South Vietnamese lot. There's so much inside rivalry among those blokes, everyone wanting to be the next boss in Saigon, I wouldn't lay any bets against a little bit of skullduggery there."

There it was again: no one trusted the Vietnamese. So why are we fighting there? Malone asked. But he knew it was too simple a question, the sort asked when lazing on the beach at Bondi, the only barrage on the ears that of the rolling surf.

"Who else is on the list?" Malone sat down beside Edgar. His light brown socks showed beneath the dark blue trouser leg, but Edgar did not seem to suffer from any aesthetic revulsion. The new shoes no longer hurt Malone's feet and he wiggled his toes comfortably in them. But the jacket of Quentin's suit was still a tight fit, not helped by the holster in Malone's armpit. "Do they suspect anyone else?"

"Us."

"Who'd give away any information in our delegation?" Malone realized it was an embarrassing question: he was talking to one of the delegation.

"Well, Phil Larter and I didn't, for a start," Edgar said with a grin. "And the boss is not the sort who makes unguarded remarks. We've had papers from the Yanks, but they've had top classification. Only the boss, Phil and myself, oh, and our military adviser—we're the only ones who've seen them."

"Where are they kept?"

"In a safe at Australia House. The boss probably brought them home to study, but he has a safe here that only he knows the combination to."

"I've seen it."

"I'm sorry for the boss." Edgar looked at the closed door of the drawing room; he spoke with affection for the man in there. "He put a lot of faith in old-fashioned diplomacy with this one. Over the past couple of years there's been too much of what I call marketplace diplomacy. Everyone yelling their heads off in public, selling influence and compromise and all the rest of it as if we were conducting some sort of public auction. Too many so-called diplomats today forget or ignore the fact that the main object of diplomacy is to get what you want without resorting to violence. That's what diplomacy means—the art of negotiation." Someone else has been looking up the dictionary, Malone thought. But now other, newer definitions had been introduced that baffled Edgar. "There's been too much diplomacy by television and press conference. So Quentin has been trying for trading behind closed doors."

"Doesn't sound as if there's much trading going on behind *that* closed door." The voices were harsh and unintelligible, like jungle cries.

Edgar nodded morosely, then stood up as the voices began to subside. "They shouldn't be accusing him. He's done more to keep this conference going than any half a dozen other men. And he's not well, have you noticed that? In the past week—why, only since you arrived—" Malone waited to be accused himself; but Edgar was only naming *when,* not *who* and *why.* "He looks as if he's aged ten years. He needs a rest. He was on the phone to the P.M. at lunchtime, I just caught the tailend of the conversation as I went into his office. Sounded as if he wanted to go back home. Has he mentioned anything to you?"

Malone stood up as the door to the drawing room opened. "Just casually, that's all."

Quentin and Larter came out with three men, one of them the thin balding man who had been there that morning. All five men were flushed; Quentin looked healthier than he had since Malone's arrival. There were stiffly formal good nights and Edgar ushered the Americans to the front door. Quentin nodded at Malone and the latter took the hint; he said good night to Larter, who nodded at him cursorily, and walked along the hall to the library. He closed the door on the troubled voices behind him. He had enough troubles of his own without listening to international ones. Treachery between nations was another part of history; it was part of diplomacy, getting what you wanted without resorting to violence. But treachery between men: it was his profession to combat it, yet he would never grow accustomed to it.

Coburn rose from one of the leather armchairs and turned down the sound on the television set in one corner of the room. He looked at the gyrating long-haired figures on the grey screen, then at Malone. "Makes you wonder, doesn't it? And there are some people campaigning to see hermaphrodites like that in *colour!* That bloke, I *think* he's a bloke, he's singing about wanting to be some bird's man. A real cry from the crotch, but I think it's biologically hopeless. When I was eighteen I wanted to look like Cary Grant or John Wayne. Now they all want to look like the Bride of Frankenstein." He switched off the set and turned back to Malone. "Well, how did it go?"

Malone told him everything they had learned at the American Embassy. "Now all you blokes have to do is pick up Madame Cholon."

"I wonder what she's cooking up in the meantime."

"I don't think it matters if we can keep Quentin out of her

[228]

way till Saturday morning. The conference should be over by then, maybe even tomorrow night."

"When are you going back?"

"Saturday."

"Is Quentin going with you? I heard his wife say to him that she would have to start packing."

"Not that I know of," Malone lied; he was instinctively still protecting Quentin. "Where is Mrs. Quentin?"

"Upstairs in her room."

"Joseph back yet?" Coburn shook his head. "Lisa?"

"I gather she's working late at Australia House."

Good, Malone thought, I'm going to get that hour alone with the Quentins. He opened the library door and looked out; Larter and Edgar had gone and Quentin was slowly climbing the stairs. "Okay, I'll take over now. You can go and have a word with your bird about purple ties."

"She said last night she wished I was younger, so's I could have a Beatle haircut. I just wish she wasn't such a dish, I'd walk out on her. Well, hooroo, mate," he said with an attempt at an Australian accent. He stopped at the front door and looked back. "She's got a sister. You wouldn't be interested in a double date before you go back?"

Malone shook his head, grinning. "I've got a wife and six kids back home. All with Beatle haircuts."

"How do you tell the boys from the girls?"

"The ones that stand up to pee are the boys."

Coburn looked around the elegant hall, then back at Malone. "Watch it, mate. You're making the old mansion sound like a vulgar music hall. Hooroo again. Have a nice restful night."

He went out, closing the door after him, a young man whose only trouble in the world was a bird who was too much with it.

Malone stood for a moment listening to the quietness of

[229]

the house about him. A car went by outside, its horn hooting derisively: someone thumbing his nose at one of the embassies. The house creaked, feeling its age. Malone began to climb the stairs, feeling his own age, all thirty-one years of it. Christ, he thought; and laughed at himself.

He knocked on the door of the Quentins' bedroom, annoyed at himself for his tentativeness. He would rather have talked to them downstairs; but Lisa or Joseph might be home any minute. Deep in the bowels of the house he could hear a radio playing: that must be the cook. He hadn't seen her in his three days in the house: she was like a pit pony, never allowed out into the light.

Quentin opened the door and said, "Come in, Scobie."

He hesitated, then stepped into the big room. Quentin closed the door and stood with his back to it for a moment; Malone felt trapped and looked back over his shoulder defensively. Then Quentin moved away from the door, sat down beside Sheila on the wide four-poster bed.

Malone stood awkwardly in the middle of the room. He wanted to turn, to fling open the door and demand that they follow him downstairs to the library: he would lock the door there against all interruptions. It still would not be neutral territory, but it would be more neutral than this. They had reduced him to the level of a private investigator; they sat facing him, holding each other's hands, as if waiting for the flash of his camera. This was the room of their secrets and he should never have allowed himself to come this far. He moved back to the door, put his hand on the knob, but Quentin said, "Sit down, Sergeant. That's what you want us to call you from now on, isn't it? Sergeant."

There was a chair beside the door covered in yellow Thai silk, a woman's bedroom chair that seemed to float on a soufflé of ruffles. Malone sat down on it, felt the Thai silk with his rough palm, thought of the dead Jamaica. Then he looked across at the Quentins and made himself think of the dead Freda. "I'm repeating my question," he said in his best formal policeman's voice. "Which of you killed Freda Corliss?"

The linked hands tightened on each other. "I don't think we have to answer that," Quentin said after a moment. "I have admitted causing the death of my first wife and you have a warrant for my arrest. That's all there is to it. I'll reserve my plea till we get back to Sydney and I'm charged in court."

That should stop me dead, Malone thought. But he heard himself go on speaking, the Celtic tongue that never knew when enough was enough: "When I get up in court to give evidence against you, I'm going to have to tell everything that is in the file on you."

"I don't know what is in the file. But if there is anything that implicates my wife, they would have issued a warrant for her, too."

Malone looked at Sheila. "You must have been afraid that there was something in it that implicated you. Otherwise why did you try to open my briefcase?"

She did not even attempt to deny it. Her face tightened, the jaw coming down, as Malone had seen women's faces tighten in the moment just before they screamed; he tensed, ready to jump forward and slap her face as she went into hysteria. But again her control came back, just in time this time; she shuddered like an old woman with the ague, and Quentin raised an arm and put it about her trembling shoulders. He glared at Malone and almost shouted, "Leave us alone! Get out and leave us alone!"

Malone shook his head, not at Quentin but at himself: why the hell was he persisting, torturing himself as well as them? But he knew the answer and he could not understand why Quentin did not know it: "Christ Almighty, can't you see I'm trying to help you!" His own voice was as anguished as Quentin's had been.

"How can you help me, trying to bring Sheila into this?" He held her closer to him; her trembling communicated itself to him. "I tell you she had nothing to do with it! I killed Freda—it was an accident—but I killed her! You understand, it was me! Me!"

Malone stood up, began to walk about the room. He passed a dressing table loaded with bottles: Arden, Rubinstein, Revlon could no longer offer much to disguise the crumbling face of the woman on the bed. He saw himself and the Quentins reflected in the mirror: they were watching him, like caged animals watching their keeper. He stopped, looked at the photograph on the dressing table: Quentin with a beard and in naval uniform, Sheila in a dress that now looked ridiculously long and with the upswept hair of twenty-odd years ago. They looked happy, carefree; but that might have been only for the benefit of the photographer. But he knew that the camera could lie, or anyway could be tricked: it could never be used to authenticate the emotions it showed. He nodded at the photograph and said, "Were you really as happy as that?"

Quentin seemed to realize that Malone was not going to be dismissed. He slumped a little, still keeping his arm round Sheila. "There were occasional days. Sergeant—" He looked up, a note of pleading now in his voice. "What is in that file?"

Malone sat down on the dressing-table stool, his back to the mirror. "It's not so much what's in it, but what's not in it. The omissions. What you can read between the lines, if you like."

"That sort of evidence is never admitted in court," Quentin said. "Juries aren't expected to read between the lines."

"A Crown prosecutor is."

"Nobody else seems to have read between them. Why did you?"

Malone looked at Sheila. "You weren't careful enough,

Mrs. Quentin. I wasn't trying to trap you, I didn't even suspect you. But you gave yourself away. You were the one who started me reading between the lines."

Sheila spoke for the first time, her voice no more than a croaking whisper. "How?"

"You told me about the coolibah tree when you were a child. You tried to cover that up by saying your grandfather had brought it over from the eastern States. And I swallowed it—I guess there are some coolibahs in the West. But in the file on you they say you were brought up in northern Queensland. There are coolibahs there, at least as far north as Townsville."

"None of that proves anything," said Quentin. "What if my wife did come from Queensland instead of Western Australia?"

"Why tell lies about it? There was one other thing. This morning at breakfast, just before that man from the American Embassy was announced, Mrs. Quentin said something that didn't register with me right then. She said, 'We knew it couldn't last.' *We*. You told me the night I arrived here she knew nothing about it, that she didn't even know about your first wife." Suddenly his anger came back: "I trusted you! I've gone out of my way to help you, put myself out on a limb!"

"I didn't ask it for myself," Quentin said tonelessly. "I told you it was for the conference—"

"To hell with the conference! I was trying to help *you*—" He caught the trembling note in his voice just in time; he hated to sound querulous. He suddenly felt that his anger was artificial; what he really felt was sadness, a sense of loss. But what had he lost? A friend? There hadn't been time for that. And yet perhaps there had been. He had felt admiration, respect, yes and pity, too; and pity, he sensed rather than knew, was a part of love, of friendship. Whatever it was, he had lost *something;* and Quentin had caused him to

[233]

lose it. He said, quietly now, "We three will be on that plane for home on Saturday and the conference and everything else that's occupied you for the past twenty years will be behind you. You're not going to be any hero when you get into the dock. All that's going to help you is the truth."

The Quentins sat in an attitude that could have been shock or despair: they were stiff, brittle: one felt they could have broken with a touch of the hand. Again Malone had the image that they were waiting for the divorce photographer's flash globe. This was the bed where they had made love, whispered their secrets, waited in the well of the night for this dreaded moment that had finally come. Sheila was the first to move. She stood up, moved to the window and looked out. It was still light and the last of some homing pigeons scratched a silent scrawl on the sky.

"Are you prepared to listen to the truth, Sergeant?"

They are no longer calling me Scobie; slowly I am becoming less and less involved. He warned her: "I'll be listening officially. I've done enough of the other sort—" He looked at Quentin, who turned away with what could have been shame.

"You can take it all down if you like," said Sheila. "And I'll sign it."

"No," said Quentin, but there was no real argument in his voice. "You'll sign nothing."

"Please, darling. We had this argument all those years ago." She looked back at Malone. "Do you want to take it all down?"

Malone hesitated, became involved again. "I'll see. Tell me what you have to say first."

Sheila sighed, then began to talk, calmly and with something like relief: "I killed Freda, but it was an accident. I had gone to see her that day to ask her to give John a divorce—"

Malone interrupted: "How long had you known each other before that?"

"Three months, perhaps a little longer. I did come from Queensland, from Charters Towers. My parents were dead and I came down to Sydney to work. I worked for Manly Council as a typist and I met John one day when he came into the Town Hall on business. We started meeting each other secretly—I had no friends and neither did he, so there was no one to recognize us when we were together. There was only Freda." She turned to Quentin. "Do you want me to tell him about her?"

Quentin, shoulders slumped, looked sideways at Malone. All his dignity was gone: dignity requires some hope, some belief that not everything is lost. "I was never in love with Freda nor she with me. I realized that a month after we were married. I was young and lonely, a boy from the bush. I'd just had my twenty-first birthday. She was a good-looking girl and, well, I suppose you could say she had the attraction of being foreign. Australians in those days didn't meet many foreigners. And perhaps I was sorry for her, I don't know. She didn't love me, she told me that a couple of years after we were married. We didn't sleep in the same room after that. I'm not blaming her for anything, trying to make out she was calculating or anything like that. She was just as lonely as I was, and more than that, she was scared. She'd come from Europe—well, I've told you all about that. Our marriage was some sort of haven for her. And she never wanted to leave it. When I told her about Sheila, she just didn't want to know. She'd lock herself in her bedroom and not talk to me for days."

He looked at Sheila and she nodded sympathetically. Then she took up the story again: "John and I went away for a week together. We decided we'd go away together for good. I'm not trying to excuse ourselves when I say we were truly in love, which John and Freda never were. I'm just giving it as the reason. When people are in love they do a lot of things without worrying too much about the consequences for others."

"We did worry," Quentin protested, but weakly.

She nodded. "I know we did, darling. That was why I went to see Freda that Monday afternoon. I'd never met her up till then," she said to Malone. "That was the one and only time. If I hadn't gone to see her, tried to be—well, decent, I suppose—she'd still be alive. John was at work, he didn't know anything about my being there. Not till he came home and found—" She stopped, her mouth open in a half gasp; it was as if she had just opened a door on that scene of twenty-three years ago. Quentin moved to get off the bed, but she shook her head and he sat back. She swallowed and went on: "I pleaded with Freda to give John a divorce, but she wouldn't listen. She called me names—and I don't say I didn't deserve them. But I got angry then, told her we were going away anyway. She had been sewing when I called on her—we were in the front room and she had a sewing basket on the couch beside her. When I got angry, so did she. She picked up the scissors, threatened me with them and told me to get out of the house, to leave John alone and not break up her marriage. I don't even know now if she intended hurting me with the scissors. She might even only have been trying to frighten me. All I know is that I grabbed them and we struggled and the next thing—"

Again there was the half-gasp. This time Quentin came off the bed quickly, moved across the room and took her in his arms. She buried her face against his chest and sobbed quietly. He held her to him and looked over her head at Malone.

"She sat there with Freda till I came home a couple of hours later. We did nothing then for at least another couple of hours, perhaps longer. All I can remember was that it was

[236]

dark. Both of us wanted to go to the police and each of us talked the other out of it. If we'd gone to them, told them the truth, do you think they'd have believed it? Australians are puritans about marriage—they are now and they were then. The wife could be a Gorgon or a—a Madame Cholon, but if the husband had a mistress, no matter how much he and the mistress might be in love, all the sympathy is going to be for the wife. Especially if she had been killed by the mistress."

"Don't you think Freda deserved some sympathy?" Malone said.

Quentin shook his head in despair. "You don't understand, do you? So how could we have expected"—he changed the tense—"expect a jury to understand? I felt more than just sympathy for Freda. I *grieved* for her—not just for her death but for her whole life—"

"He wept for her." Sheila turned in her husband's arms. "Because he didn't love her and loved me instead, didn't mean he had no feelings towards her. But maybe you wouldn't understand that, Sergeant," she added bitterly. "Policemen never have much time for charity, have they?"

Malone looked at Quentin, not defensively but sardonically. He was surprised when Quentin said, "Don't say that, Sheila. Not about him."

Malone gazed steadily at him, trying to hold up his own defenses. But something began to crumble them: the roots of friendship? he wondered. He said with real regret, "There's nothing I can do to help you now."

"You can," Quentin said quietly; he seemed to realize that all of Malone's antagonism had now gone. "Just forget everything my wife has told you."

"No!" Sheila pushed herself away from him. "We've got to tell them everything. It's the only way, tell them the truth!"

"Darling." Quentin's voice was gentle, not bitter. "I've

[237]

seen this past week how little the truth counts. People believe what they *want* to believe. They are only interested in the truth if it's convenient."

"Convenient to what?" She was past understanding compromise: now the truth had been told she wanted nothing less.

Quentin shrugged. "Their politics, their morals, anything. Scobie has said"—he was Scobie again, the friend—"he's said no jury would believe it was an accident. Not after so long, not after we ran away. One of us has got to pay for it. And it's not going to be you," he said firmly. "The warrant is for me and that's the way it's going to remain."

Sheila shook her head, but she was weeping now, beyond words. There was nothing left of the beautiful, poised woman Malone had first met only three nights ago. Quentin took her in his arms again and looked at Malone.

"Would you leave us alone, please, Scobie?"

Malone went to the door, opened it. He turned and said hesitatingly, "You won't try anything foolish?"

"Suicide?" Quentin didn't even seem shocked by the question. He shook his head. "No. I've been waiting twenty-three years to pay this debt. I'm not going to run away again."

4

Lisa said, "I got the cook to take them up something on a tray. What's going on, Scobie? Is there something wrong between them?"

"It's personal, I think. They've had some bad news." He was disgusted at his fluency: lying was becoming his second language. But he had committed himself again to the Quentins; no matter how he felt towards Lisa, he was not committed towards her. "He said something about going back to Australia on Saturday."

They were dining alone in the big dining room, sitting together at one end of the long table. Lisa, joking, had in-

[238]

sisted that Malone take the head of the table. He had not argued, but he was acutely aware of the unconscious irony of the joke: he *was* now head of this house.

Lisa looked up from her plate, a forkful of food stopped halfway to her mouth. "Back to Australia? *Saturday?*"

"Don't broadcast it. He asked me to keep it quiet. He'll tell you about it later." Everyone would have to be told sooner or later; he wondered how *she* would react to the truth when she learned of it.

"But I'll have to get them tickets—are they *both* going?"

He nodded. "He's got the tickets. You don't have to worry about those." Quentin's cheque was in his pocket. The envelope had been lying sealed on his bed when he had gone upstairs to wash his hands just before dinner. He was not going to argue about it any more. The money meant nothing to him right now, but it meant less to Quentin. And it would mean still less again in the future. "They're on the five-thirty plane Saturday."

She looked at him shrewdly. "And you too?" He nodded. She put down her fork, trying hard to contain her impatience with him. "Scobie, what *is* going on? You know more than you're telling me."

He didn't reply at once, dodged behind a mouthful of food. He was hungry, but he had no taste; Lisa had told him he was eating Osso Bucco, but it could have been dog's meat. At last he said, "I can't tell you anything, Lisa. Not yet, anyway."

"I know you're a security man," she said impatiently, "but what's security got to do with their personal problems? They're not going to *sack* him, are they?" The thought seemed to horrify her. She had her own idea of treason, a government betraying an individual.

"I don't think so." Quentin would resign before they sacked him. He turned the conversation: "If he does go back—for good, I mean—will you stay on here?"

She picked up her fork again, began to eat without relish. She had worked long enough in government to recognize censorship: Malone was going to tell her nothing. "Stay at Australia House or stay in London? I don't think I'd want to work for any other High Commissioner, not after him. I might go back to Australia for a visit, see my parents. Why?"

"They're in Melbourne, aren't they? Would you come to Sydney?"

"Why Sydney? I thought you worked in Canberra."

He was getting careless. "We have a branch office in Sydney. I work out of there most of the time."

"Somehow I can't see you as a spy."

"I'm not a spy. I'm a security agent." He was fluent again.

"It's the same thing. You have to be deceitful to be successful at it. And you don't seem the deceitful sort."

"Only professionally," he said, and hoped it was true.

"I was deceived once," she said, remembering the physics lecturer. "I shouldn't want it to happen again."

He hoped she would understand when he explained to her why he had deceived her. He might even have to call Quentin as a witness for the defense.

"There's the reception tomorrow night at Lancaster House," she said. "Can we be partners again? If you're going Saturday—"

"I was going to ask you."

"I got in early." She smiled. "How's your Osso Bucco?"

"Great." His taste had suddenly come back. He grinned at her, picked up the bone and began to chew the meat from it. "I saw them do this in some Italian film. It's the sensible way."

"To hell with decorum." She laughed and picked up the bone from her own plate. They were munching on the meat, slobbering gravy down their chins, grinning with pleasure at each other, selfish in their forgetfulness of everyone but themselves, when they heard the front door open. Lisa put

[240]

down her bone, wiped her chin and looked over her shoulder at the door that led into the hall. "Is that you, Joseph?"

The butler, in dark suit, his Homburg held in his hand, came to the door. His professional eye automatically checked the table; he pursed his lips when he saw the wine bottle without a napkin wrapped round it. He would speak to the cook in the morning. "You wanted something, miss?"

Lisa shook her head. "No, it's all right, Joseph. Have a nice afternoon?"

"Yes, thank you." It had been one of the worst afternoons of his life; nothing in Budapest had been worse. "Good night, miss. Good night, sir."

Joseph withdrew and they heard him going down the lower stairs that led to his room in the basement. Lisa picked up her bone again, but Malone said, "What was the matter with him, I wonder?"

"What do you mean?"

"He looked ill. Or anyway unhappy."

"Hungarians always look like that underneath. I've never believed all that propaganda about their being so gay and happy. They're not all Zsa Zsa Gabors." She looked at him soberly over the gravy-dripping bone. "He might have personal problems, too. Butlers do, I suppose."

CHAPTER TEN

1

Joseph stood for a moment at the top of the stairs that led up from the basement. Below him he could hear the cook complaining to the daily charwoman about cooking breakfasts for people who did not eat them; she was tossing pots and pans about in tinny chords of protest. In the hall Quentin, hat in one hand, briefcase in the other, was saying good-bye to Sheila. Both of them looked tired and worried; Quentin leaned forward and kissed his wife comfortingly on the cheek. Sheila raised both hands and seemed to clutch at him through the shoulders of his jacket; she said something and Quentin shook his head sadly. Joseph stood studying them and for the first time since he had come to this house he began to have some feeling for them. It had been part of his training that he should never become involved with people and up till now he had avoided any traps. He had even avoided marriage, though once or twice he had been tempted: he was not incapable of love. He felt no love for the couple standing at the end of the hall, but he felt sympathy. And that was the beginning of involvement.

Then the front doorbell rang and he walked along past the Quentins and opened the door. Larter stood there; the Rolls was at the curb. "Coming," said Quentin, and looked up at Malone as the latter came down the stairs. "You'd better cash that cheque today. There may not be time tomorrow."

Malone nodded reluctantly. "This reception tonight, sir—what's the dress?"

"I've already told Joseph to lay out my extra tails for you. I'm afraid it's full dress again. Decorations if you have any."

Malone grinned, but his joking was an effort this morning. "I have my Bondi surf club's bronze medal."

"I'd wear it, Mr. Malone," said Sheila. "It means as much as some of the other decorations you'll see tonight."

Joseph was aware of some sort of atmosphere between the Quentins and Malone; you could not live in other people's houses and remain insensitive to currents in relationships. Quentin kissed his wife again, then led Malone out of the house. Joseph closed the front door and turned back as Sheila spoke to him. "Joseph, would you bring up the three large suitcases from the storeroom?"

He hid his surprise. "You're going away, madame?"

He noticed her hesitation, as if she hadn't quite decided what to tell him. "Just a short holiday. My husband needs a rest."

"He does look tired. And you, too, madame. When will you be leaving?"

"Tomorrow, if the conference finishes."

"I thought it was to finish today?"

"There's an extra session planned for tomorrow morning." She began to move up the stairs. He had always admired her because she was a beautiful woman and he had a Hungarian's eye for beautiful women; but this morning she looked old and almost ugly. "Bring the cases up to my room."

Joseph went down to the basement and through the kitchen. The Cockney charwoman and the Spanish housemaid were sitting at the table having a cup of tea; they gave him a cool look as he went by, dismissing him as a snob. The

[243]

cook, a middle-aged woman with goiter-affected eyes and a low boiling point of injustice, was still clashing pots and pans; she hurled them into the sink, splashing water over Joseph as he passed. A transistor radio was turned up full blast as another protest: Radio Caroline warned fishermen to look out for squalls. Joseph went on into the storeroom, glad that he would not have to put up with the cook much longer.

He put two suitcases in his own room, then took three large ones upstairs. He knocked on the door of the Quentins' bedroom and Sheila opened it; he was shocked to see that she had been weeping, but he said nothing. She had obviously tried to hide her tears, but he had seen enough women weeping to recognize the signs: Budapest had been full of sorrowing women in 1956. He went past Sheila into the room, set down the suitcases and returned to the doorway. "Will that be all, madame?"

"The clock, Joseph—when will it be fixed?"

"I am to pick it up today."

"It's getting old and it wasn't expensive to begin with. Perhaps I should get a new one." Then she shook her head, as if she had decided there was no sense in what she had said.

"I shouldn't do that, madame," Joseph said, and tried not to sound too emphatic. "The watchmaker thought it a very good clock. It was just a minor fault."

Sheila nodded carelessly, as if the clock no longer interested her. Joseph studied her for a moment, then closed the door and went back downstairs and down to the basement. He went through the kitchen, ignoring the three women still there, and into his own room. He locked the door and sat down on the bed and took the cheque from his pocket. It wasn't riches, but it was a good price for murder. Especially when the alternative was a sort of bankruptcy.

He hadn't quite believed it when the small Oriental man had come up beside him yesterday in Knightsbridge and said, "Would you come with me, sir? I have a gun in my pocket—"

He had looked down and saw that the man had one hand in the pocket of his cheap, ill-fitting jacket. It was incredible that people could be shot in Brompton Road in broad daylight, but England could no longer be relied upon. Decorations for pop singers and ducal castles turned into circuses: murder outside Harrods was consistent with such a new way of life. If the Russians would only be patient, the West would defeat itself. . . . "Where are we going?"

A taxi drew up beside them and Harrods' commissionaire held open the door for them. My God, Joseph thought, even Harrods are in the conspiracy! "Where to, sir?"

"Avenue Road, St. John's Wood," said Pham Chinh, and sat back as the taxi driver, arrogant as any duke, did a U-turn and held up traffic in both directions for at least four blocks.

"I don't know anyone in St. John's Wood." Joseph showed no sign of being afraid, but his hand was clutched tightly on the clock in its brown paper bag. It was a poor weapon, but it was the only one he had; if he hurled it into the face of the other man, the man would surely be knocked out. But by then the bullet would just as surely be in his own gut. "Are you from one of the embassies?"

"Mr. Chen wants to see you," said Pham Chinh, watching him closely.

Joseph pursed his lips, started to say something, then sat back. "Why the gun, then? Did he think I wouldn't come?"

Pham Chinh shrugged and smiled. "One never knows. We had to see if you were the man we wanted. You have just proved you are."

Joseph was puzzled, but said nothing. The two men sat in silence all the way to St. John's Wood. Pham Chinh gave the number of the house in Avenue Road to the driver and the taxi pulled into a gravelled courtyard in front of a large neo-Georgian house. Joseph got out and waited while the man paid the driver. Up till now he had always met Chen and Pai in shabby restaurants at various main-line railway stations around London; the Russians had chosen slightly better meeting places, such as the restaurant at Festival Hall. Neither of them had ever asked him to meet them at such a stylish rendezvous as this. He was impressed, though still puzzled.

The taxi drove away. Pham Chinh opened the front door and Joseph went ahead of him into a hall that impressed the Hungarian as much as the exterior of the house had done. A Dufy hung on one wall: an original, not a print, he noted with approval. A silk-seated armchair stood beside a small wall table: he classed them both as Regency and also genuine. The Chinese, it seemed, were making the most of the evils of capitalism while they were here in London.

Pham Chinh led the way into a large drawing room, but stood aside as soon as he entered the door. Joseph was one step past him when he realized he had been tricked. He stopped and half-turned, but the woman standing by the window said, "Sit down, Joseph, unless you want to be hurt. Pham Chinh's gun has a silencer on it and silencers do ruin the accuracy—but I hardly think he could miss you at that distance." She looked at Pham Chinh. "Is he the man we wanted?"

Pham Chinh nodded. "As soon as I mentioned Chen's name, he knew who I meant. He's the one, all right."

Madame Cholon introduced herself, then sat down and waved Joseph to a chair. "Do I call you Joseph, or have you another name?"

"Liszt," said Joseph. But Madame Cholon made no comment: she knew little of Western music, and Hungarian rhapsodies were as nothing compared to what had been practiced in the Hall of Mirrors brothel in Saigon. But

Joseph made his own comment on Madame Cholon: "I've heard your name mentioned."

"Where—at the High Commissioner's house?" She was interested, but not alarmed. Pallain had told her that Scotland Yard was curious about her. But the years with Bay Vien had taught her nothing but contempt for the police. "How much have you heard about me?"

Joseph looked at Pham Chinh, still standing with his hand in his jacket pocket. "If we are going to talk, does he have to stand there like that all the time? I'm not used to discussion under the nose of a gun."

Madame Cholon smiled. "You have a certain *sang-froid,* Monsieur Liszt. I wonder if you have enough to do what I want you to do?"

"What's that?"

"Kill your employer."

Joseph's *sang-froid* deserted him for the moment; he heard himself say, "Which one?"

Her smile widened. "An understandable question, monsieur. You have several, haven't you? It must be confusing at times. But I'm only interested in one of them. Mr. Quentin."

Joseph recovered his poise. He sat back, shook his head. "Definitely not. I'm not a murderer, madame."

"But you're several other things, aren't you?" Madame Cholon's tone was sweet, too sweet: she could have been practicing her brothel wiles. "A double agent, for instance. Working for the Russians and also the Chinese."

Again his poise slipped: "Who told you that?"

"An American friend." She thought of Jamaica lying dead on the bed upstairs; he had proved to be useful after all.

Joseph could feel himself beginning to sweat. He looked at Pham Chinh, who had taken his hand from his pocket but still stood leaning against the door jamb, blocking any escape. He licked his lips and looked back at Madame Cholon. "Who else knows?"

"No one—as yet." She was enjoying his disquiet; anyone else's torture was her pleasure. "But I'm sure the Russians would not be pleased to learn you were also working for the Chinese. That isn't part of your contract with them, is it?"

"This American—" He wondered who it could be. "How much did he tell you?"

"Everything he knew. And he seemed to know a lot."

That was one of the dangers of the game: that you could be exposed by people whose existence you never even suspected. "But why did he tell you?"

"We—er—persuaded him." She ran her tongue over her lips, as if recapturing a taste. She had been surprised that Jamaica had told her as much as he had; but perhaps at that stage he had still hoped to leave the house alive and thought that the information about Joseph was a small price to pay. After all, as he had said, he had stumbled on Joseph's activities only by accident. He had been watching Chen to see if *she* would meet him, and instead Joseph had turned up. Then he had followed Joseph and seen him meet a Russian. "Do you want me to tell you what I know?"

Joseph tried again for some poise. He sat back again, crossed one leg elegantly over the other. "Since you are evidently going to make a proposition to me, I'd like to know how much you have to bargain with."

Madame Cholon's eyes came as close to twinkling as was possible with her. "I do admire you, monsieur. I can see why you have lasted as long as you have. Well, your history. Our American friend knew nothing of your early life, but that really doesn't interest us. You were working for the Russians in Budapest before 1956." She did not know how Jamaica had got his extra information; she could only assume that, given a clue, he had known where to go next. "You

[248]

got out of Hungary, ostensibly as a refugee, and came here in December, 1956. You worked for two years for Lord Porthleven, another eighteen months for the Duke of Isis, then you went to work for the previous Australian High Commissioner, Sir James Gable. You can't have had much to pass on to the Russians up till this conference. The Australians like to think they are important, but they are nobodies in world affairs. Don't you agree?"

"A good butler never discusses his masters," said Joseph, who had never worked in a royal household nor been approached by Sunday newspapers.

"And I'm sure you're a good butler. I just hope you won't discuss me when our little business is done. Shall I go on?" Joseph nodded. He was playing for time, though he did not know what use time would be to him. "Some time in the past month the Chinese found out you were working for the Russians. When it became apparent that Quentin was to be one of the leading men at this conference, they approached you. I don't know whether they blackmailed you or bribed you, perhaps both. In any case you began to work for them. I don't know what you were able to tell them—our American friend hadn't got on to that."

"So his information on me must have been very recent?"

"I gather it was. He may not even have transmitted it to his superiors. I don't know." She smiled again. "But that's your worry, monsieur, not mine. All I can tell you is that if you don't do as I ask, then *someone* will be told about you. It would be very awkward for you, wouldn't it, if the Australians, the Russians and the Chinese were all disillusioned about you? Traitor to three countries, not counting Hungary. That would be some sort of record, wouldn't it?"

Joseph sat for a while in silence, one leg still crossed over the other; but there was a stiffness about him now that no longer made him look at ease. He remembered all the years of training, at the Marx-Engels school at Gorky, then at

Verkhovnoye and finally at Gaczyna. They had taught him all the uses of guns and explosives, but no amount of teaching and propaganda could make one a killer unless the urge to kill was already there, like a seed waiting to be nurtured. They had never recognized that the seed was not in him and he had never told them. His primary use was as an agent, at which, up till now, he had been good; and an agent, if he is really good, should never be in a situation where he has to kill. But now the situation had at last arrived.

"I couldn't kill him in cold blood," he said.

Madame Cholon had no reservations, other than tactical ones, about how the murder was to be committed. "It would be best if we could devise some way that wouldn't implicate you." She smiled at him again. "Just in case we want to use you again."

"You're very sure I shan't double-cross you," said Joseph, with a side glance at Pham Chinh. "What if I should go to the Chinese—or the Russians—and tell them what you've just proposed? It mightn't fit in with their plans. And they might decide to—"

"Kill me?" The thought seemed to amuse Madame Cholon; she was afraid of nothing, not even death. "Are you threatening me?"

Joseph looked again at Pham Chinh: the Vietnamese had straightened up, taking the gun with its fitted silencer from his pocket. Joseph uncrossed his legs, straightened the crease in his trousers and looked back at Madame Cholon. "No, madame. I'm just stating my side of the bargain. Whatever way Mr. Quentin is disposed of, I don't think either of my other employers is going to have much use for me in the future. I'll be, to say the least, suspect. Not only to Moscow and Peking, but to Scotland Yard, the CIA, the FBI and any other security organization you care to name. In other words, I shall have to look around for a new life. And for that I shall need what the Americans call a stake."

[250]

"How much?"

Well, he thought, if I'm going to die I may as well do so with dreams of wealth. "Twenty-five thousand pounds."

It was Madame Cholon's turn to lose poise. "Out of the question!"

"Had you intended paying me at all?" She hesitated, then nodded. "How much?"

"Perhaps five thousand pounds."

Joseph smiled. He had become fatalistic: he was going to be killed anyway, if not by this woman, then by the Russians or the Chinese. "That, too, is out of the question. Madame, when the Chinese approached me they blackmailed me, just as you are doing. But they also knew they could trust me, well, just a little, if they paid me a figure that put a fair value on what I was doing for them." He sighed, looked around the richly furnished room. He knew the number of agents who spent their lives in mean surroundings; he had been one of the fortunate ones. "I've become accustomed to good living, madame. And even though I was to go on being a butler, according to my employers' plans, I should have been living in a beautiful house, eating the best of food, drinking the best of wine and whisky. If I have to vanish—as seems probable—after Mr. Quentin has been, er, disposed of, I don't want to spend the rest of my life in a shabby room in some remote South American village, exchanging reminiscences with some ex-Nazi."

"Where would you go—Australia?"

He wrinkled his nose. "Hardly, madame. No, I have several retreats in mind. One always has them in mind, just in case." He looked at the gun in Pham Chinh's hand, then back at Madame Cholon. She, too, was a beautiful woman, but in her way she looked just as ugly now as Sheila Quentin had looked this morning. This woman was ugly inside and she would order him to be killed without being in the least disturbed. He had nothing to lose by holding out for as much as he could get. "I shall need a minimum of fifteen thousand pounds. Payable in cash on a Swiss bank—I take it you have money there?" She nodded, just as he had guessed she would. The Russians and the Chinese paid him through Switzerland: neutrality had its uses. "I'll take the cheque with me today."

"And if I refuse?"

He sat back, playing his biggest bluff. "Then you will have to find someone else to do your dirty work. And you will have the trouble and inconvenience of disposing of me." The Hungarian in him came to the surface, the weakness for gestures; he would even die with *sang-froid*. "It might not be so easy."

"It would be no trouble at all," said Madame Cholon, thinking of the dead man upstairs. It would not be much more difficult to dispose of two corpses than to dispose of one. She wondered if the Chinese would appreciate the joke if she planted a Russian spy, as well as an American one, on their doorstep. The Chinese sense of humor had changed since the Communists had taken over, but perhaps some of the older men would laugh behind their hands at it. She studied Joseph, tempted by the idea of the vengeful joke on Chen and Pai; then she dismissed it, she hadn't come all this way to play jokes. "Fifteen thousand, then," she said, and saw Pham Chinh lift his head. His price would go up now, but she could deal with him. It would be even less trouble to dispose of him than of Joseph and Jamaica. Dead men were always floating down the Mekong River. "But how will you kill Quentin?"

"I thought you would have had that planned," said Joseph. "You seem to have command of so much else. How did you first get on to me? Did the American proffer the information voluntarily?"

"No." Madame Cholon could not help boasting: "I had

a visit this morning from your Chinese employers. They did not give their names, but it wasn't difficult to find out who they were. All I had to do was call a friend in another embassy, describe them, and he gave me their names. They told me, though not in so many words, that they had someone working for them. It was not hard to guess where that someone was. They knew all about the attempts on Quentin's life— What's the matter?"

"I just hope I am more successful than you have been," Joseph said. "The attempts so far don't seem to have been very professional."

"Oh, they were made by professionals," said Madame Cholon with a contemptuous glance at Pham Chinh, whose face remained expressionless. "But as you say, they were not successful. Where was I? Oh yes. It was not hard to guess that they must be getting their information from someone in Quentin's house. There were not many to choose from. We eliminated Malone, the cook, the housemaid, the members of the delegation. It *could* have been Mrs. Quentin, but why should she have wanted to betray her husband? That left either you or the secretary. Then Mr. Jamaica paid us a visit and we questioned him about you."

"The Russians or the Chinese could use you."

"Thank you. The prospect doesn't appeal to me at all. I like being my own boss." She stopped for a moment; a sense of power coursed through her like a drug. Then she went on, as calmly as before: "It was not difficult to contact you. Pham Chinh has been watching the Quentin house for the past two weeks. He has a key to the garden in Belgrave Square. He began life as a pickpocket in Saigon, didn't you, Pham?" Pham Chinh nodded, still expressionless. He's thinking about that fifteen thousand pounds, she thought; then turned her back on him again. "No one knows him and it has been easy for him to sit there in the gardens among

[253]

the nannies and the children, reading a book and watching your house. The English have a pleasant habit of minding their own business if you mind yours."

"What did he discover while he was busy minding his own business in the gardens?"

"That you are a man of habit. Every afternoon, even on your afternoons off, you emerge from the house at the same time and go for a walk. Pham Chinh has never bothered to follow you until today. I hope bringing you here has not kept you from some appointment? Perhaps with one of your other employers?" She smiled. "You must be one of the most employed men in London just now. Four bosses. I wonder what the British Minister for Economic Affairs thinks of that."

"I had no appointment," said Joseph, and held up the brown paper bag. "I was just taking this alarm clock to be fixed. It belongs to Mr. Quentin."

Madame Cholon held out her hand and after a moment's puzzlement Joseph handed her the bag. She took out the small clock in its blue leather case and studied it. Then she went out of the room and Joseph heard her on the phone. He caught only the word "bomb," but it was enough. When she came back into the room he knew what she was going to suggest.

"Leave the clock with me. It will be mended. Pham Chinh will meet you tomorrow morning and return it with instructions. I shall phone you at ten o'clock."

Joseph stood up. "There is one more thing. I shall take the cheque now."

She stared at him for a long moment, as if debating whether the gamble she was taking on him was too big. Then she moved to a desk in one corner of the room, wrote out a cheque and brought it back to him. "There has to be a certain amount of trust in this, monsieur. I must confess it is not a condition I usually accept."

[254]

"Nor I, madame," said Joseph. "We are each in a position of being able to double-cross the other. But each of us, I think, could soon repay the other. I think you have become desperate. That's why you need me. And I"—he kissed the cheque, another Hungarian gesture—"I need this. Good-bye, madame."

His poise had left him as soon as he had left the house. He had noted the address, then walked down Avenue Road to Regent's Park. He had sat in the park all afternoon, taking out the cheque time and again to look at it, not with appreciation but with something like fear, as if the cheque itself might blow up in his face. At last he rose and walked on through the park, hearing the lions roaring across in the zoo, listlessly and bronchially, like tired old men who knew their rage was hopeless. Young mothers, proud as mares, manes bright in the sun, strode by with their children; old ladies peg-legged by with their brood of dogs. He had come to like England and its way of life; the English amused him with their self-deception but at least they were civilized. He would have been sorry to leave London when the order came for him to move on to Washington.

It had been a long-range plan, this planting of him as an "illegal." The three years as a waiter in the Hotel Duna, doing the occasional small job for Western espionage agents but always letting his Russian bosses know; the manufactured "escape" during the 1956 rebellion; the several years with the innocent lord and duke; then the position with the Australian High Commissioner. The eventual aim was for him to be taken on at one of the principal embassies in Washington, the British, French or German; it might take years, but Moscow had been prepared to wait that long. And he, too, had been prepared to wait: after all, he could have been planted as a mechanic and spent the waiting years in some dirty garage in the Midlands. But now all the Russian plans for him were finished, even if Moscow did not yet know. In

[255]

two days' time, for he had now made up his mind, he would be on his way to South Africa. It was not what he would call a civilized country, but its wines were good, he would be able to afford a servant to look after *him,* and it was a country where Russian agents found it difficult to operate. And he did not want his retirement interrupted by some agent from Moscow seeking revenge.

Now this morning he was waiting for Madame Cholon's telephone call. He got up, began to take some of his clothes out of a closet. He folded them neatly, putting tissue paper round each garment; he had learned his job well as butler-valet, took pride in it. He packed only his best things: the Sulka shirts, the Peal shoes; it had been one of his nightmares that he might be recalled for duty in Moscow, would be reduced to wearing Russian-made clothes. He looked around his room at the items he had collected: the small Dresden piece, the three pewter mugs, the old matching pistols. They would have to be left behind, along with the leather-bound set of *The Thousand and One Nights,* the good Gauguin print and the small Persian rug. If a man was going to start a new life, he should start it with no identification at all. He already had a new name and a new passport. They were a precaution the Russians had known nothing about; another old Hungarian saying (he smiled to himself, recalling the conversation with Malone) was, "Just in case . . ." He would bequeath his belongings to the Spanish housemaid: they might wean her away from the cook and Radio Caroline.

Then the cook knocked on the door and snapped, "You're wanted on the phone. Some woman."

2

The Rolls-Royce, the small Australian flag fluttering from its tiny mast on one fender, sailed majestically through the rapids of traffic up past Buckingham Palace. Other cars gave way to it. Malone, sitting in the back seat, could not tell whether the other cars were being deferential or just prudent; after all, a lightweight Ford would be foolish to take on something that weighed over two tons. But he enjoyed the feeling of being given way to; not even police cars got this sort of respect in Sydney. Then the slight feeling of pleasure died at the thought of home. He looked at his watch: seven o'clock. In a little over sixty hours from now the man beside him would be stepping into a police car in Sydney.

"Something troubling you?" Quentin said.

The two men were alone in the back of the car and the division separating them from Ferguson was closed. Malone nodded and said, "Yes. You. Are you going to persist in leaving your wife out of this altogether?"

"Don't let's discuss it, Scobie. I've made up my mind." He looked at Malone, shifting in the seat so that he directly faced him. His voice was flat, neither threat nor plea: he wanted to hope, but thought it fruitless: "You're not going to tell them in court what you heard last night?"

Malone shrugged. He did not mean to be non-committal; he honestly did not know what he would do when the time came. "Depends what questions they ask me."

"But you won't proffer the information voluntarily?" His words were stiff, an echo of the conference table.

"I don't know. I like to see justice done, that's all."

"You mean you want to see my wife punished? That you don't believe what she did was an accident?"

They were caught in the pack-ice of traffic at Hyde Park Corner. A bus stood right alongside them: dozens of people stared in at them, trying to lip-read what was being said behind the glass. "No, I believe her. And I don't want her to be punished—I mean I'm not vindictive. All I mean is, I don't think you should chuck your life away. Tell them the truth. They *might* believe it."

"The way you say that proves you don't think they will. No, Scobie." He shook his head, looked out at the passengers in the bus. "There's a jury for you. Do you think they would believe the story? Look at that woman in the pink hat, the one with all the feathers. Do you think she would ever have any compassion for a man's mistress?"

Malone and the woman stared at each other through the windows of the car and the bus; she pursed her lips, then turned away with something that looked like resentment. The bus moved on, going up towards Knightsbridge, taking the woman on to the home that she would defend tooth and nail against besieging mistresses. The Rolls turned down Grosvenor Place towards the mistress now besieged by the ghost of a wife. Malone sat further back in the seat and changed the subject: "How did it go today?"

Quentin was not accustomed to having younger, junior men turn the conversation on him. There was a momentary spark of anger, but it died quickly. He, too, sat further back in the seat, almost slumping. His time of authority was over; he and Malone were not even equals. He spoke listlessly: "It's finished. We meet tomorrow morning, but it's just a formality to draw up the communiqué."

"Did it turn out the way you wanted?"

"Couldn't have gone worse." He looked sideways at Malone, permitted himself a little malice: "Can I trust you to keep quiet, at least till tomorrow?"

Malone tried a little malice of his own: "You know who's been the one to be trusted these past few days."

Quentin flinched, then nodded. "Don't let's quarrel."

The two men were silent for a while, each regretting his moment of malice. It was as if each knew he was tarnishing something that had never been valued but had shown promise.

Then Quentin went on: "That African I told you about yesterday, the one with the Chinese accent, he got up today and spilled the works. Said that the Americans had plans, if the conference failed, to build up their forces in Vietnam for a large-scale war. He knew all about it, even used an American term. Said they were going to 'escalate' the war."

"And are they?"

Quentin nodded. "That's their idea. But no one was supposed to know it but ourselves, the British and the South Vietnamese."

"What effect did it have when everyone else learned of it?"

"The natural one. No one trusts the Americans any more. The irony is that the Viet Cong were probably planning exactly the same thing. It's just plain common sense insurance. But the Viet Cong kept their secret better than the Americans. Now they're sitting back smug as cats and saying 'I told you so.' The whole conference folded up in a matter of minutes. There were a dozen so-called neutral delegates on their feet at once, all of them shouting that this proved the Americans didn't want any sort of terms in Vietnam but their own. We tried arguing, but we might just as well have tried arguing that our skin was the same colour as theirs. The room was suddenly divided into the 'imperialists' and the 'independents.' And the 'imperialists' were out-numbered ten to one." He sighed on a personal note. "I've always thought of myself as a liberal, with a small *l*. I really have been sympathetic towards the new countries, thought they've had a poor deal in the past and tried to do something for them. I've worked harder than anyone to make the Colombo Plan a success in Asia. But today they branded me, called me principal spokesman for the 'imperialists.' "

"They know that's not the truth."

"Circumstantial evidence." He looked up as the car drew up in Belgrave Square. "It's a hard thing to beat, don't you think?"

CHAPTER ELEVEN

1

"The English have conveniently short memories," said the Indian, choosing caviar in preference to curry. "That way they can enjoy only the better aspects of their history."

"He's so charming," gushed the wife of the junior Foreign Office official. "Of course, he's not civilized enough yet to be bad-mannered."

"Importance is a matter of occasion," said the man from the American State Department. "A king sitting on a john is only a man on a hollow throne."

"She calls it cleavage," said the wife of a Cabinet minister, "but at her age I think it looks more like erosion."

Malone listened to the remarks, some obviously rehearsed, others flung with sparkling spontaneity, as if the speakers were surprised by their own wit or wisdom. He kept one ear cocked for a remark on Australia and was not disappointed:

"Australian women are so crudely unsophisticated," said the man from Commonwealth Relations; he had been transferred from the Foreign Office as not being virile enough. "I do believe they use Airwick as a perfume."

Righto, mate, I'm going to do you, thought Malone; and moved forward. But Lisa came out of the crowd and caught his arm. "Careful, Scobie. Don't break up the Common-wealth."

"But he's insulting you and every other Aussie girl I know!" He grinned at her. "Including me old Irish mum."

"You're quite old-fashioned in lots of ways. Are you always so chivalrous towards women?"

"Not always," he said, and across the room caught a glimpse of Sheila Quentin.

Lisa took his arm and they began to move on through the crowd. Her taking of his arm had a natural intimacy about it, was more than the gesture of a girl identifying herself with her escort for the night. Their relationship was easy and warm now, but Malone was still uncertain how much further to take it. It might all end tomorrow.

"I'm going to miss you," she said, as if reading his thoughts.

"I don't think I'll ever get back this way again. You'll have to come home."

"I might, if—"

"If your boss doesn't come back here?" He won't, he said silently; but he couldn't tell her that just yet.

She nodded and looked around the crowded room for Quentin. They were in the Great Gallery of Lancaster House and the long high-ceilinged room was burning with colour. Voices and glasses clinked with the same light inconsequential sound; diamonds and eyes sparkled in competition. Mirrors on opposite walls reflected the scene in each other: gaiety spread away into infinity. It was impossible to imagine that the conference had failed; the soldiers in the paddy-fields of Vietnam still had their hopes. Lisa looked back at Malone.

"I can't see him or Mrs. Quentin."

"He's over there. Sergeant Coburn is keeping an eye on him. I'm having a breather."

"You still don't expect—?" She didn't finish the sentence.

[261]

"No." He shifted his arm, conscious of the holster; guns had never been meant to be worn beneath tight-fitting tail-coats. "But just in case—"

Then he looked over her shoulder straight at Madame Cholon, in a green *ao dais,* looking as beautiful and unpredictable as some jungle bird that had strayed into a city aviary. She came out of the crowd on the arm of the portly African Ambassador whose father had dined on missionaries. Lisa saw the surprise on Malone's face and she turned as the Ambassador spoke to him.

"Just on our way to supper." He smiled and winked broadly; but Malone knew he would not be entirely unsubtle. "This one is put on by the Foreign Office. Theirs are always so much better than Commonwealth Relations'. *They* serve such bottled jokes as Tanzanian champagne. The worst of the lot is Economic Affairs. They put on some sort of budget supper."

"May we join you?" Malone said, and took Lisa's arm as he introduced her to the Ambassador and Madame Cholon. "I remember you set me a fine example the other night, sir, on what to choose at the table."

The Ambassador laughed, shaking hugely. "What he means is I showed him how to overload a plate without spilling any. Gluttony is only a sin where dieting is a religion. That was one of my father's aphorisms. He ate the last dietitian who came to my country."

He led them through into the Music Room, still laughing like a whole chorus of merriment. Lisa, holding Malone's arm tightly, whispered, "What is *she* doing here?"

As if she had heard the question Madame Cholon turned to them as they reached the supper tables. "His Excellency's wife is back home in his country—"

"Always goes home for the English summer," said the Ambassador, supervising a waiter as the latter heaped two plates. "She can't stand it."

"I happened to mention to His Excellency how much I'd enjoyed *his* reception—"

"So here we are." The Ambassador turned back with two loaded plates. Madame Cholon took hers without protest, but had to hold it with two hands. "Cementing Afro-Asian relations, eh, madame?"

Madame Cholon smiled in agreement, and Malone wondered what had happened to her colour bar: the Ambassador was much darker than Jamaica had been. "Have you seen Mr. Jamaica tonight?" he said.

The smile froze on her face, but only for a moment. "Mr. Jamaica? Oh, the American gentleman. No."

"Nice fellow," said the Ambassador, eating heartily. "Told me his great-great-grandfather came from my country. Must have been my great-great-grandfather who sold him." He laughed again, almost choking on his food.

Malone handed Lisa a plate and began to eat from his own. Other guests had come into the room, had taken up plates. Lisa looked around and said, "This reminds me of British television. The screen always seems to be full of people eating. People and dogs."

"You're so right, my dear girl," said the Ambassador. "I'm a TV addict, sit in front of the set for hours. I've become an expert on the gullets and teeth of British people and dogs. Oh, and cats, too."

Oh Christ, thought Malone, listening to the talk. Doesn't anyone have a thought for the poor bastards who had hopes for this conference? He looked about the Music Room. The big conference table had been taken out, replaced by smaller tables; order papers had been replaced by plates of smoked salmon. Brittle silly conversation was the echo of the hard serious debate that had taken place here only a few hours ago. Malone looked about him and once more, as on his first night in London, had the feeling of being an

[263]

outsider. Smug hypocritical bastards in their tails and rib-
bons . . .

"Something bothering you, Mr. Malone?"

The Quentins stood beside him. "No," he said, glad of
their arrival just at this moment. He did not enjoy being
bitter and cynical; he *wanted* to put his faith in men. And,
whatever Quentin might have done on his personal level,
he could be trusted as a statesman. Malone knew that he, at
least, was sick with despair at the wreck of the conference.

The Ambassador greeted Quentin; then, despite his bulk,
bowed with grace to Sheila. "May I present Madame
Cholon?"

The polite smiles on the faces of both Quentins did not
alter; they were locked in behind their diplomatic façade
tonight. They exchanged greetings with Madame Cholon,
whose own smile was as polite and unrevealing as theirs.

"I've heard a lot about you, Your Excellency."

"Oh?" Quentin seemed to be watching with dry amuse-
ment this woman who had been trying to kill him. She had
failed in her aim and now he seemed able to look at her
with cool detachment. "All good, I hope."

She nodded, then said, "Has the conference been a success?"

Quentin looked at the Ambassador and the latter said,
"There is one more session to go, my dear. We still have
hopes, eh, Quentin?"

Malone looked at the Ambassador with new respect. He
was not the buffoon he played; that was *his* façade. The
conference was dead, but the delegates were keeping their
bad news to themselves till they had agreed on the communiqué. Something might still be salvaged, something
to keep alive, no matter how faintly, the hopes of the men
who had to fight the war. Malone glanced around the room
again, silently retracting his opinion of at least some of the
guests.

[264]

"You are quiet tonight, Mr. Malone." Madame Cholon had put down her plate untouched.

Out of the corner of his eye Malone saw Sheila Quentin watching Madame Cholon with a sort of horrified fascination: her eyes never left the Vietnamese woman's face. If Madame Cholon was aware of Sheila's stare, she gave no sign of the fact. After the first greeting with both Sheila and Lisa she had ignored them. Malone recognized her type: she was the sort of woman not interested in other women, the true professional harlot. Yet somehow he could not see her in a brothel, not the brothels he had raided in Sydney.

"Just tired," he said. "London is an exhausting city."

"How true. I'll be glad to return home."

"When are you going?" Sheila asked.

Madame Cholon turned her head, seemed to look at Sheila for the first time. Sheila's dress was almost the same colour as Madame Cholon's *ao dais,* but the antagonism between these two women went far beyond mere resentment over a fashion note. But her voice was as cool as Sheila's had been. "Tomorrow afternoon."

Sheila glanced at Malone, then said, "Not on the Qantas plane through Singapore?" Madame Cholon nodded, a slight crease of puzzlement spoiling the smoothness of her brow. "Then you'll have Mr. Malone as a travelling companion."

Madame Cholon looked at Malone, turning away from Sheila, dismissing her. "How pleasant! And how coincidental. Ah, good evening, Mr. Chen. And Mr. Pai, too."

The two Chinese, in hired dress suits that did not fit them, had come to the table. "Caviar, sir?" said a waiter.

"Is it Russian?" asked Mr. Pai.

"Oh, yes, sir."

"No, thank you," said Mr. Pai, bringing politics to the table. "What is that?"

"Clam chowder, sir," said the waiter, no diplomat. "A very tasty American soup."

"No, thank you. What is that?"

"Onion soup, sir. French."

"Yes, please."

Chen, meanwhile, was talking to Madame Cholon and the others. Malone was aware of a certain tension on Madame Cholon's part towards the two Chinese, but Chen did not seem to reciprocate it. He was completely at ease, except for the inconvenience of his dress coat, which was at least a size too big for him. He kept shooting his arms down, as if trying to prove that he had hands; but then the coat sleeves would creep down again to cover everything but his short stubby fingers. Pai, for his part, stood nervously in the background, staring steadily at Madame Cholon through his glasses that kept misting up from the heat of the bowl of soup he held.

Sheila drew Malone aside. "Do you think she plans—?"

Malone shook his head. "Not here. She's shot her bolt, I think. Otherwise she wouldn't have come out into the open like this."

"Isn't there something you can do?"

"What? Arrest her? On what grounds? Suspicion isn't enough. I've had a little lecture from Sergeant Coburn on that." He saw Coburn standing in the doorway and nodded to him. "Here he comes now. Maybe he is going to arrest her, after all."

Coburn came up to them. "There is a phone call for you, Mrs. Quentin."

Sheila was puzzled. "For me? Here?"

"One of the waiters brought the message. He's over there." Sheila, still looking puzzled, excused herself and went over to the waiter standing in the doorway. When she had gone Coburn turned to Malone, jerking his head dis-

[266]

creetly towards Madame Cholon. "She's quite a dish, isn't she? I fancy the Oriental stuff."

"I wouldn't let your girl hear that. Is Pallain here to-night?"

"He's around somewhere."

"Do you think one of us had better stick with Mrs. Quentin, just in case?"

"You mean the phone call? He wasn't the one who called her—I saw him just before I came in here. But I'll go down and keep close to her. What about Quentin?"

"I'll look after him. I think we're okay now, but you never know. Denzil would chop our heads off if something did happen this late in the piece. Where is *he* tonight?"

"At the Yard. He never comes to these sort of do's. I'm always the mug for this sort of game. Actually, I don't mind." Coburn looked around appreciatively, at the huge chandelier, the carved wooden pelmets, the richly decorated ceiling. "It's a bit different from the Hammersmith Palais. I must bring my bird one night."

He moved towards the door and was stopped by Pallain as the latter came into the room. Pallain said something to him and the two men stood talking for a couple of minutes, Coburn looking as if he were impatient to break away. At last he nodded abruptly to Pallain and went out the door, pushing his way through the tide of guests now flowing in for supper. Pallain saw Malone across the room, gave an exaggerated bow of his head, and moved across to another supper table. He knew of Madame Cholon's plan of the bomb in the Quentin alarm clock and thought it ingenious and bound not to fail. The one weakness was that someone else, the butler, had had to be recruited to implement the plan. He knew from experience that the most successful assassinations were those in which there were as few participants as possible. Just in case the butler should be caught and should talk, he had already bought his air ticket and would be leaving London tonight. But he had not mentioned that precaution to Madame Cholon.

Malone watched him for a moment or two, then turned back to Quentin and the others.

"Where is my wife?" Quentin asked.

"She's gone downstairs. There was a phone call for her. Sergeant Coburn has gone down to keep an eye on her."

Madame Cholon and the Ambassador had been caught up in the whirlpool of guests and swept away; Chen and Pai were trapped in another current and they, too, were gone. Quentin, Lisa and Malone, sticking close together, fought their way out of the room on to one of the balconies. They looked down into the Staircase Hall and saw Coburn moving aimlessly about. He crossed from one side of the wide hall to the other, then disappeared into one of the side galleries.

"I don't think I'll stay long," Quentin said. "I'm tired."

"What time is the session in the morning?" Lisa asked.

"Ten-thirty. I think I'll sleep late, forget about setting my alarm. Would you wake me at nine, Lisa?"

They saw Coburn reappear from the side gallery, looking worried and puzzled. He stood for a moment, then looked up and saw the three of them standing on the balcony. He ran up the stairs to them, his concern apparent even at a distance.

"I'm sorry, sir, but your wife seems to have disappeared!"

2

Quentin stood stock-still, his hands gripping the balustrade. Guests went by, throwing greetings like confetti, but he did not hear them. His face had turned grey again; Malone thought he was going to faint. Then he drew a deep breath, collected himself. "Perhaps she is in the ladies' room?"

"I'll go and see," said Lisa, and went quickly down the stairs, her long blue gown held up in front of her.

"We'll look around, too," said Malone. "Will you be all right, sir?"

Quentin nodded, his face still ashen. "I'll stay here. Find her, Scobie." It was a cry for help.

Malone and Coburn moved away from him along the balcony. "Try everywhere downstairs," Malone said. "And check with Ferguson. He's outside with the car. I'll scout around up here."

"I just hope she *is* in the loo," Coburn said, and went down the stairs at a run.

Malone went round the balcony and back into the Great Gallery. He pushed his way through the throng, swatches of conversation catching at his ears, irritating him again:

"Sexwise, she's just foolish—"

"It was rather a nice pasteurized orgy—very American—"

"Darling, I'm talking about my *horse,* not my husband—"

People looked at him curiously as he went past them; he was not a conference delegate, so he was not expected to look so worried. He saw Pallain, who moved towards him to say something; but he shook his head and moved quickly on. He saw other faces he knew: Larter, Edgar, the Americans who had been at the house this morning. And he passed close by Madame Cholon and the Ambassador.

"You look worried, Mr. Malone," said Madame Cholon.

"I'm looking for Mrs. Quentin. You haven't seen her?"

Her expression was almost too innocent. "Should I have seen her?"

Then she turned away from him, excused herself from the Ambassador and slid away like a green bird into the thicket of the crowd. The Ambassador looked after her, then at Malone. "Never trust the Orient, my father used to say." He was not laughing now; Africa was not as simple as so

[269]

many thought. "I wonder how right he was? What do you know about that woman, Mr. Malone?"

"Enough not to have any trust in her at all, sir."

"Care to tell me about her?"

"Could I see you later, sir? I must find Mrs. Quentin."

But he didn't find her. When he got back outside to the balcony Lisa and Coburn were already there with Quentin. Lisa had drawn a blank in the ladies' room.

"She's nowhere downstairs," Coburn said. "And the car has gone. There's no sign of Ferguson."

"Well, if he's with her, that's some comfort." But Quentin hadn't convinced himself. He bit his lip, thumped his fist on the balustrade. "But why did she go off without a word?"

"Perhaps she's gone home," Lisa said. "She might have felt ill—she didn't look well—"

"But who phoned her?" Malone said.

"Call the house." Quentin moved down the stairs and the others followed him. "Joseph should be there."

Lisa went away to telephone the house. Coburn went out through the vestibule towards the front doors again, and Malone and Quentin were left alone. Quentin was looking about him, peering at women as they passed, as if he expected them to take off the mask-like faces they wore and turn into Sheila. Behind them the marble smile of the Duke of York had now turned sardonic: he had lived in a time of cruel jokes. Quentin said, "What I can't understand is why she just disappeared without a word. If anything has happened to her—no good-bye, nothing—"

"Don't sound so—so *final*," Malone said, distressed for the other man. "Like Lisa said, she may just have felt ill. She's had enough happen to her, Christ knows—"

Quentin nodded, but he was still unconvinced; his despair had reached a momentum where nothing could stop him now from expecting the worst. Today was a day of disasters: first the conference, and now this, the worst that could possibly happen. "If they've harmed her—" he said, but even his rage was helpless.

"*They* are still here," Malone said. "Cholon and Pallain— if he's connected with her. I checked on them both before we came downstairs."

"They could have someone else—"

"If they have, we've also got Cholon. But don't start thinking like that. You're being too pessimistic—"

"Do you blame me? Christ, Scobie—" It was the first time Malone had heard him swear. "What grounds have I got for being optimistic about *anything?*"

Malone's apology was interrupted by the return of both Lisa and Coburn. Lisa said, "The phone's engaged."

"She's all right!" Coburn's relief made him look comical; the quizzical eyebrow twitched excitedly. "Ferguson's just come back. He took your wife home, sir."

Quentin sagged visibly; Malone stepped close to him to catch him as he fell. But the older man hadn't lost all his strength; again the control came back. He straightened up, managed to smile. "Lisa, will you go up and tell Mr. Larter I've gone home. Tell him I felt a bit off-colour."

Lisa stared at him. She loves him in some way, Malone thought; but felt no jealousy. "Hadn't I better come home with you? In case Mrs. Quentin—"

Quentin pressed her arm comfortingly; she might have been the one despairing and he the one with confidence at what the world had to offer. "We'll be all right, Lisa."

"I'll go with you," said Malone; and Quentin looked at him as if to protest. "I have to, sir."

Quentin hesitated, then nodded reluctantly. He looked at Lisa and smiled wearily, resignedly. "You see, Lisa? Mr. Malone won't let anything happen to us. Go upstairs and enjoy yourself. There are a dozen Second Secretaries wanting to talk to you."

[271]

She grimaced, then looked at Malone. "Call me if you think I'm needed."

She went up the stairs, brushing past the first of the Second Secretaries who tried to speak to her. Quentin stared after her, then turned as Malone said to Coburn, "I'll go back with His Excellency. You'd better stay here and keep an eye on Madame Cholon and our mate Pallain."

"Be a pleasure," said Coburn.

"And would you keep an eye on Miss Pretorious?" Quentin said.

"That will be even more of a pleasure," said Coburn. "And, sir—I'm glad Mrs. Quentin is okay."

"Thank you, Sergeant." Quentin seemed surprised at the personal note Coburn had introduced. It was almost as if he had begun to feel himself cut off from public sympathy; he had already closed the gaol gates. "That's very kind of you."

Coburn, having offered his sympathy, now seemed embarrassed. He gestured awkwardly, then turned quickly and went up the stairs almost at a run. Quentin said, "Why am I surrounded by *decent* policemen? Aren't there any bastards left?" He was getting closer to home, becoming more Australian: even the vowels had slipped a little.

Malone grinned, also embarrassed now. They went out through the vestibule and met Denzil as he came up the front steps. "I've just come from the American Embassy, sir. I'm afraid I have some bad news—"

"This is the day for it, Superintendent. Can't it wait? I have to get home to my wife at once."

Denzil said, "Could I ride with you, sir? This *is* important."

He gestured to the police car that had brought him to follow the Rolls-Royce. The three men then walked across to the Rolls and Ferguson opened the door for them. "Mrs. Quentin is at home, sir. She's all right. Just seemed a bit upset—"

"Better hurry then, Ferguson." Quentin jumped into the car and gestured impatiently for Malone and Denzil to follow him. "You'll have to forgive me, Superintendent, but I'm worried about my wife—" Denzil mumbled a word of sympathy, but it seemed abstracted. Quentin for the first time seemed to become aware that Denzil, too, was worried. "What is it?"

"It's your butler, sir. Joseph Liszt." Denzil was suddenly embarrassed; it was not easy to tell an ambassador his security arrangements were lax. "I'm afraid he is an agent. For both the Russians and the Chinese."

"Joseph?" Quentin shook his head: it was hard to tell whether he was surprised at what he had been told or disgusted for having allowed himself to be duped. But his second question was tinged with surprise: "*Both* the Russians and Chinese?"

"I gather the Russians didn't know he was working for the Chinese."

"Where did you get this information?"

"From Royston at the American Embassy. It had just come in from Washington. Evidently Jamaica had cabled it to CIA headquarters yesterday. They decoded it, took some time about their decision, then sent it back to Royston to pass on to us."

"But why all the rigmarole?" Malone asked. "Why didn't Jamaica come straight to you? Or go to Royston direct?"

Denzil shrugged. "I'm afraid that's the way security organizations work. There is as much red tape and inter-department jealousy as in any other Civil Service set-up. I don't know whether Jamaica didn't want Royston bossing him or whether he was under instructions not to tell us anything till Washington had vetted it and okayed us—" He shrugged again and sighed. It had been different in Kenya years ago; trust had been a man-to-man thing. "In the spy game nobody trusts anybody else, even your allies. Anyhow, the delay has been only something over twenty-four hours. We can still pick up this man Liszt. Is he at the house tonight?"

"He should be," Quentin said.

"I don't like him being there alone with Mrs. Quentin," Malone said. "I wonder if he made the phone call?"

Quentin shook his head. "Why would he call her? No, I'm not worried about him—not as far as my wife is concerned, I mean. He's a spy— God, why didn't I check closer on him! I'm sorry—" He looked at Denzil. "I've been pretty lax. But there's never been even a hint of anything suspicious until these past couple of days. I should have been suspicious then, I suppose. But there's been this other thing—"

Malone didn't feel this was the time to talk about the ancient murder. "What were you going to say about Joseph and Mrs. Quentin?"

"Oh yes. Well, I don't think he'd harm her. He's a cold fish, but I think he had a lot of time for my wife. And for me, too, I think. Whatever else he's done, I don't think he would harm us personally."

Then the car was drawing in before the house in Belgrave Square. Malone, sitting on the jump seat, was first out. Instinctively he looked quickly around; the night was dark enough to hide a dozen assassins. Quentin was next, hurrying across the pavement and up to the front door. He fumbled with his keys, then pushed back the door and went into the house. Malone and Denzil, still on the pavement, heard him calling for Sheila, his voice echoing in the hall.

"I don't have a warrant for this fellow," Denzil said to Malone. "I'll have to phone the Yard and have one sent. But do you have your gun?"

Malone patted his armpit. "I don't think he's the violent type."

"You never know. When a man's faced with years in prison, he might try anything."

Yes, thought Malone. And a woman, too: if she were faced

with years in prison, would she try suicide? He felt suddenly cold inside. He crossed the pavement on the run, went up the steps and into the hall as Quentin, trembling like a crazed man, came stumbling towards him.

"She's not here! And neither is Joseph!"

3

Madame Cholon dismissed the African Embassy car that had brought her home and let herself in the front door. She felt apprehensive, and the unaccustomed anxiety began to manifest itself as a rising fury. When Pham Chinh came into the hall to meet her she snarled at him. "Is she here?"

He nodded towards the drawing room. "In there." He was both puzzled and afraid; too much had gone wrong in the last few days. "I didn't know whether to let her in—"

Madame Cholon waved a curt hand of dismissal and went by him and into the drawing room, still wearing her mink stole over her *ao dais*. The night was warm, but she still felt the chill of the English summer; now, unaccountably, she felt even colder. She stopped just inside the door, drawing the stole round her, as Sheila Quentin rose to meet her. Sheila wore a green silk evening coat buttoned high to the neck; it gave her a slightly Oriental look, but for the auburn hair above it. The two women stared at each other for a while in silence.

Then Madame Cholon snapped, "I hope what you have to say, Mrs. Quentin, is important. I was enjoying myself at the reception—"

"What I have to say won't take ten minutes," said Sheila, and drew back the sleeve of her coat to look at her watch. "A little less."

Madame Cholon turned to Pham Chinh, who stood in the doorway staring uneasily at both women. "You may go, Pham."

"I'd rather he stayed with us," said Sheila. "If he was concerned with you in the attempts on my husband's life, then he must stay."

Madame Cholon stood half-turned away; she stiffened and looked over her shoulder at Sheila. "Accusations like that can get you into trouble. Your country has laws—"

"And yours doesn't?" Sheila smiled, but there was no humour in her. Her face was stiff and white, and the smile was no more than a tensing of muscles; the hazel eyes seemed to have a tinge of yellow in them, adding to her look of illness. She no longer gave the impression of being tall, looked even a little stooped; she looked old and defeated and ready to die. But not just yet: some spirit was still alive in her: "From what Joseph told me, I don't think you care about the laws of any country."

"Joseph?" Madame Cholon's voice was icy; it gave her away. "Who is he?"

"Our butler. Or ex-butler now. When he called me at the reception he didn't say where he was, just that he was leaving the country. So I think he must have been at the airport then."

"I don't know what you are talking about." She would phone the bank in Zurich first thing in the morning, have them stop the cheque. But the money was not the important thing. Another attempt on Quentin's life had failed, this time through treachery: the man must bear a charmed life. She shivered as the fury began to increase in her.

Sheila shook her head wearily. "Don't waste our time. He told me everything. It's hard to forgive him for going as far as he did. But in the end he couldn't go through with it. You see, madame, you overlooked one thing. There are people who have respect, even affection for my husband. I don't know what it is that Joseph feels, but it stopped him from murdering my husband. And me, too, I suppose. Because the bomb would have killed both of us there in the bedroom. It was ingenious, having it in the alarm clock. My husband

[276]

would have set the time of his own death. And you would have been miles away, safe from suspicion. I just wish I had had your forethought. No, I don't," she said, and sounded horrified at what she had heard herself say. "I never meant to kill anyone. Not Freda."

"Who?" The woman was crazy. "Who is Freda?"

"No one you'll ever know." Sheila regained some control. She smiled again, once more without any humour. "You didn't have to kill my husband, you know. That's the irony of it. The conference is a failure, didn't you know that?"

"I don't believe it!" She was trembling now, her face turning ugly.

Sheila bent down and picked up a black handbag from the couch beside her. It was a large bag, one that did not go with her evening wear. "I went home when Joseph phoned me. Somehow I couldn't believe him. But I found the clock, took the back off it to make sure."

Madame Cholon's curiosity at this strange woman was too much for her. "Weren't you afraid of being killed?"

Sheila shook her head. "That intrigues you, doesn't it? No, I didn't care. If it had gone off, it would have solved a lot of things. But it didn't. And then I got my idea. If I had died, you would still be alive. Still able to make more attempts on my husband's life—"

"I wouldn't be interested in him," Madame Cholon snapped. "Not if the conference has failed!"

"Perhaps. But there would still be the attempts you did make to kill him. I believe in justice, Madame Cholon—perhaps I'm a little late—"

Outside in Avenue Road Coburn sat in the police car that had followed Madame Cholon from Lancaster House. "I wish I knew why the bitch left the reception in such a hurry. Try the Yard again, get them to phone the Super at the Australian High Commissioner's house, ask him does he want me to barge in on her."

[277]

The detective beside the driver got through to Scotland Yard on the radio. Coburn sat in the back of the car, frustrated and worried by a sense that something was about to happen that could and should be stopped. Once more he wished for the freedom that the KGB enjoyed. He looked at his watch: 10:24 . . .

Sheila opened the black bag. "My one regret is I did not say good-bye to my husband. But that would have ruined everything—" She was crying now, the tears running down her face, killing her beauty, killing her. "I had twenty-three years, and not all of us have that much happiness. In a way it was a sad sort of happiness, but it was enough—"

Madame Cholon felt the fear suddenly take hold of her. She lunged towards Sheila, screaming at the top of her voice for Pham Chinh to help her. Sheila now had her hand in the bag; she snatched it out and showed the small leather-cased clock. She fell away from Madame Cholon, wrenched the case open and fumbled with the alarm release.

"Twenty-five past ten!" Sheila was hysterical now, swaying and moaning, holding out the clock like an offering. "I'm sorry, Freda—"

Coburn heard the scream. He fell out of the car, was half-way across the road when the windows of the front room of the house blew out in a red explosion.

CHAPTER TWELVE

"The shock will wear off," Quentin said. "But I'll always go on missing her."

Malone said nothing, having only awkward words that would have embarrassed both himself and Quentin. The small restaurant, dark and a little shabby, in which they sat was a long way from the glittering style of Lancaster House; but Quentin himself had suggested it and Malone was glad. Somehow it suited the mood that he knew would close in on both of them as soon as they met.

"I'm going to Malaysia," Quentin said. "There are several Colombo Plan teams there and I'm joining one of them."

"What will you do?"

Quentin smiled, catching the critical surprise in Malone's voice. "You forget I was once a surveyor. I'm qualified, and I was a good one. At least I thought I was," he added. The old air of confidence had gone, and with it gone he looked older. "I'll need some toughening up to plod up and down some of those jungle roads. But it should do me good."

"Have you seen the Prime Minister—I mean again, since that time when you first got back?"

"No. I think it would have been too painful for both of

us. When I saw him three months ago, handed in my resignation and told him the truth about everything, he didn't take it very well. Oh, he wasn't angry or anything like that. Disappointed—but perhaps that wasn't it, either, it was more than that. Anyhow I couldn't face him again. I wrote him and he was the one who fixed this Malaysia job for me. But I don't think we'll meet again. He's an old man—" He stirred his coffee, looked down at it for a few moments. With his head tilted forward the grey hair showed one or two streaks of white; the once tight skin now looked wrinkled and slack on the bones of the face. "Too old to have time to forget recent disappointments."

Flannery had been disappointed, too, but for different reasons. The morning after Sheila's death Malone had phoned Leeds, told him what had happened and asked for a few more days. Quentin would be wanted by Scotland Yard for routine questioning on the attempts on his life and the death of his wife, Madame Cholon and Pham Chinh. It would be hardly possible for him to leave London at once.

Malone had also told Leeds about Sheila's confession. "I believed her, sir. It may or may not have been an accident, but I do believe she was the one who killed Freda Corliss. Quentin had nothing to do with it, except as an accessory after."

"Do you have any sworn statement?"

"No, sir. It was just verbal." He didn't tell Leeds that at the time of Sheila's death he still had not made up his mind what his own statement would have been when he finally appeared in court.

There was a long silence at the other end of the line. Then at last Leeds said, "This could solve a lot of things, Sergeant."

"I've thought of that, sir." Malone was relieved that the Commissioner had suggested it. It would not have done for a detective-sergeant to argue for turning a blind eye to legal justice.

"All right, tell Quentin we'd like him home by next weekend. But stick close by him, Scobie."

"I'll do that, sir," said Malone, thinking not as a policeman but as a friend.

"In the meantime I'll see the Premier," Leeds said. Then he permitted himself a personal comment, betrayed by the ten thousand miles between himself and his junior officer: "He's going to be disappointed if it works out the way I hope."

"Yes, sir," said Malone, careful not to say too much. "But I hope it does work out."

A week after that Quentin and Malone left London for Sydney. Among others Denzil had come to the airport to see them off. He took Malone aside. "We've found no trace of that butler chap, Joseph. He could be anywhere in the world now."

"What about Pallain?"

"We had nothing on him. All we could do was offer him a polite hint to leave the country. Which he did."

"I hate the thought of both of them getting away."

"You can't catch them all." He looked around to make sure they wouldn't be overheard, then said, "I had a call from your Commissioner—"

"He told me he would be phoning you."

"Sounds a decent chap. Asked me if I could forget what you had told me about the High Commissioner and that business of twenty-odd years ago. Evidently they are going to forget it out there."

"That's the idea, sir. They accept now that Mrs. Quentin was the one who killed the first wife. There are very few people who know why I came to London. The warrant I have is made out in the name of John Corliss, so even the

[281]

records will show nothing. Proving that John Quentin is John Corliss—what good will it do now?"

"What about your State Premier?"

"I gather he didn't like the idea at first. But he's too shrewd to go through with bringing it out into the open now. The papers back home have made Mrs. Quentin into something of a heroine. A woman finds out her husband is to be killed, goes looking for the killers herself—"

"Do you think that was what she was trying to do? Bring them to justice?"

Malone shook his head. "No. But I'm not going to contradict them. Would you, sir?"

"As I said, you can't catch them all. And sometimes it's for the best." He smiled and put out his hand. "Good-bye, Sergeant. It's a pity you're not staying on longer. We could have gone and seen a few cricket matches together. I could have told you again how I bowled Wally Hammond for a duck." He winked and smiled more broadly. Why, the old bastard can even laugh at himself, Malone thought. "Sergeant Coburn sent you his best. Said to tell you his girl—he called her his bird—she's just given him a present to celebrate his escape from that bomb. A purple weskit to go with his purple tie."

Malone grinned. "He'll look good in that at the Yard."

"Over my dead body he will," said Denzil, and with a final wave of his hand walked away, stolid, dependable, eroded only by memories of other days.

Lisa was the last to say good-bye to Malone. "I'm coming home," she said. "But not for a few months. Mr. Quentin has asked me to stay on till the new High Commissioner is appointed. I'll be training a new girl to take my place."

"You might like the new High Commissioner."

She shook her head. "It wouldn't matter who he was, what he was like. I couldn't stay on, not after—" She took his hand, began to walk towards the passengers' entrance with him.

[282]

They had been in the V.I.P. lounge, the last time, Malone knew, that he would ever receive that sort of treatment. Two days from now he would be back to his proper status. "I think I'd like to try Sydney for a while."

"Sydney? Not Melbourne, with your parents?"

"Sydney," she said, and lifted her face and kissed him for the first time. "Will you write me each week till I come back?"

"Every day," he said, and returned her kiss. "I like that perfume."

"I'll douse myself in it just before I get off the plane." She had gazed at him for a moment, then nodded, as if satisfied she had made some sort of right decision. Then she had turned away and gone across to say good-bye to Quentin.

Now Quentin, in the small restaurant in Sydney, said, "Are you ever going to tell Lisa the truth?"

Malone waited while Quentin paid the bill, then they walked out into the bright spring sunlight of Macquarie Street. The lunchtime crowds were hurrying reluctantly back to their offices. Flushed, tousled-haired girls who had been playing basketball in the Domain went by in their brief bright skirts; it was difficult to imagine that in ten minutes they would be cool, modestly clad typists. A tanned healthy-looking street singer stood in the gutter telling the passing girls he couldn't give them anything but love; nobody dropped any money in his upturned hat, nobody believed in his destitution. Sydney in the spring was a city where people were too gay, too preoccupied with their own awakening sap, to want to know the truth about other people. The street singer's sign said: Heart Disease, Unable to Work; but no one believed him. They laughed, were sure he was joking, and passed on.

Quentin stopped by the singer and dropped two shillings into his hat. "Thanks, mate," said the singer. "And good luck."

"Thank you," said Quentin with a touch of his old grace.

He and Malone walked on and at last Malone said, "No, I'm not going to tell her. Lisa, I mean. I told her I'm a policeman, I was on special duty. But that's all."

"Why?"

"I don't know. When I was in London I thought the truth would help you and Mrs. Quentin. Now I don't know that it's going to help anybody. It won't help Lisa. She had—has a lot of time for you. Why disillusion her?"

Quentin walked in silence for a while, then he said, "Are you going to marry her?"

"I'm going to ask her. It's another thing whether she'll say yes."

"She wants her head read if she doesn't. And if you don't ever tell her the truth about me—well, thank you. But you don't owe me anything, you know."

"Well, let's say I owe it to myself," said Malone.

They came to a corner. Quentin stopped and put out his hand. "I have a doctor's appointment. I have some vaccinations to be done. Good-bye, Scobie. If I write to you from Malaysia, will you—?"

Malone nodded. "I'm a poor letter writer, so Lisa tells me. But I'll write. And like that bloke back there said—good luck."

Quentin nodded his thanks, started to say something, then seemed unable to get the words out. He put his hand up to his moustache and tugged at it; behind his hand his mouth quivered with emotion. Then abruptly he turned and walked off up the street. Malone watched him go, a man who might have been great, till he disappeared, anonymous and alone, into the careless, incurious crowd.